THE LONG PIVOT HOME

THE LONG PIVOT HOME

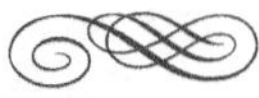

Based on a true story of love and loss in Oklahoma

JIM WILLIS

ArtStrings Press, LLC

Other Books by Jim Willis

Tinkertown: A Wheatfield, an Airbase, and Us
The 1960s on Film (with Mark Miller)
Daily Life in the 1960s Counterculture
Tweeting to Freedom
Documents Decoded: 1960s Counterculture
From Twitter to Tahrir Square: Ethics of Social and New Media Communications (Vols. 1 & 2)
(Bala Musa & Jim Willis)
Daily Life Behind the Iron Curtain
100 Media Moments that changed America
The Mind of a Journalist
The Media Effect: How the News Influences Politics and Government
The Human Journalist
Prelude to Greatness: Sooner Football in the 1990s
(with Jay Smith)
Images of Germany in the American Media
Reporting on Risks (with Albert Adelowo Okunade)
The Age of Multimedia and Turbonews
The Shadow World
Journalism: State of the Art
Surviving in the Newspaper Business

Dedication

To the strong people of Oklahoma
and to those who came and helped

Acknowledgements

I would like to thank so many people who have encouraged me to do this book, starting with my wife of the last quarter-century, Anne Kindred Willis. She has been my muse in this endeavor. A more loving and patient soul has never existed on this planet.

But there are many others to thank as well including my good friends and fellow writers Joe Bogan and Joe Hight out in Oklahoma; John Maruskin, Bill McCann, Marie Parsons, Jeanine Grant Lister, and Julie Maruskin in Kentucky, Roger A. Brady, in North Carolina, and Alan Rifkin in Los Angeles. Editorial consultants David Sanford and Annie Bomke were also helpful in establishing my concepts.

A special thanks goes to Bev Allen who is one of the survivors of the Murrah Building bombing on April 19, 1995, and who was working in the building when the bomb exploded. Bev related his eyewitness account to me, and it is in this book. The irony is that while Bev and I were both in Oklahoma City during the bombing and aftermath, we never met until 2024 at a church we now both attend in Winchester, Kentucky.

Thanks also to my former editor at *The Edmond Evening Sun*, Carol Hartzog, and to that paper's publisher, Ed Livermore, Jr. And finally, thanks to my fellow reporters and editors in news organizations like *The Oklahoman*, the BBC News World Service, the *Los Angeles Times*, Associated Press, and others.

Many journalists covered the events and people of the Oklahoma City bombing in April, 1995, and some excellent stories were written as reflective pieces even years later. Few were as good as a *Los Angeles Times* story by Hailey Branson Potts, whose vivid story about the officer who made the April 1995 arrest of Timothy McVeigh is featured in

Chapter 20. This entire copyrighted story is reprinted with permission of the *Times*. My thanks to Hailey and her newspaper for this.

--Jim Willis

Contents

FOREWORD: BLENDING GENRES

PART ONE

PART TWO

PART THREE

Grief

"Life is full of grief, to exactly the degree we allow ourselves to
love other people."

Orson Scott Card, *Shadow of the Giant*

Foreword: Blending Genres

Sometimes real life is stranger than fiction, sometimes it's the other way around. *The Long Pivot Home* is a historical novel containing elements and names of both fact and fiction. At least two people I care deeply about are not in the story at all. The description of what took place in Oklahoma City in April and May 1995 -- are real; some other things happened a little differently, or not at all. They are meant to underscore why feelings were so intense at the time. I have my reasons for writing it this way. In the end, the *essence* of the story -- how one person among many dealt with sorrow -- is true.

It is a story that, as the subtitle says, is *based on a true story of love and loss in Oklahoma.* At least that's where the pivoting from the past to the future *began* for its focal character, Luke Jarrett. Hopefully readers will find the story engrossing, even humorous in places, but also helpful in surviving times of personal tragedy and darkness. If you're looking for some role models there, you might start with the people of Oklahoma who refused to let a mass killing by two right-wing terrorists prevent them from going forward and emerging stronger because of the fight they won.

Part One

LOST

I

Arizona

It was a warm and sunny March afternoon in 1995, and I, Luke Jarrett, was in a reflective mood as I drove my Isuzu Rodeo SUV north on Arizona's Interstate 17 through the Coconino National Forest. The city of Flagstaff, one of America's best-kept secrets, loomed about 50 miles ahead. I looked forward to seeing it again, even in passing. I remembered how beautiful a setting it was amid the mountains, pine trees, and cooler temperatures of northern Arizona.

Although its population is only 76,000, Flagstaff is a busy place. For one thing, it is the gateway city to the Grand Canyon, lying some 45 minutes to the north and, unlike a stereotypical hot Arizona town, experiences a four-seasons climate.

The city also has a university that I've always liked, mostly because of its environmental programs and because the campus itself fits so snugly up against the foothills of those mountains. Its name is Northern Arizona University, and the whole campus has embraced the love of the great outdoors and the dense forests of pine trees and evergreens. Even the NAU athletic teams go by the name Lumberjacks.

I had been on the road about three hours after leaving a little-known Apache Junction, east of Phoenix, earlier that morning and was going ... well, that was the question, wasn't it?

I wasn't sure *where* I was going.

At this point in my life, I was a walking wreck of a 49-year-old man in the middle of an emotional, midlife crisis that had been my worst nightmare come true. It had already caused me to contemplate suicide a couple months before. It was late night in the St. Louis Airport as I awaited a flight to Oklahoma City and stood at the terminal windows watching planes take off and land outside.

How easy it would be to slip down the stairs and through a maintenance door that had been left open to the runway's apron, I thought. Then just walk out into the middle of the dark runway as one of those 727s was coming in for a landing. It could be over in a second. I am not meant to live the rest of my life alone, and yet here I am without Selena. It might just be better to end things now.

But that airport door closed quickly, both literally and figuratively, and I survived the night. I've heard often that the *act* of suicide is a product of the moment – of the impulse -- and not a long, drawn-out reasoning process. That night in St. Louis made me realize the truth in that assertion.

So here I was today on this Arizona highway. I was following instincts at this point, subconsciously trusting them to tell me where to go. On this bright sunny day, it was as if I was just feeling my way along in the quietness of a nearly empty Saturday highway. If I listened, I could hear writer Rod Serling's distinctive voice from 1960s television intoning, *"There's a signpost up ahead; your next stop, the Twilight Zone!"*

I've always paid a little too much heed to my emotions for my own good, but I had the gut feeling then I should make a turn onto I-40 when I got to that intersection in 40 more minutes. The thing is, I was unsure whether to turn west or east. I also had the feeling the decision would be an important one, although I had no idea why. After all, if it didn't matter where I was going, why should I turn at all? Why not just keep going north toward Canada?

I had just spent a week in an otherworldly wilderness, doing something completely different from my Boston routine, something designed to remove me from the nightmare of the present and propel me to grope for my life's reset button. I had ridden horses into the rugged Superstition Mountains seven days ago, and just emerged back at base camp early this morning.

The dark reality tearing at me was that I had lost *Selena,* the love of my life. The call from the first responders had awoken me about 1 a.m. three months ago. It was a Friday night, snowing in Boston where l was living with Selena in a renovated condo on Gainesboro Street in the historic city's Back Bay section. She was a little late getting home after anchoring the 11 p.m. news on a local television station. Matters at the station often required her attention after her show, so this wasn't all that unusual.

"Dr. Lucas Jarrett?" the woman's voice began.

"Yes," I replied, only half awake.

"I am Sergeant Lucy Markham with the Boston Police Department."

A pause ensued as I struggled with the cobwebs of my mind. She continued, "There has been an auto accident, and your wife Selena is in Massachusetts General Hospital. Do you have someone who can drive you here? If not, I can send a police unit to escort you."

I was in immediate shock, but I felt around and found my voice. "I'll be right over. But how is she? And why would I need someone to drive me, unless ... Selena will be all right, won't she?"

Again a pause, and then the officer's voice. "Dr. Jarrett, your wife's car was broadsided as she was driving through Copley Square. The hit came on her side, and she was transported by ambulance to Mass General. That's all I can tell you at this point, but the attending resident and I will be in the emergency room to meet you when you arrive and tell you more. I'm sorry."

I did not take time to respond. I clicked the phone off, swung out of bed and found my pants, shirt, and shoes, grabbed the car keys and headed out into the darkness. My SUV was parked just outside on Gainesboro. I jumped in, started the engine and sped off in the direction of Mass General, hoping my worst fears about Selena weren't true.

At that moment, I didn't know I would never see Selena alive again. Ten minutes later, I was essentially being told that by the resident who met me at the door of the ER.

"How is she?" I blurted out. "How is my Selena?"

The resident was a young man of about 26, and I doubt he had had to convey news like this very often in his young career. He hesitated, took a deep breath, then said, "I am sorry, Sir, but we lost your wife just moments ago. The damage from the wreck was too great ... she had lost too much blood, too quickly."

I gasped for breath as I reached for the wall to keep me from falling over.

"Selena!" I shouted. "Where is she? I want to see her!"

"I'll take you to her," Dr. Jarrett, but is there someone you can call to come and be with you? A family member, perhaps?" Or a close friend?"

"No. Please just show me where Selena is. And, by the way, have you caught the driver who hit her?"

"Unfortunately, we don't know who hit her," Officer Markham said. "This was a hit and run. Boston PD is starting to look for the other driver now."

Then she said, "Your wife was apparently stopping to help a female motorist whose engine had stalled on the street. When she got out of her car on the street side, another car hit her, taking the door clear off her car."

I felt my blood pressure rise as we walked toward the room where Selena was lying still, already in another realm, oblivious to all of this. Worse yet, oblivious to me.

As I thought about what the cop had said, I thought to myself, "That is so much like, Selena. Stopping to help a woman in need, even if she was a stranger and it was the middle of the night in Boston."

And that was that. Just like Elton John's *Norma Jean*, Selena had been as fragile as a candle in the wind. And, this night, that wind gusted, the flame vanished, and she was gone.

I spent the rest of the night at the side of Selena's lifeless body, unable to tell her again all she had meant to me in our 17 years together, 15 as husband and wife. At some point, I did find myself uttering those words as I dug my face into her silent torso, and I hoped -- pretended, maybe? -- that she heard them. It made me feel just a bit better to think her soul absorbed them and perhaps even tried to console me.

"I'm okay, Bear," I imagined she said, calling me by her pet name for me. I imagined it so hard that I thought I actually heard her say it. I wanted to imagine it into reality. In my heart, she continued, "I'm in a good place, and I will always love you."

Somewhere around 5 a.m., I was awakened by a hand on my shoulder. It was the duty nurse, coaxing me awake from the fatigue that had allowed me to sleep a couple hours, still at her side, holding her hand in both of mine.

And then it was over, and the stark reality of a new normal -- a life without Selena -- began its long descent into my consciousness.

The problem was believing it. I couldn't imagine life without her. When she wept, I tasted salt. I would taste it for many years to come.

Now, three months later in Arizona, here I was, driving alone. Interstate 40 was just a half-hour ahead now. I felt that my decision on which way to turn could change my life.

Frankly, I didn't care.

2

Columbia

The flood of memories began filling the deep trenches of my mind, overflowing for as long as it would take for this pain to somehow soak into the soil where it could hurt me no more. Behind the wheel of my car, it was if I was sitting at a railroad crossing, waiting for a long train to pass. All I could see as I looked left down the tracks was an endless number of freight cars. Only in this case, each of those cars contained box after box of memories of my beautiful wife and our life together.

Selena was named for the Greek goddess of the sky who was known for pulling the moon across the heavens in her chariot. She was celebrated mostly on nights of a new moon and – true to my Selena's persona – she was usually akin to mystery and seduction. Perhaps she even encouraged those perceptions.

She and I had begun much like a romantic movie back in 1978, when we each came separately to Columbia, Missouri, from different parts of the country to begin a new chapter in our lives as graduate students at the famed University of Missouri School of Journalism. I was 32; she was 28. Up to that point, we were strangers and neither of us knew our two paths were about to cross, and then blend into a single trail. I had left my newspaper job in Dallas, and Selena had left her high school teaching job in Seattle.

She was pursuing a master's degree in journalism, and I was starting my Ph.D. in the same field. I had also been hired as a full-time instructor in the J School, where my job was to serve as a supervising editor on the school's daily newspaper. It was a dream come true for both of us, and a trifecta for me because I could continue practicing my daily journalism, as well as teach, all while pursuing the doctorate in that field and doing it with a faculty paycheck and deep tuition discount.

Although I often look back on this current Arizona time as the decision that would change my life, the truth is life is made up of several such choices, no? One of them was made in 1977, when I chose to leave the newsroom in Texas and head back to school for a doctorate. Another was when I chose the University of Missouri School of Journalism to get that Ph.D.

I had already been accepted into the graduate program at the University of Iowa and considered going there. If I had, there would have been no Selena. Life would have tracked differently for us, and the deep love I had experienced with her would never have materialized at all.

But it did happen, thanks to the fabled butterfly effect of Chaos Theory. In my case, the butterfly effected its landing in Columbia, Missouri, instead of Iowa City, Iowa. Now, years later here I was out on the Interstate coming to grips with the legacy of my choice in grad schools.

Both Iowa and Missouri have fine journalism schools, but since I was a *working* journalist, I preferred Missouri's *applied* journalism approach to Iowa's more theoretical approach. It's a hands-on academic program, and that fit well with the decade of newsroom experience I'd already accumulated in Oklahoma City and Dallas.

In Missouri's journalism program, students' classroom work was enhanced by real-life lab experience working as reporters for *The Columbia Missourian,* a newspaper based in Columbia, the largest town in central Missouri with a population then of about 70,000. Today it is home to 120,000 people.

The Missourian was then published six days a week and is "affiliated with" (in reality it is part and parcel of) the Missouri School of

Journalism, and is owned as a 501c3 non-profit under the Missourian Publishing Association. It dates to 1908, which is the date the journalism school itself was founded.

It's even more unique in that the newspaper – as well as the area's network affiliated television station KOMU – are the newsroom labs for undergrad and graduate students of the Missouri School of Journalism. This was very important to Selena and me, because it is how we met and came to spend a lot of working hours together; more so than if she had just been in my traditional classroom 3 hours a week. Missourian reporters work until their stories are done and filed.

All the *Missourians'* reporting is done by these students, all of whom pay tuition for the semester-long experiences. Further, the editors and other managers are all professors in the journalism school. My assignment was night city editor, and my reporters were my journalism students. So far as I know, it's still the only program like it in the country. Adding to its distinctiveness, the Missouri School of Journalism is the oldest school of journalism in the world, founded in 1908 by Walter Williams, whose name still graces one of the main journalism buildings on campus.

As if that weren't enough, the city of Columbia may be the only town of its size in America that is served by not just one, but *two*, daily newspapers. And they are probably two of the best small dailies in existence. When I was there, the *Missourian* was (and I presume still is) in full-fledged competition with the afternoon daily, *The Columbia Daily Tribune*.

That newspaper was founded seven years before the *Missourian*, in 1901, and its founder was Charles Monro Strong, with assistance from Barratt O'Hara, as the city's first daily. Strong was a University of Missouri grad, although there was no journalism school there when he graduated.

The two newspapers produced a competitive battle like any other mid-size town in America. Both newsrooms were staffed with dedicated and gifted young journalists hungry to show that they deserved a career in big-time journalism. The list of reporters who moved on to larger news organizations in New York, Chicago, L.A., and capitals of the world is quite impressive. The same is true for the graduates of the school's KOMU-TV news station.

As editors in Columbia, we used to joke that if you threw a stone in any direction in the city, you'd hit a dozen journalists covering stories somewhere at that time. Depending on what was happening around town, that was not too great an exaggeration.

Indeed, while some newspapers struggle to send one reporter regularly to city council and school board meetings, *The Missourian* was able to send a half dozen, since they were all journalism students needing to publish stories for their grades. On a given night, we would often assign one reporter to each action item on the agenda of the council or board. Once that item was finished, that reporter would come back to the newsroom to write that part of the story, followed by another, and another, etc.

The Tribune, on the other hand, could only send one – or at most two – reporters on a given night, because they were traditionally paid positions and the only city hall reporters the paper had.

Add to that the fact that *The Missourian* was aggressive in pursuing advertising revenue against the family-owned *Tribune,* and some perceived an unequal playing field for the cross-town competitors. The system remained intact, however.

If you were a journalist living and working there, it was a lot of fun.

Selena, who had been a Phi Beta Kappa in college, was not only smart, but she was intrepid in her reporting and writing skills. She could take even a routine feature story and turn it into must-read copy. I remember one story which she enterprised that did just that: A fine feature on eating places in the area where you could get a filling lunch for less than $2. How do you make a fun read out of that? Just read the one that Selena wrote!

I was single and moving up from Dallas where I had resigned my position as managing editor of a suburban daily newspaper. I was doing what I do best: I was looking over the next hill for the next great adventure.

I would find it quicker than I expected in the wooded hills of Columbia, Missouri.

Columbia is a city lying halfway between St. Louis and Kansas City, on I-40 along the northern edge of the Ozark Mountains. It is a lovely area, especially in fall and spring, but can be bitter cold during the harsh winter storms that visit the region.

It is, first and foremost, a college town (and often called College Town USA) where the University of Missouri campus is the focal point, although not the only college in town. Two smaller private schools, Stephens College, and Columbia College, add to the progressive, educational, and research interests of the city.

In some ways, Columbia is a microcosm of the city from which I was now taking a leave of absence in 1995. That city is Boston, and it boasts more colleges per square mile than any other city in the country. The joke, in fact, is that Boston has more colleges than McDonalds restaurants. I believe that to be true.

I had moved from Texas to Columbia in the summer of 1978 to start work on my doctorate in journalism and to work on the university's paper, *The Missourian*. I had just come out of a long-term relationship with a woman there and was still feeling my way, unattached, for the first time in several years.

I had been in Columbia only three months before I met this new graduate student from Seattle who arrived on campus to start the fall term. The first day of class in early September, she was one of the students assigned to the basic reporting course, and that put her into *The Missourian* newsroom, where I served as night city editor. It was my faculty assignment as an instructor at the University of Missouri.

This, then, was Selena Williams. I would be her editor and mentor, and she would be my graduate student reporter on *The Missourian* during our first semester there, covering her assigned beat in Columbia.

I met her one afternoon when she walked into the newsroom to start her first shift as a student reporter. There was an easiness and breeziness about us right from the start. We were both adults who had decided to become college students again.

Selena had driven her Mazda cross-country from Washington State to Missouri. Her decision to move to Missouri to pursue a master's degree in journalism was her way of moving on to a new chapter in life. She had left her high school teaching job where she taught English and Journalism, and she was excited about moving from teaching it to practicing it as a career. She, too, had recently come out of a failed romantic relationship.

In short, Selena and I were both very vulnerable people at that time, and we had unknowingly put ourselves into a situation where our defenses would crumble. And they would do it quickly.

We felt the same sense of adventure and possibilities that we had felt back when we started college more than a decade before as freshmen. We talked a little that first night in the newsroom, and I learned she was originally from New York. That was a good fit, I remember thinking, because she reminded me of the Marlo Thomas character, Ann Marie, from the 1960s TV sitcom, *That Girl,* which also was set in New York.

Selena and I didn't know what the future would hold for either of us or even if there would be a future. But neither of us shied away from the possibilities in front of us. Within a month, we were excited about exploring a close relationship.

I realized I now had two reasons for being excited about what was to come: a new journey in my life and perhaps a woman, who seemed to walk right out of my dreams, to travel it with me. It was at least a possibility, and neither of us seemed to fear taking the first step.

For me, there was a feeling that Selena was the woman I had been seeking since ... well ... forever. Before long, she was telling me she had the same feeling about me. I felt a sense of rightness about it, and she did, too.

It's odd the things you wind up remembering, but there was this one night when a few of us were just walking to the parking lot and Selena's arm inadvertently brushed lightly against mine. Such a small thing, so innocent, but one never forgotten.

The one signature moment that convinced me -- in every way possible -- that I wanted to marry this woman, came when I was studying in the school's library, and she came in looking for a particular journal. I wasn't having the best day and often that shows in my face, or so I've been told by others. She must have seen it, and she sat down across the table from me, saying hello and asking if I was okay.

As she was doing so, she smiled, reached across the table, and touched my right arm. I had never experienced a moment like that in my life, and her touch sent electric ripples throughout my entire body. Our eyes met and bored into each other and, from that point on, Selena and I knew we were going forward together.

Although we'd only known each other for a few weeks, I believed that the feelings I had for her were exactly the ones missing in my life. I didn't know if she and I would really have a chance together, but I did know I was going to go for it.

It wasn't long before Selena and I took advantage of being able to see more of each other. I called her one evening to see if she would go out for a walk around campus with me, and she said yes. I picked her up and we strolled over to a campus park called People's Park, we would come to rename it Peace Park because of the peaceful, easy feeling we felt with each other while there.

That first night we sat on the lush grass beneath the trees and just talked. We talked about our pasts, about school, and about our lives in general. About an hour into the talk, our fingers inadvertently settled on the same twig on the ground between us. We smiled at that and, as we looked up at each other, our fingers inched closer to the middle of that twig until flesh touched flesh. It was a breathless moment, and we tumbled over backwards on the lawn, locked in each other's embrace. I lost track of the number of kisses we shared after that.

Our first official date came a week later, and the waiting seemed like an eternity. I spent most of my time thinking about that Friday night when she would come to my townhome for dinner. I felt comfortable cooking only two things – spaghetti and lasagna – so I planned the menu and spent the night before getting ready to cook the lasagna and tossed salad the next afternoon.

I bought both red and white wine, and cleaned the place from top to bottom, rearranged my LP collection by artist, bought a few candles, tuned up my guitar for a planned serenade later ... pretty much all the things a love-struck guy in a rom-com movie would do.

Just before we sat down to eat, I turned on my stereo to listen to Neil Diamond's new album, *I'm Glad You're Here With Me Tonight,"* which seemed totally appropriate. We started our dinner to the strains of Diamond's song, *You Don't Bring Me Flowers.* I have no memory of what the lasagna tasted like; I have every memory of Selena's glowing eyes over the dinner candle flame.

It all seemed to work to perfection, and I felt I had set foot on TV's *Fantasy Island.* Later, we went out for a walk in the neighborhood and encountered the next-door neighbor's friendly collie, *Whistler.* He walked with us the rest of the way and even wiggled his way past us through the door and into my townhome. Since this had happened before and since his owner said he didn't mind if Whistler visited me, I let him stay.

As the inevitable happened later, Selena and I willingly took the relationship to the next level in my bedroom. Whistler went along with us.

"Luke," Selena told me, "I don't know what's happening. I am developing these deep feelings for you. I do know I want to enjoy what you and I have found, however."

Somewhere in the early-morning hours when I awoke after a night of lovemaking, I discovered Whistler was sprawled out across both Selena and me. I took him downstairs and sent him home and went back upstairs.

Selena and I spent the rest of that weekend together, and we talked about plans for the immediate future. In short, we really had none, other to enjoy the time we would have together in Columbia.

Monday morning came, and I found myself recalling singer-songwriter John Prine's song, *Illegal Smile.* It seemed to fit my countenance perfectly from that first date forward. Sometimes friends at school would catch me smiling and ask what I was so happy about.

"Oh, just happy to be here at such a great school on such a pretty day," I would usually say.

About a month after that, Selena and I were living together, and we continued doing that through the remainder of our two-year, on-campus life until she graduated with her M.A., and I reached the ABD (all but dissertation) stage with my doctorate.

That summer, in 1980, we formalized our relationship into marriage, then moved to Chicago where she became a news anchor and reporter at the ABC television affiliate, going professionally by her maiden name of Williams. She had already established that name on-air with her work at the University of Missouri's TV station which she anchored while a student there.

I was hired as assistant professor of communication at DePaul University, along an extension of Chicago's Miracle Mile. It was there that I finished my Ph.D. dissertation, long-distance from the University of Missouri, in 1982.

We were on our way into a marriage that I felt would last forever. But then, doesn't nearly every newly-married couple believe that?

There would be many good years ahead and too many good moments to count. From Chicago, we would head to Boston two years later, where I snagged a faculty position at Northeastern University while Selena was hired by a network television affiliate to report and anchor the news. The news director there hired her on the spot when she interviewed, then told her to go home, think about (honest to God) how much she wanted the station to pay her, then come back and let him know on Monday. She could start whenever she wanted.

She started a few days later as weekend news anchor and weekday reporter. Overnight we became financially solid, we loved our new city of Boston, and we felt on top of the world. We were very much in love and happy in our careers.

Within a year, Selena was promoted to evening news anchor – the best job in television news – and I was developing a graduate program in journalism at Northeastern. All that would last for four years, and they were wonderful ones. We purchased our first home together, a lovely Victorian cape, in the nearby town of Winchester.

About four years later, however, Selena felt she'd had enough of the station's politics and intense, internal competitive pressures, so she decided to leave television and join me on the journalism faculty. Such a bold move was unheard of among the ranks of big-market television news professionals who let money, fame, and celebrity status muscle out everything else in their lives.

Some thought Selena had lost her mind in giving up a $200,000 salary for a $30,000 job teaching college. She was more than qualified academically for teaching, holding two master's degrees from the University of Chicago and the University of Missouri, and racking up several years of experience as a journalist.

After several months in the classroom, however, I could tell she was missing her anchoring career, and I witnessed what television celebrities are up against when they try for more balance in their lives and take a lower-profile job. It happened one afternoon as we were walking on a sidewalk in front of the Northeastern campus.

A woman was walking past us, then stopped as she saw Selena and said politely, "Excuse me, but weren't you once Selena Williams?"

Startled, Selena replied, "Er, I think I still am!"

It was then I realized a celebrity has two identities, one public and one private, and when she is no longer in the public eye, one of those identities dies, and part of the self-esteem dies with it.

So, I set about trying to get Selena back into television, serving as her agent and scouring the various broadcasting job sites. I came across an anchoring position at a Cleveland television station, and I sent Selena's audition tape and resume'. I heard back from the general manager within a few days, and not long after that, Selena and I were flying to Cleveland where she would do a formal interview and audition, and I would scout out teaching jobs at local colleges. We both struck pay dirt, as she was offered the prime-time news anchor slot, and I was offered a faculty slot at a nearby university.

What seemed to be a perfect arrangement, getting Selena back into TV in a less-stressful station that was ecstatic about having a top-caliber news anchor, would eventually prove otherwise. There we would find new and daunting stresses and strains that often occur in two-career marriages. I often wondered if I'd made the right decision in suggesting we leave Boston, but that *what-if* was fruitless to ponder.

In 1993 I received an offer to go back to Boston as chair of the Communication Studies Department at the prestigious Boston College, but Selena was understandably reluctant to leave her job and life in Cleveland. Fate intervened, and another Boston station reached out to her to lure her back to the city where she had made a name for herself. She agreed to go, mostly because she knew I wanted to, I believe. So, we resigned our positions, loaded up, and headed east again later in the year.

I've second-guessed that move many times since then, because a year later, Selena would lose her life on that city's streets. I had been so full of wanderlust, a trait that I had developed as a kid growing up in an Air Force town in Oklahoma where people were always going and coming from different parts of the country. As much as we loved each other, Selena was built to plant herself in one place, grow, and develop long-term friendships. But she gave that up to be with me, and it would cost her life.

Now, here I was in 1995, out in Arizona alone, deeply saddened, and headed to some unknown destination. The "forever" dream of our marriage had ended abruptly three months ago.

As I drove on through north toward Flagstaff, I could still feel her first touch in the library 17 years ago, and I would never forget that first date. I seriously doubted I would ever experience anything like either of them again. I had already told her ghost that I didn't think I had enough years left to find anyone I could love as much as I did her.

I felt utterly lost, I had no idea how this trip was going to help me find myself, but I also felt I had to continue the journey.

I was in the middle of one of the most iconic of western states, 2,500 miles and several cultures removed from my city of Boston and my faculty position at Boston College. I was graciously being granted a leave of absence from its ivy-covered campus to do exactly what I was doing on this Saturday afternoon: dealing with my grief. The past week, arduous and different as it was, deadened the pain for a while, but now it was coming back as I neared what would forever be a fateful intersection ahead.

I was driving north past some of those beautiful landscapes Dad had ever painted. In fact, he still was. At the time of my Arizona adventure, both Dad and Mom were hard at work with his artwork, creating and selling it. They were still out there on the western highways themselves somewhere, their travel trailer in tow, looking for the landscapes that would become Dad's newest paintings.

I realized I had inherited his wanderlust as well as his love of the West. But Dad had felt the weight of his family responsibility too much to act out his wanderlust, choosing instead to keep us all in the same town, the same home, and the same schools through our graduation. It wasn't until his retirement that he and Mom hit the open road with their newly acquired travel trailer, paint, and easel in the cargo hold.

As for me, nothing could keep me from moving around the country. I wasn't yet 50, and I had already lived and worked in six different cities, in five different states.

I scanned the desert, the multicolored mesas, and distant mountains that were all laid out around me as I pushed toward Flagstaff. Past that, who knew? I supposed I'd figure it out when the time came. The liberty to do that, as well as the endless openness of Arizona, all enhanced my feelings of – and love for – freedom. Or, at least, the *idea* of freedom. I was in a state of being free, yet finding that freedom problematic. When the Kris Kristofferson song, *Me and Bobby McGee* queued up on my CD player, the lyrics fit my mood perfectly. *"Freedom's just another word for nothing left to lose,"* Kris would croon in his slow, craggy voice.

And it was true: I was free to do whatever I wanted, but the price was losing the person I wanted to do it all *with*. Here I was, out on the open road both literally and figuratively, looking to anyone else like freedom personified. Yet across every mile of that long journey, I was hearing Kris sing of lost love.

I was a freaking mess.

3

The Superstitions

Sunset over the Superstition Mountains

This had been an adventurous week; I'll give it that. It was why I came out here to this rugged outback, looking forward to a challenge that would capture and require my near-constant attention. I had spent the past seven days on horseback in one of the wildest and most untamed places in America: Arizona's Superstition Mountains.

I had two Appaloosas assigned to me, and I had spent each day navigating narrow and often treacherous trails high above the canyons below, where a single slip could send you and your mounts sliding down the rocky canyon wall to an uncertain ending far below.

I was loving every minute of the ride, mostly because it was my version of a ropes course at a time I needed to feel self-reliant. And, of course, it also helped take my mind off my troubles. For the most part, anyway.

I was in a state where I would not have been surprised to pass John Wayne out riding one of his 17-hands-tall horses by the roadway. "Howdy, Pilgrim," he would say. About ten days ago, I had stopped off in Tombstone to soak up a sense of history at the famed OK Corral where the Earps shot it out with the Clantons and McLaurys.

Arizona *is* the West.

I have always loved long road trips because they give me a chance to go deep into thought about my future, and even come up with creative ideas and – sometimes – solutions to problems vexing me. I was open to all three on this cross-country tour from Boston to Phoenix.

Countless memories of the years with Selena were competing for my attention as they pushed, shoved, and maneuvered their way toward the front of a long line. Once there, they would await my reflection and interpretation, wondering how I could have prevented this tragic ending.

This reflective stream seemed to flow on to infinity. That's especially true for those images of the past year when it became harder for me to allay my fears that many other good-looking guys from the television news world would gladly take my place as the object of Selena's affection if somehow our marriage hit rough waters. The bits and pieces of evidence would just keep appearing, like occasional flakes of confetti falling from the sky.

That parade of images was akin to a full-scale assault by enemy troops against whom my senses and I were vastly outnumbered. Having lived in Texas and visited the Alamo, I had pictured the 200 brave Texans in that isolated mission, surrounded and attacked from all sides by 1,800 hardened soldiers of the Mexican Army led by General Santa Anna. The *Texicans* knew it was hopeless but, for many reasons, they still fought on until death.

It seemed that I had done the same thing in this war for a lasting love, probably needlessly, but such was my fear of losing the woman I loved dearly. I never dreamed that, if I did lose her, it would be because she died. Selena knew my fears, and I knew it must have hurt her that she couldn't convince me she wasn't going anywhere. I had just seen such scenarios play out with other celebrity couples we knew over the years. Then came her sudden death in Boston, she was gone, and our wonderful marriage was now over.

It was my love for Selena, and the pain over losing her, that would take a very long time fading.

After her funeral, however, my plan had been simple: to return to work at BC and bury myself in the responsibilities I had there. Or so I thought. After trying that for a couple months, and failing miserably to keep the grief at bay, I knew the time had come for me to get away from Boston.

I needed a break to sort things out.

I had been sitting in my office at Boston College, seemingly working through my department leadership tasks but inwardly working with grief from the love I had lost. It was then that I picked up a copy of *Outside* magazine I had just bought at a newsstand. *Outside* describes itself as, "the quintessential magazine to everything adventure-oriented. As one of the biggest outdoor publications the world over, this magazine is a one-stop source for everything outdoor related."

That's what I was looking for at this point in my life: a way out of my pain, and I had a feeling that taking to the outdoors in some far-off mountains might provide that.

I thumbed through its pages and came to the ads in the back of the book announcing getaway adventures. That's when I saw the notice of the Superstition Mountain trail ride in a few weeks. I picked up the phone and paid to join the expedition. My feeling was a cross-country road trip to a week in the wilderness might help clear my mind's cobwebs and put me on the road back to sanity.

The lure of Arizona, a state I hadn't spent much time in but one which my dad had always loved painting in his oils, was very strong at that moment. Boston was beautiful, but Boston held way too many painful memories for me now. Plus, it had been a while since I'd spent time on horseback, and I missed the experience after having owned two appaloosas when I lived in Texas and Missouri. In short, it all pointed me toward Apache Junction, Arizona, and the Superstition Mountains.

I resolved that day in February, 1995, to just flat get away. I approached my dean at BC about taking a paid leave, and I confided in him the reason for it. He was a compassionate man, readily understood, and told me to take as much time as I needed. A couple weeks away would do me good, he said, and told me to let him know if I needed more. As it turns out, I would need more. A lot more. In fact, although I didn't know it then, I would not be returning to Boston nor Boston College.

A couple weeks later, I was entering Arizona's Superstition Mountains. Originally called by their Spanish name of *Sierra de la Espuma* (Foam Mountains), the Superstitions are encircled by U.S. Route 60, on the south Arizona State 88 on the northwest and the Arizona 188 on the northeast. The mountains exist in a desert climate where the days are hot, and the nights can be downright cold. They are a utopia for wilderness lovers, and you have to take food and other provisions in with you because there are no stores nor gas stations, even if you owned a vehicle strong, rugged, and nimble enough to drive into the wilderness.

Although driving is allowed through parts of the area (but paved roads are a rarity), most travel is either by horse, or donkey, or on foot, and the complete trails can cover as many as sixty miles roundtrip. Motorcycles are allowed, but nothing short of a surprised rattlesnake shakes up a horse and rider more than a speeding and bounding motorcycle.

Several hiking and horseback riding trails snake through the mountains, and the one I took with three other riders began at Apache Junction, which is the main trailhead town of the wilderness area. It was there I met with my trail companions, and our group was small, indeed. There was the lead guide, Sam, and his partner, Curly. Their only paying customers on this trek were a spunky 30-something British woman named Janet, and me, just a tick away from 50. Janet and her husband were on a drive across America and, while he was spending the week at a Formula One racing fantasy camp, she was going to see the American west from horseback. They would rendezvous at the end of the week and return to England.

Sam and Curly had clearly planned for a larger trail-riding party, but the four other riders were all coming together, and they all canceled at the last minute, much to the chagrin of the partners. This expedition would wind up as a financial loss for them, but they kept their bargain with Janet and me, and the adventure was on. Sam's wife, Jane, was the outfitter for the trip. While Janet and I brought our own clothing, sleeping bags, and personal items that could fit on a backpack, Jane brought two horses for each of us and all the needed tack. While not rivaling the looks of a Kentucky Derby entry, these were the horses you wanted if you were going into this wilderness. They were calm, steady, and extremely sure-footed. But any horse would grow tired after three or four straight days on these steep trails, necessitating a change in mounts at mid-week.

Jane was also in charge of the food and tents. She would load all that into her 4x4 pickup and take it to pre-determined camping sites along the trail in the mountains. When we riders arrived in late afternoon, we would pitch our tents, water and feed the horses, take a brief rest, then dig into the dinners that Jane prepared. As darkness set in, the hot daytime temperatures began cooling and, within an hour, we were putting on jackets. High-desert nights can get flat out cold.

We riders were up early in the mornings, checking our mounts, feeding and watering them, then sitting down to one of Jane's delicious breakfasts. We packed up our gear, saddled up, and rode off onto the trail again to find the adventures awaiting us that day. The morning ride was more comfortable since the heat of the day hadn't yet reached its summit.

Communication with the outside world is tricky in these isolated mountains, and dead cell phones are often the norm. So, if you fall, break a bone, or get bitten by one of the 13 different species of rattlesnakes that populate the area, you may find it difficult to get help in time to do you much good. This is a mountain range where rattlesnakes far outnumber the humans passing through and, for that reason alone, First Aid kits are at the top of the survival list for those who enter the Superstition Mountains.

Our trail ride took place over the first week of March, just before the start of the official snake season which kicks off early that month. Unofficially – but too official for us – some rattlers were making an early appearance. I will never forget the time when Curly, who was not averse to impressing Janet, saw a rattler crossing our trail just ahead of us late one afternoon. He signaled us to stop, dismounted and, armed only with a lead rope from his horse, stalked into the tall grass after the venomous reptile. All we heard was one whack! of the heavy rope buckle, and then Curly comes out of the brush dangling a 6-foot dead rattlesnake from his right hand and holding the fatal lead rope in the other. His wide grin bespoke the pride of his achievement.

"Can't let these rattlers hang around the trail and cause trouble for the next unsuspecting horse and rider," he said.

He opened his saddlebag and dropped the dead snake in. But he wasn't through with it. It was late afternoon and we stopped shortly after that for the night. The first thing Curly did after dismounting was to open the saddlebag, remove the snake, pull out a knife from his scabbard and cut the snake open.

"It may sound strange to you guys," he said as he looked up, "but sometimes these snakes have another live snake inside them that they've devoured earlier in the day. Those snakes can crawl out and be just as deadly. So I always check the snakes I kill."

If Curly's intent was, indeed, to impress Janet and me, mission accomplished. Bizarre as moments like this were, they also worked the trick of keeping me alert on the trails and – just as important – took my mind off Selena so I could enjoy the rest of the ride.

Before leaving Boston, I had done some reading on this wilderness area, and what I found had convinced me that this was a perfect place for me to go get lost for a while and turn my attention to the challenges the mountains posed to its visitors. The Superstitions cover an area of 160,000 acres or 250 square miles and a maximum elevation of 6,266 feet at Mound Mountain on the far eastern side of the range.

These mountains were once home to the Apache, and some of the tribe's cliff dwellings are still there. I remember the day we found one, hollowed out a couple hundred years before, in a sandstone cliff above our trail. We took our mid-day rest and climbed up the cliff to the dwelling. Entering it, I found myself transported back to the days when this part of Arizona belonged to the Apaches and when life must have been much simpler before the Anglo-Europeans began moving in to "tame" the West. This was the country that the last of the free Apaches roamed under the defiant warrior Geronimo before even he could not continue with his remaining starving band of fewer than 50 warriors. So, he surrendered and lived out his long life as a reservation farmer in Florida and Oklahoma.

The mountain range lies in the middle of a larger federally desig-nated Superstition Wilderness Area, and it has many rock outcroppings that are the remnants of past volcanic eruptions. One of these is the rock formation called Weavers Needle, which sits just behind Super-stition Mountain itself, and it draws many rock-climbing enthusiasts throughout the year. Weavers Needle plays a key role in the legend of the Lost Dutchman's (Deutschman's) Gold Mine, named after German immigrant Jakob Waltz who, before dying in 1891, purportedly discov-ered a mother lode of gold near it, but didn't reveal its location until he reportedly confided in Julia Thomas, the owner of the boarding house who looked after him for his remaining years.

Waltz had been a miner at the Vulture Mine, and many believe he probably stole the gold from that mine's owner and made up the story of his own mine's discovery to turn suspicion away from his theft. Many mines have competed for the title of the Lost Dutchman's Mine, but none of the claims have been verified.

Another legend associated with the mountain range is believed by some Apaches who say that the hole that leads down to the "lower world" or hell, can be found in the Superstition Mountains. A part of that belief is that the strong winds blowing out of that hole are the probable cause of so many severe dust storms in that part of Arizona.

The Superstition Mountains are a good place to go get lost, and stories continue to circulate about those who did just that, ultimately disappearing. Many adventurers have come looking for the legendary Lost Dutchman's Mine, and some of those searchers' stories have ended in heartache and death. One story often told is of Adolph Ruth, an amateur explorer and treasure hunter who set out searching for the mine in the summer of 1931 and wound up making the gold mine into a national sensation. Ruth came into possession of a map that was purported to lead him to the lost mine.

Ignoring the advice of a local rancher who told him, "the area and the mines are cursed and full of devils," Ruth took off for a two-week trek into the mountains. He was never heard from again, although his skull, containing two bullet holes reportedly fired at point-blank range, was found some six months after he went missing. When the *Arizona Republic* broke the story, the legendary mines became a magnet for every adventurer who read the account.

Other disappearances and deaths would follow. One was a prospector named James A. Cravey, whose headless remains were found in the mid-1940s. Other tragedies would follow. In 2010 three Utah hikers (Curis Merworth, Ardean Charles, and Malcolm Meeks) were reported missing in the mountains as they, too, searched for the lost mine. A year later, searchers discovered the remains of three men, believed to be those Utah adventurers. Then, in 2012, the remains of Colorado treasure hunter Jesse Capen were found, wedged into a crevice. He had told others he was obsessed with finding the lost mine.

Were all these deaths really the result of a search for some lost mine, or did these men simply meet their fate at the hands of outlaws who are known to flee into these mountains, trying to escape the law? The question just adds to the tapestry of mysteries that engulf the aptly named Superstition Mountains. Add to this the reported screams, unnatural lights, and shadows of Apache warriors – and even bands of cannibals said to be roaming through the mountains – and you have the legend of the cursed Lost Dutchman's Mine. And that, of course, makes this whole mountain range more intriguing with each passing generation.

As for my small band of trail riders on this week in 1995, it all made for great campfire stories at night, where Curly would entertain us with his surprisingly good cowboy poetry. This was a genre unknown to me and, I dare say, to most other sojourners in the southwestern states. Although I had grown up in Oklahoma, I hadn't heard this kind of poetry before. That is, until I realized it's where some lyrics came from for country-western music. But in Arizona I discovered these rugged, rough-and-tumble outdoorsmen do, in fact, have a softer side that warms up to this form of artistry.

Cowboy poetry has even been institutionalized and, since 1985, its devotees have assembled in Elko, Nevada, for the National Cowboy Poetry Gathering. The art form is often known by poems that have been deemed classics by these cowboy poets. Three of the most beloved are *Tying Knots in the Devil's Tale, When They've Finished Shipping Cattle in the Fall,* and *Strawberry Roan.* All of these were eventually put to music, and famed western singer Mary Robbins had a hit with *Strawberry Roan,* a story known by most cowboys about a bucking bronco that refused to be ridden. This was the one our trail guide Curly regaled us with one night. It's a long one, but it winds up this way:

I lost my stirrups, I lost my hat,

I was pullin' at leather as blind as a bat
With a phenomenal jump he made a high dive
And set me a-winding up there through the sky.

I turned forty flips and came down to the earth
And sit there a-cussing the day of his birth

I know there's some ponies that I cannot ride
Some of them living, they haven't all died.
But I bet all money there's no man alive
That can ride Old Strawberry when he makes that high dive.

Curly was good at his delivery and intonation, and we all went to bed thoroughly impressed. Before going to sleep, each of us made sure we had a loaded gun near our bedrolls and that the flap of our tents was zippered shut – as if that would do much good if trouble arose in the form of mountain lions, wolves, or even some resourceful snakes.

For me personally, it was a whole week of stepping far outside my comfort zone and the familiarity of urban Boston. The adventure of riding the mountain trails aboard sure-footed mountain horses, the magnificent wilderness, and the perils that might exist around the next bend all made for a much-needed distraction from heartache and the pesky "why?" questions.

But they were patiently awaiting their return, and they would go unanswered for a long time to come.

4

⸚

Decision Time

Those questions were still haunting me after the trail ride as I drove north on I-17 past the signature saguaro cactus plants that adorn this part of the country. I had certainly encountered many of them on my journey through the Superstition Mountains, and I had the small wound scabs to prove it.

Inhabiting the same landscape as the saguaros are the "jumping" cholla cacti, and we had seen plenty of both on the trail ride. One thing I learned about both plants is that, while the needles don't actually *jump* out at you, they are so loosely attached to the arms of the plant that they will snag you even if you just lightly brush by. In the case of the chollas, their needles can latch on to you like fishhooks, penetrate your clothing, and are not the easiest things to remove.

I felt that was a pretty good analogy to my thorny thoughts of Selena. All I had to do was get close to them, and they would sense my presence and attach themselves like hooks. All while I was listening to the CD player churn out Joe Cocker's musical pleadings about the pain of walking away from love in his haunting ballad, *Letting Go:*

Take my fears away
Lift me high above the sky
I'm out here on a limb
Like a bird that's forgotten how to fly.

As usual, I was lost in thought as I approached Exit 171 and the I-40 crossing. From the immediate landscape stretched out on both sides, the western vista looked just like the eastern one, I couldn't see how it could make any difference at all which way I turned, or even if I should turn at all. I had not yet mapped out the rest of this magical mystery tour, which was my respite from reality.

I had a sense this had been a good idea, although I also knew there was a danger in dwelling too much in the past and wallowing in the grief. But these western states were a welcome change of scene from the places Selena and I had shared east of here, where the sight of even a street or a building could bring back instant thoughts of her.

I did not feel I was ready to return to Boston, and I was strongly considering turning west on I-40 and heading for California. Wasn't that what my predecessors from Oklahoma had done decades before to escape the Dust Bowl? And didn't it work for them? At least, eventually?

With the exit a few hundred yards away, though, I realized that turning east didn't necessarily mean I *had* to return to my life at Boston College. In between Arizona and Massachusetts was my native state of Oklahoma where Mom, Dad, and my big sister Elaine still lived. Within the span of the last couple miles, something in me equated returning to my roots with resetting my life. And maybe, surrounded by loved ones, childhood friends and familiarities, I could answer another question I found myself asking:

Am I okay as a person, or is there something inherently wrong with me –
perhaps some missing character link?

I was at Exit 171 now.

It was 11 a.m. on March 10, 1995.

I turned east. The sun was at my back now, and I was going home to Oklahoma. Maybe I would find clues to my future there.

5

Man in Motion

Journalist Anderson Cooper once noted in his biography that, as a world-trotting reporter, he sometimes felt as if he were a shark. The reason? Most sharks have to keep moving to stay alive. Their forward motion forces water in and across their gills, allowing them to breathe. Cooper felt the same way about his own life. He needed to be a man in motion.

Such has been my life, as well. I have chosen a life of movement and, as a result, have lived and worked all across the nation. Selena once said that I have made a hobby out of changing jobs every few years. That is true, although my career has always been filled with jobs in journalism, whether practicing it or teaching it. That constant motion has not always caused my resume' to resonate with employers, but it has made for an interesting life.

I had been on this particular stretch of I-40 twice before. Both those times were college road trips from Oklahoma to San Bernardino, California, and back again. My destination had been Arrowhead Springs which was, at that time, the international headquarters of a campus ministry I volunteered with at the University of Oklahoma. In my college years, I had wanted to go into the campus ministry, and I enjoyed being around others my age who were considering the same career.

After graduating OU, I spent three semesters at Dallas Theological Seminary and found ample evidence that my square peg of ambition wasn't fitting the round hole of the vocational ministry. I decided to give God a break and do something else.

I became a journalist, which was my major at OU. I likened that profession to the ministry in that both practitioners were chasing after the truth so they could pass it on to people who could use it, even though they might not want it.

After spending a decade as a reporter and editor for the *Daily Oklahoman* and *Dallas Morning News,* I returned to school for a Master's degree at Texas A&M, and the Ph.D. in Journalism at the University of Missouri.

I had also moved from right to left along the spiritual and ideological spectra. I was still trying to cling to the basics of Christianity (not always an easy job), but I found my *interpretations and applications* of those beliefs were changing. I had become, as the conservative right would say, a *liberal.* Living in Boston for almost a decade can do that for a man from Oklahoma, but so can critical thinking. So, while this drive east through Arizona and New Mexico might have been familiar, *I* was different from the guy who drove it back in the late sixties.

Travel can also do that for you. You take a trip or move out of state to a new job, and you think you're just going to have a change of address for a while. But what you find is that the new address winds up changing *you.* Maybe it's an incremental change, maybe it lasts forever; depends on where you go, what happens when you're there, and what resonates with you.

As a writer, I probably have paid a little more attention to the uniqueness of places I've seen, and I've turned around and written about them. Travel has always inspired me to write.

The fourteenth century explorer Ibn Battuta, often called the Islamic Marco Polo, once noted:

"Traveling: It leaves you speechless; then turns you into a storyteller."

Now, looking out over the vast New Mexico deserts and highlands, I recalled how much I have always loved traveling and what I discovered along the way.

Ever since I was a kid, I have often dreamed about being someplace else. All my life I've dealt with wanderlust, and I have spent time feeling guilty until I finally came to peace with it. Over the years I've admired friends who stayed home and built something, like George Bailey in *It's a Wonderful Life*. Instead, I've been like George's brother Harry who left home and family for other adventures.

It wasn't that I had an unhappy home life; it was very good and safe, and I felt secure in my parents' love. And it wasn't that we lived in a rundown shack with a leaky roof. Ours was a small middle-class home, and my sister and I each had our own bedrooms. It was fine. Still, all this satisfaction lived alongside my wanderlust, and it was my unbounded imagination -- often unleashed in the Narnia of my own bedroom -- that allowed me to go places and experience adventures. They may have been virtual trips, but they were better than anything Oculus has come up with in the VR age.

Case in point: my dad's catalogues from the Alaska Sleeping Bag Company. This was a now-defunct outdoor outfitters company that fell to the other giants of Eddie Bauer, Orvis, and L.L. Bean. But in the 60s, it was king. Every few months, this book would arrive in our mailbox, and my dad (apparently with his own case of wanderlust) would devour it and then turn it over to me.

The company's narrow name belied the fact that it featured so much more than sleeping bags. Inside were page after page of everything a hearty soul might need to live and survive an outdoor adventure in the Alaskan wilds. All manner of camping gear, clothing, survival gear, rifles, bows and arrows ... the works.

What could be better than grabbing my dog, Laddie, packing up all my neat gear from the Alaska Sleeping Bag Co., and heading off to the Klondike? It was the stuff my dreams were made of, and there were plenty of those dreams.

When I got my driver's license and went to college, my virtual trips began turning into real travels. Before I graduated, I had crisscrossed the Southwest three times, from Oklahoma to California and back, either by car, plane, or bus. Route 66 both the old and new versions) was becoming my new best friend, and those road trips would prove to be only the precursors of countless more in the future.

That would be particularly true of many drives across the Southwest. I got to know every wide spot in the "Mother Road" intimately. I considered having "Route 66" tattooed across my chest but opted instead for a good t-shirt saying the same thing. I still toy with the idea of, when life is over, having my ashes scattered out on a stretch of the road somewhere in New Mexico.

But it was my first trip to New York City that opened my eyes to the enlightenment that travel provides. I was teaching at the University of Missouri in 1978, when I agreed to drive 11 journalism students to a Society of Professional Journalists convention in Manhattan in a 12-passenger van. We were all excited about rubbing shoulders with A-list journalists and hearing from the bow-tied iconoclast Charles Osgood: the man CBS called the poet-laureate of radio news.

Our expectations were all exceeded, although the road trip itself hinted at disaster more than once. It doesn't take much imagination to realize what could go wrong with a mini-busload of 20-year-olds, especially when the spirited coeds in the group decided to strike up flirtatious chats over the CB radio with passing truckers, some of whom we'd run into at a couple truck stops down the line.

There's a *Halloween* movie in there somewhere.

About the City itself, New York was the first of my future destinations to actually send a jolt of electricity through every fiber of my being. Rubbernecking with my students out on Broadway, late at night after an out-of-body experience called *A Chorus Line,* I felt my life had just begun at age 32.

If I hadn't already become hooked on traveling, I was on this night.

Continuing to freelance my writing after I left the daily newsroom was a decision that boosted my frequent flyer miles as I chased off after stories far away. In 1985, I was on assignment covering the one-year anniversary of the aptly named Bhopal Disaster in India, which occurred on Dec. 2, 1984. That was when a Union Carbide pesticide plant exploded, sending toxic fumes into the air and ultimately killing upwards to 8,000 people and injuring another half-million.

I was doing a story for *Nieman Reports*, the Harvard-based publication for the Nieman Foundation which honors top journalists, and Selena was along with me on the trip. I was asked to interview journalists around India on how that disaster was covered. Part of my journey took me into Sikh regions where violent outbreaks had occurred, and I discovered halfway through my three-week trip that the Indian government was keeping tabs on me. I never found out why, although some people I encountered thought I was with the CIA.

I remember the night I realized that this level of suspicion was real. My host in Chandigarh – a Sikh of some importance in the region – had asked me to deliver a talk on American journalism to an area journalistic society. When Selena and I arrived, we found the hall packed and were told most of them were reporters and editors. I took the dais, and Selena sat next to me. Since she was helping me do the story I came for, she wanted to jot down some of the interaction I planned to have with the journalists in the room.

I delivered a few remarks about press freedom in America, and then I asked the audience to describe their challenges with press freedom in India. But instead of a rush to respond from those gathered, a silence fell over the room for what seemed like a few minutes until my host got up and made and made an observation related to my question.

As he was speaking, however, another man got up and rushed the stage where Selena and I were. He raced toward her and the notepad she had in her lap, grabbed it, and ran off as quickly as he had come. He ran completely out of the hall with the notepad, and two of the men in the audience got up and chased after him.

Again, silence fell across the room until our host came up on stage and apologized profusely to Selena and me, and then to the audience, and adjourned the meeting.

Coming over to us afterward, the host told us, "I am so very sorry and embarrassed. One of the men who chased the thief caught him and retrieved your notebook," handing it to Selena "You see, he thought you were with the CIA and that you were spying on us and planned to give your notes to our country's security forces."

Although India's Constitution allows for press freedom, it was then (and I suppose still is) a right that the government can suspend in a time of crisis, and there was plenty of tension at the time between the Sikhs and Hindus in India.

When we left Chandigarh, we took a bus trip through the treacherous terrain of northern India to the city of Shimla, nestled into the foothills of the Himalayas. I recall vividly thinking, as our bus driver was making harrowing hairpin turns a few thousand feet up, that this might be one trip I'd never return from. I was able to catch my breath for only a minute when our bus arrived in Shimla near midnight.

As the overhead lights went on in our packed bus, we were mobbed by a horde of hungry hands and arms lowering our windows and reaching inside for any handouts we might have. Then the driver opened the door, and we were thrust out into this throng to fend for ourselves.

Fortunately, the natives were friendly, and we wound up enjoying ourselves immensely over the next few days, which happened to be Christmas week. Riding a yak up a mountain trail proved interesting, as did sharing beers with three Russian soldiers on a wintry night.

In 1988 and 1992, I made two trips to Asia. The first was to Seoul to the Summer Olympics, and the second was to Bangkok where I had accepted another freelance reporting assignment. There was trouble in that part of the world, and my job was to try and make sense of it for the magazine's readers.

As I drove, I scrolled over my past travels – and knowing more lie ahead – I thought of poets like TS Eliot who wrote:

"Only those who risk going too far can possibly find out how far one can go."

I knew I would spend the rest of my life finding that out.

For the immediate moment, however, I was thinking of how the terrain and landscape of eastern Arizona and western New Mexico are exactly the same, yet it's not hard to tell when you pass into the Land of Enchantment on I-40. That's because of the large red rock cliff dwellings of the Navajo you pass on the north side of the interstate right after you cross the New Mexico border.

Of course, right below those reminders of centuries past sit the icons of the 20th century: souvenir stores, a diner, a reptile attraction, and a gas station. The love of history itself is not enough of a reason for most travelers to stop, unless you can pick up a rubber snake and cap pistols for the kids, and a Navajo dream catcher to hang in the kitchen window.

As I drove east through the Southwest, these were the thoughts that made the miles fly by. They were agonizing at times, enlightening at others, but mostly they were all-consuming. If there were answers to my questions of life and sudden death, I knew they wouldn't be coming soon; possibly not until I lost the need or desire to even ask them anymore.

Much like the border crossing from Arizona to New Mexico, you cannot tell from the endless flatlands when you cross from New Mexico into the Texas panhandle. If you've lived in Texas, as I had years before, you do know there are probably more rattlesnakes here than in New Mexico.

As if I needed any more reminders of snakes after Arizona, I did cut my rest stop picnic short when my peripheral vision caught a rattler about to come out from his hole in the ground under the table, when he saw me and jerked his head back underground.

Lunch was over for me, and I was back in my Rodeo SUV and on the road again. One last night on the road, in Amarillo, and then I'd be home in Oklahoma the next day.

A few weeks after that, I would encounter a challenge that made the Superstition Mountains look like a Sunday afternoon walk in the park.

6

Oklahoma

If you're a Route 66 traveler headed east and your destination is Oklahoma City, you know that when you hit Amarillo, you're only three hours away. I felt peace about going back to the place I grew up and still called home. The feeling was growing in me that, somehow, I could become re-centered by going back to where my memories of childhood began. Maybe, in those memories, I could discover a little more about myself as I mulled over a life I was too busy living at the time to analyze.

I've always considered Oklahoma to be my native state, even though I was born in Columbus, Ohio, before my family moved west exactly 60 years after the state was opened to settlers in the famous land run of 1889. The state still celebrated *89er Day*, every April 22 in fact, and I always loved it as a kid. Each and every town in Oklahoma would return to its wild west roots that day, donning western gear and joining family and friends at giant cookouts and carnival midways. Also known as the 89er Festival, its epicenter is the town of Guthrie, which was the state's first capital before some political scalawags stole the state seal and moved it to Oklahoma City.

The festival is held each year to commemorate the opening of the

"Unassigned Lands." This was the name the federal government gave to 1.8 million acres of land that bordered reservations of the Chickasaw, Cheyenne, Arapaho, Shawnee, Sac & Fox, Iowa, Pawnee and Potawatomi reservations). Before it became the state of Oklahoma in 1907, it was commonly known as Indian Territory where these tribes lived. "Oklahoma," in fact, is the Choctaw word for "red people." As the westward movement picked up steam, this large strip of central Oklahoma was assigned to non-Indian settlement by 1889.

Local 89er Day festivals are still held in various towns and cities contained within the historic boundaries of these Unassigned Lands.

One of those celebrations I remember, and which my dad wished he could have forgotten, took place up our Lockheed Drive at Jarman Junior High School. I was about 7 or 8 at the time and, after we downed a plate of beef ribs, Dad took me to the carnival games where he lovingly tried to shoot enough plastic ducks to win me a huge Teddy bear. I really wanted that bear and I kept pleading with Dad to buy another ticket, fire off a few more shots, and win me the stuffed animal.

This went on until Dad was almost broke, whereupon he himself began pleading with the vendor to just let him *buy the damn bear!* The guy relented, knowing he had already made three times what the bear was worth in tickets, and sold Dad the bear for another $5. I was happy, but Dad just took me home and went to bed without saying another word.

After spending a restful night in Amarillo, I arose early that next morning to finish the final leg of this journey. When I crossed the state line into Oklahoma, moving from one vast prairie into another, I did feel I was home. It's odd how a simple geographic boundary can make you feel that way, but if it's your home state's boundary, it does. Selena once told me early in our relationship that she found little of interest the first time she drove across Oklahoma on her trip from Seattle to Columbia Missouri.

"It's so flat, and it just goes on forever!" she said.

I agree with that, but it is that vastness that has always spoken of endless possibilities to me, and I love it. Every time I drive through this stretch of western Oklahoma, I'm reminded that a lot of successful people have started out their lives here. Astronauts Tom Stafford, who grew up in Weatherford, is one; Roger Brady, who rose to the rank of four-star general in the Air Force, spent his earlier years in Elk City. And, in the entertainment world, singer Roger Miller was from the small town of Erick, with a population only 991.

I have never passed by Erick on I-40 without exiting and cruising its Main Street, stopping to look in the windows of the Roger Miller Museum. That Museum, by the way, is located at the intersection of Sheb Wooley Street, so named for the singer/actor who had a massive hit in the 1950s with the novelty song, *Flying Purple People Eater*. He would become a regular trail drover named Pete on the hit series, *Rawhide* in the 1960s, alongside Clint Eastwood's Rowdy Yates. So, Erick is always a fun walk back through time and the heroes of my childhood years.

I thought about all the other entertainers who began their lives and careers in Oklahoma, too. Those include Vince Gill, Reba McIntire, Garth Brooks, Toby Keith, Blake Shelton, and Carrie Underwood, among others. This state knows how to line dance, for sure.

I was passing the skyline of Oklahoma City now, moving on to the southeastern suburb of Midwest City, which was my destination. My folks still lived in the home I grew up in at 301 E. Lockheed Drive. My street was in the city's "original mile," and the half century of its age was starting to tell on the neighborhoods.

The town's claim to fame is Tinker Air Force Base, the largest military aircraft maintenance facility in the country. In fact, Tinker was the reason there *is* a Midwest City in the first place. The two were born at the same time in 1942, and grew up together. Many Midwest City residents worked and served there, and a lot of us kids used their athletic facilities because of our parents' connection to the base. I lifeguard at the NCO swimming pool one summer in college.

As I pulled into the driveway at 301, Mom and Dad were glad to see me and to have me back in my old bedroom for at least awhile. They knew I needed some TLC but also didn't need to be crowded, and it was enough for me just to be surrounded by their love. This home I grew up in was always a safe haven for me, and I loved hanging out here, even in those teenage years when a spirit of rebellion and the generation gap kept other teens from embracing home life.

I told Mom and Dad what I was going through with Selena's sudden death, and they just listened and offered me their support. I also told them of my recent adventure in the Superstition Mountains, and they were glad I finally had a chance to live my childhood dream of becoming a cowboy, even if it was just for a week.

Lucas C. and Irene Jarrett always tried their absolute best to be the parents my sister Elaine and I needed. Like all parents, they made a few mistakes along the way, but my sister and I knew they were always trying hard, and their efforts paid off in raising two secure kids, sending them to college, and putting them on their paths to success.

Over the years, I've realized how impossible it is to be everything your child needs. Parenting is the toughest jobs on the planet. The best you can do is to try and do your best, which is what both Mom and Dad did with Elaine and me.

The years have only caused me to appreciate my mother more than ever before, and I had entered that phase of thanksgiving by the time I decided to come home and let Mom and Dad help re-center me. I think I realized that I could learn a lot from remembering what a fighter and achiever my mother really was. All I had to do was think back on all the things she did for us and for her own self-fulfillment when Dad moved us all to Midwest City back in 1949.

One of the memories Mom had kept in my room was a photo from 1950 of me and some of my friends in the inaugural class of her very own Jack & Jill Pre-school. Now *there's* a whole slew of memories, and Mom was at the center of them all.

One thing she used to tell me when things weren't going well was, "Bad beginnings make for good endings," Son. As I realized I was entering a new phase of my life and that the beginning was less than spectacular, her message was a ray of hope. I know Mom was pulling from her own life experiences when she made those declarations, and that added credibility to the statement for me. It wasn't just an abstract concept to her.

Mom's mom was a loving woman named Cecelia who had also seen her ups and downs. She was divorced from a shady kind of character who Mom never talked about, in a time when you didn't talk about divorce itself either. Grandma Cecelia made the best of what was left for her and her two daughters, and she had this whimsical impulsive streak that sometimes got her into trouble and made the family finances shaky. Like the time she bought a snazzy and pricey new car right off the auto show platform, even though she didn't drive. Or the time she won a jackpot, then lost it.

I trace my own impulsiveness to the tree branch named Cecelia. I mean, we gotta blame *somebody* for our flaws, right?

Through it all and because of her rock-solid determination, Mom landed on her feet in life. She did it again, and again, and again, even threatening to defy gravity and live forever. She almost made it, if you count her 103 years as an effective protest of death.

In 1949, Dad moved us all from Columbus to Midwest City, Oklahoma, a town that had been an uninhabited wheat field seven years earlier. I was 3, Elaine was 5, and Mom faced the task of raising us in a small rented duplex with two bedrooms, driving a one-star used car whose tires needed filling three times a week. Within a year, we moved to a three-bedroom brick home of our own and -- a year after that -- Mom had implemented a vision she'd had of starting a pre-school, which was not only Midwest City's first, but also the first one with a structured curriculum in the entire area. She named it Jack & Jill Preschool, after the nursery rhyme, and planted it in the back den of our already-small 1,200 square-foot home. It was a rough start, but it became a wonderful success.

In Midwest City, Mom saw a town with this big Air Force base and a burgeoning population with a lot of families and small kids. While some entrepreneurs might have just envisioned a day care center, Mom's vision was greater. She built a school that would be the first step of a structured educational journey that would take its students as far as they wanted to go. She planned Jack & Jill carefully, worked out a deal with Dowling's (a major educational materials supplier in nearby Oklahoma City), hired two teachers, built the curriculum, did all the marketing and recruiting of students, bought a used "woody" station wagon, set up a pickup and delivery system for the students, and began teaching everything from spelling, to basic math, music, and art. Our backyard became the playground for recess, complete with all the climbing, sliding, and swinging paraphernalia.

If all that wasn't enough, J&J had two stage productions each year, held at a local elementary school, and each year ended with a commencement program complete with caps, gowns, diplomas, and scrapbooks of students' accumulated work.

My sister was already in first grade, but I became one of J&J's first recruits, a reluctant student who would wind up staying in school through a Ph.D. program and ultimately making a career of higher education myself. But I was only one of many success stories that came through Jack & Jill. My sister graduated from college as well, and went on to her own career in teaching and co-founded a thriving home school business after retiring. In fact, most of Mom's students would go on to college and many wound up in professional careers. Over the years as I've gone back to town, I keep bumping into former J&J alums. At Mom's funeral a few years ago, four or five people came up to greet me and let me know they had been Mom's students.

Nothing lasts forever, though, and in the late 1950s Mom received notice from the city stating that Jack & Jill was in violation of city zoning laws. Our street, Lockheed Drive, was not zoned for business, and some neighbor had made a complaint. Mom could have fought it and won, but she felt it was time she devoted more time to her own kids, so she closed the school voluntarily, much to the dismay of many families in town.

I remember those two years when Mom was unemployed and doted on Elaine and me, probably spoiling us in the process but happily so. I recall my pastor saying once, "Isn't it about time we realized that the best gift we can give *is time*?" I know Mom knew that, and she acted on it.

Still, Mom was a woman of action and a couple years later she was chasing a new venture: going to work for the Air Force. By this time, 1960, Midwest City had grown to about 40,000 residents, and Tinker Field was the largest military aircraft maintenance facility in the country with a huge payroll. Mom had worked for the government earlier in life, so that gave her an inside track to being hired, but she first had to take and pass an exhaustive Civil Service Exam, for which she would need to study long and hard. This she did over a period of months. Sadly, she failed to pass the test. But again her determination and never-say-die spirit took over, and she took the test again. Same result. Once more into the breach, she passed it a month or so later on the third try.

Mom went to work at Tinker in the medical records division, and I remember the mammoth building she was ensconced in. It has the government-gray name of Building 3001, and was built to withstand a nuclear attack. How appropriate for Mom, I remember thinking, because that's how she's built, too.

Thus began Mom's second career and, before it ended some 15 years later, she had risen in the ranks to a GS 13, the civilian equivalent of a Lieutenant Colonel on the military side.

When she retired, Mom helped Dad co-found and run a series of galleries called Artisans 9 in Oklahoma City and Norman. She was so dedicated about keeping Dad's artwork secure after hours, that she kept a cot and a baseball bat in the storeroom of one gallery and slept there on occasional nights to take a swing or two at any late-night thieves. Did it matter that she was in her 80s and might not be able to finish what she started with the miscreants?

Hell, no.

After all, *"Bad beginnings make for good endings, Son."*

Maybe these memories were closer to the surface with me than I realized as I made my decision to come back to my roots and hang out with Mom and Dad for a while. Maybe I realized I could use some more of Mom's grounded wisdom as I searched for a way forward. In any event, I was glad I was home.

It was also during this visit home that I realized what an influence my dad was in my life, as well as Mom. For while she was, by all appearances, the dominant parent in the family, Dad's lower profile had a quieter way of influencing me.

My dad and I shared the same name of Lucas Calvin Jarrett (he was the junior and I was the third), and we both served in the Navy, but since his passing I've realized we shared so much more in common. I only wish I had recognized it while he was still alive; it would have helped make us closer than we were.

Although Dad was in the communication business, as am I, he wasn't much of a talker, at least when it came to handing out life lessons. Neither is his son. But his actions have come to speak loudly to me. I suppose my own two sons would say the same thing about me. Funny now that modeling influence works out.

In several nonverbal ways, Dad taught me that actions do speak louder than words. He was a kind man who sacrificed for Elaine and me, and he also had this sweet habit of being kind to strangers in times of stress. One image stands out in my mind more than any other I can easily recall about Dad, and I recounted it when I spoke at his funeral. It was on a hot summer day in Oklahoma, and Dad had taken Mom, Elaine, and me to the local Dairy Queen.

Outings like this didn't occur everyday for our family, because this was a time earlier in his career when money was tight around the house. We had all placed our orders and were already enjoying them at a picnic table as Dad waited to pay at the DQ window. As he was walking over to us, a little boy who had just bought his own double-dip cone tripped on the way to his bike. Both he and his cone hit the pavement at the same time, the ice cream starting to melt instantly on the hot blacktop. The boy began to cry over his lost treat. Dad saw and heard the whole thing, and then he went over to help him get up. Then he walked back to the DQ window to place another order.

"One double-dip cone, please," Dad told the server.

He laid down the last of his money, took the cone and walked back over to the boy who was up and drying his tears. His expression turned instantly to a broad, ear-to-ear smile as he began downing his new cone.

"Thank you, Mister!" he said, between licks.

"You're welcome, Son. Be careful with that one!" Dad replied.

Then Dad walked over to our table, sat down, and ate his own ice cream in silence.

I don't ever remember being more impressed with my father than I was at that moment, on that hot summer day at the Dairy Queen. I began to realize what a single moment in time could accomplish. A father could teach his son the biggest lessons in life when he doesn't even realize his son is watching what he's doing. And that action doesn't have to be dramatic or monumental to have its effect. Dad was every bit the hero to me for simply helping a kid in need who was a total stranger to him.

Such lessons don't take preaching or require a planned, articulate speech. In fact, I remember only one such planned talk that Dad gave me. It came when I was 21 and Dad was driving me to Will Rogers World Airport in Oklahoma City, where I was flying to Los Angeles. I was starting a three-month midshipman summer cruise aboard a Naval destroyer based in Long Beach. I could tell Dad had something to say and that it was a hard thing for him to blurt out. So I just sat quietly as we drove and waited for it to come. For his part, Dad waited until we entered the airport parking lot to unload it.

"Son," he began, "You're headed to the Navy and you will be in a lot or ports. Just remember that there are two kinds of women in this world, and you want to make sure you don't get mixed up with the wrong kind."

I waited to say anything, figuring there must be more to come. There wasn't. Dad was finished with his speech.

"Thanks, Dad," I finally said. "I will remember that."

What I didn't say is that I'd already figured that much out. Quite awhile back, actually. I'd already met both kinds, dated both kinds, and even a couple other kinds that Dad didn't mention. But I appreciated his concern, and I knew it wasn't an easy thing for him to say.

Over the decades since, that memory has always brought a smile to my face. But it's the image of Dad's helping the kid at the Dairy Queen that has left me feeling warm all over.

Dad was a wordsmith who plied his skill at the head of public relations for a legendary Oklahoma City television station, WKY, now KFOR. It was Dad who often looked over my own early attempts at writing, be they my English homework or my stabs at creative writing. These usually took for the form of short stories I would write, usually about a dog in the wilderness. So, my love of writing could clearly be traced back to Dad who was really my first editor in life.

But that wasn't the entirety of his legacy; not by a long shot. As I looked around my bedroom, my gaze fixed on the northwest corner where I could still visualize the photographic darkroom I had set up and used for years in my teenage years. I had draped the corner off from daylight and, behind those heavy black curtains, I worked my magic with the film tank, enlarger, photo paper, and chemical-filled trays. Dad was responsible for that and for my hobby of photography. He had a darkroom before I did, and it was out in the detached garage.

When I was around 12, Dad bought me a camera and opened the darkroom to me. I learned the mysteries of chemical photography through him and, when we tore the garage down to build a new one, I moved the darkroom into my bedroom. I even found a way to make some spending money from photography by taking pictures of expensive homes in town, printing them out on post-card photo paper, and selling them to the owners of those homes.

My writing also took a useful form when I went to work for my high school newspaper as a photojournalist, *The Bomber Beam*. Thus were the seeds of my journalistic career planted, and those seeds blossomed into majoring in journalism at OU and then moving on into a newspaper career, authoring some 17 books and then teaching college journalism. So, just as Dad had blended his skill in writing with his love of painting,

I would blend my writing with my photography, and they would be my lifelong companions.

I felt secure as a child and teen growing up in my family, and a big part of that was my sister Elaine, who put up with her little brother in very patient ways and who became a role model for me when I got to high school. Elaine was a senior when I was a sophomore, and I saw how someone could be so popular for the right reason: just being a caring and outgoing person. Of course, it didn't hurt that she had plenty of talent as a musician and school thespian. But she never purposely sought out popularity; it just accrued to her naturally because she was such a fine friend and student. She was so popular, in fact, that she was voted a runner-up in the annual "Miss MCHS" (Midwest City High School) Pageant. Elaine would go on to college at the University of Oklahoma, return to Midwest City to teach at Jarman Junior High School and Choctaw High School, and have a long and happy marriage to a Baptist minister.

As an adult, I have never taken for granted the influences that Mom, Dad, and Elaine had on me. I felt, at least for this brief moment of time, I had come to a safe place; I had found the clutch that would allow me to shift gears and move on to my next chapter in life.

7

In My Room of Magic

I had come home to get back to my roots. I wanted to remind myself of who I was, and why, by immersing myself in a familiar place and important people from my formative years. I felt that would help me answer the question of what to do at this stage in life. So far, my plan seemed to be working, although that last question would not be answered for some time to come.

I found that spending a week in my boyhood bedroom in Oklahoma was peaceful, but also something of a time warp. Many times I've called this room my "magic room" because it was often where my imagination and inventiveness took flight. Most of the time, that was a good thing; sometimes not. As I looked around the room, which had been reconverted to its original bedroom form after I went off to college and Mom made it her sewing room, I found artifacts that reminded me of the experiences I had here.

In many ways, my imagination took root and thrived in my room, much like the Beach Boys sang in their song of that name. Brian Wilson, who with Gary Usher wrote *In my Room*, often told friends that his room was his whole world as a kid. "I had a room, and I thought of it as my kingdom," Wilson would say. later "And I wrote in that song that you're not afraid when you're in your room." In part, the song says it was a place for him to:

Do my dreaming
and my scheming ...

And I did plenty of both in that room, all the way through high school.

In this room, I wrote, I read, I rid the Old West of all the bad guys with my cap pistol gun fights, I ran my electric train, I created magic in my makeshift photo darkroom, and I dreamed of the cute red-headed girl down my Lockheed Drive.

And, speaking of schemes, I hatched plenty of them. I even tried to permanently check myself out of the entire school district in the 9th grade. It was a plan that worked for awhile until reality set in and I was confronting the grown-ups of the school who had discovered my plan and scuttled it. Then, instead of tossing me out on their own, they gave me another chance ... along with a heavy dose of counseling. I have one particular teacher, Jessel V. Williams, to thank for seeing something in me worth saving. He worked with me until I managed to ace my most difficult subject -- Algebra -- allowing me to stay in school.

The grown-ups' plan proved more effective than mine in the long run and, thanks to the unmerited grace of Mom, Dad, the school counselor, principal, and Mr. Williams, I managed somehow to graduate from that 9th grade year at Jarman and move on to high school, where life improved greatly. Gone were the three in-between years of child and young adult and the complex unease that came with them.

My sister Elaine, a senior as I entered the sophomore year, helped me through the transition and it was great having her at the same school. She later motivated me to go on to college, promising that she could introduce me to plenty of coeds since she was now working as a counselor in a freshman women's dorm. That promise came true, although to this day I blush when I tell my own students that I went to college to get – not an education – but girls.

I suppose, somewhere in heaven the voices of Mom and Dad are sighing, *"Whatever works."*

The irony is that, after spending so much time hating school so much, I went on to the University of Oklahoma, graduated, and then kept on going with an M.A. at Texas A&M and a Ph.D. at the University of Missouri. I went to work as a writer and, for the past four decades, I've been a university professor, retiring last year as professor emeritus at a private California university. And my discipline? Journalism, of course.

I often think about how many switchbacks form the road of life as I ponder those curious days home alone writing fiction and fake notes to the principal, and how they were my springboard into an adult life of writing non-fiction.

So far as I know, none of my books has contained a single lie.

So here I was, amid these bedroom memories that, collectively said, *"This is who you are, Lucas Jarrett."* And, since my reason for coming home was to rediscover that, it was a worthwhile stop. Still, as the song goes, *"Good morning yesterday, you wake up and time has slipped away ..."* Admittedly, I am glad those junior high years are gone. Whatever emotional state I found myself in now, I was in better shape going forward than if that crazy teenage Luke would have had his own way in dumping school in the 9th grade.

I was starting to regain some self-confidence by simply remembering how I had survived earlier traumas. But one inner detractor was still with me, even as an adult: self-doubt. I had been making good progress, however, thanks to my professional career, but having Selena leave me created a huge vacuum in my life, taking my sure-footedness along with it. While in my childhood home, I reflected on how I had dealt with self-doubt when I was younger.

As a teen, I discounted myself in comparison to other school kids who always seem to be more popular. It wasn't that I wanted to strive for popularity – that always seemed more work than it was worth – and I did find my comfort zone in my relatively independent world of tackling hobbies and spending my free time as I wanted to. I had my photography, and my occasional creative writing projects, and I loved playing with my collie, Laddie. It seemed that, on most days, I preferred just being alone and doing what I wanted to do. That changed somewhat, however, when I discovered girls and took my first forays into dating in my junior year of high school.

The very first girl I targeted was Margaret Palmer, a lively blonde, blue-eyed majorette in the band who occupied most of my thoughts from the first day I met her in our CYO class at the First Christian Church. My self-doubt, however, kept me reticent about asking her out (as was usually the case with the popular girls in school), but she seemed to be taking interest in me, so that emboldened me.

Alas, this budding romance ended quickly, however, when I discovered I had a rival in the form of the Junior Class president whom she fell for instantly. I was crushed emotionally, though, and stayed that way for a couple months at the failure of my first-time love venture. She and I would later emerge as lifelong friends, but the failed romance had only convinced me that I wasn't a good enough prospect for the popular girls at school.

So, I shifted my sights to the girls who – like me – tended to avoid the spotlight of popularity and just enjoy being who they were. It would not be until college, after a few more successful adventures in dating, that I began to build a new confidence and a feeling that I was as interesting as any other guy and had a lot to offer any young woman who interested me.

In many ways, I suppose my later success in winning Selena's love in Missouri represented my achievement in beating back my demon of self-doubt. When I met her, I vowed to ignore that voice of negativity and push straight ahead in my pursuit of the woman any man at the University of Missouri would have dreamed of having. Fantasy or not, I was going to marry Selena. Then, sooner rather than later, fantasy became a reality.

Shortly thereafter, I received my doctorate and a teaching post at a college in Boston, while Selena became the evening news anchor at a large television station there and, in a short time, the toast of the town.

I now had what so many other men wanted, and I was fulfilled both personally and professionally. My dreams had come true, and anything seemed possible. These were new and unprecedented feelings for me, and I accepted them without questioning my good fortune.

Now, back in my hometown 15 years later, my dream life had imploded. The love of my life had died, I had taken a leave of absence from Boston College, and I wasn't sure I wanted to return to that famed school, or teaching or even life itself.

I spent several days driving around past some old haunts, old girlfriends' homes, and past my high school – I must have done that a dozen times – and visiting with my big sister. She and I have always been close and, when it was time for tears, they flowed in those visits. I owe Elaine so much in life. She has always known me so well, and it was she who knew the buttons to push to get me to agree to go to college.

In college, my fight with self-confidence continued throughout my freshman year, and I wondered if I had made a mistake in going to college at all. I vividly recall one evening while visiting my parents when I candidly told Mom, "You know, I was watching some seniors yesterday on campus and I wondered to myself, how in the world am I ever going to even get past this year in school, let alone reach my senior year."

What I began discovering, however, was the wisdom of a saying by actor Woody Allen who said that most of the success in life comes from just showing up. So that's what I did. Day after day, week after week, I showed up where I was supposed to be. In so doing, I made it to my sophomore year, then became a junior, then a senior, then graduated.

From that point on, I found myself hooked on learning and satisfying inner curiosities. That addiction led me into journalism and then graduate school and teaching.

As I reflected on this during my stay at home, my confidence grew, and I knew I still had some gas left in my tank. I would need all of it in the years to come.

8

The Journalist in Me

This town I grew up in -- this Midwest City, named for the Midwest Air Depot (now Tinker AFB) -- was a young, brash place when my family moved there in 1949. Only seven years old, the town was all laid out before it was built, and it was designed for young families with kids.

In elementary school, there were two choices in town when I was there. One was Eastside Elementary, and the other was Westside. The town had two other pre-existing elementaries, Sooner and Soldier Creek, but they were on the outer borders of the townand drew a lot of students from outlying neighborhoods and villages.

East Lockheed Drive was the dividing line for kids going to Eastside and Westside. I lived on the north side of Lockheed, so I went to Westside Elementary. My best friend Marcus DeHart lived just across from me on Lockheed, so he went to Eastside.

I've often wondered if I had lived on his side and gone to Eastside, whether I would have chosen writing as my career or chosen another path. That question may sound like a non sequitur (how could a career choice depend on what side of the street you grew up on?), but here's why I ask it: Each day, Markey would walk east to school, while I walked west. It was only a four-block stroll to school, but my route took me right through the city hall plaza. In that plaza were city hall, the fire station, the police station, *and* the library.

Now, maybe had I been prone to stop and chat each day with the firefighters, I might have developed enough interest to fight fires for a living; had I stopped to talk with the police desk sergeant, would I have become a cop? But I didn't. Instead, my regular afternoon stops on the way home from school were to the public library.

It was there that I developed an intense interest in reading. I clearly remember reading most of Walter Farley's *Black Stallion* books (*The Black Stallion, The Black Stallion Returns, Son of the Black Stallion, the Island Stallion, etc., etc.*) and I also remember being enthralled by Jack London books, especially *The Call of the Wild* and *White Fang*. But I also loved reading biographies, especially of early Western figure like Wyatt Earp. Buffalo Bill Cody, and Wild Bill Hickock. And this was all while I was still in grade school.

It wasn't long before I tried my hand at writing my own stories, not surprisingly about dogs, horses, and wilderness adventures. While some of this growing passion for reading and writing was undoubtedly fueled by the fun way of learning my mom introduced in her Jack & Jill Preschool, and while some was inspired by my dad's creativity as a writer and sketch artist, the Midwest City Public Library had even more to do with it.

If I had needed to go out of my way to get to that library, however, I may or may not have troubled myself in doing it. After all, I did know that reading took some focused mental energy while playing sandlot baseball or catching crawdads at the creek did not. But it was just so darn easy and fun to stop at the library on my way home from school and, once my fuse for reading and learning had been lit, there was on snuffing it out.

In later years, my mother made it her avocation to assemble scrapbooks of the work Elaine and I had done and of the experiences we'd had in our earlier years. Over the years, those books have become very meaningful to me, and I will always appreciate this labor of love that

Mom carried out. As I sat in my boyhood room, pouring over a couple of those scrapbooks containing collections of my earliest news and feature stories, I recalled how zany my early years as a journalist were and how my whole career may have begun on a day when I fell out of my chair in Mrs. Householder's high school journalism class.

It was November, 1963, and I was a high school senior in her class, leaning my chair backwards against a doorway and daydreaming about being the next Richard Harding Davis, a famous journalistic adventurer of bygone days. Suddenly, the tilt proved too much for the chair as its rear legs shot forward across the slick tile floor. My body went in the opposite direction, and I reached out frantically for the door jamb where the ring on my right finger caught on the metal plate as I was continuing my downward descent to the floor.

I lost most of that ring finger just before my butt slammed against the unforgiving tile. My right hand was still outstretched against the lock plate that the ring had snagged, cutting through skin, tissue, sinew, and bone. Blood dripped from the door frame, and the memory of the remaining bit of finger still attached to my hand is a hard one to forget. And today, six decades later, that finger still stings if I rap it against anything hard.

As the pain shot through my hand, a question shot through my head. Could I learn to write left-handed and salvage a writing career? Or would it all end right then and there as a staffer on the school's newspaper, *The Bomber Beam?*

Since seventeen-year-olds are resilient, my hand healed (though the scar remains), and six weeks later my future was looking brighter. My hand was not healed enough to do a scheduled swim meet, however, so I instead went on a field trip to the McMahon School of Journalism at the University of Oklahoma.

I ended up winning the day's reporting contest, and my story about OU parking woes was featured in the *OU Daily* newspaper. If I'd had any doubts before about journalism as a career, they were erased when I saw my first byline. It might have never happened if I hadn't carved up that hand. I was accepted as a journalism major at OU the next year, and four years later I had my B.A. I was ready to rock the newspaper world.

The world, however, would have to wait, because my first reporting job offer came from the *Muleshoe Journal,* in that eponymous and isolated West Texas town of 5,000 latter-day pioneers where the distinctive feature was the *National Mule Memorial.* As the story goes, the town was eager to build a memorial to all mules for their strength and sparse eating habits, both traits that western pioneers admired

Oddly, the isolation of Muleshoe interested me, even if it was knee deep in rattlesnake country, but I wasn't sure this was the place to get my work seen outside of Bailey County, Texas.

So I waited a couple days and went with Offer No. 2. That was the *Edmond Sun & Booster,* in Edmond, Oklahoma, a northern suburb of Oklahoma City and a college town of about 30,000 to boot. The paper came out on Mondays and Thursdays (the latter because grocery stores ran "double-truck" ads for the weekend). The newsroom had a staff of four, comprised of an editor, news reporter, sports editor, and "women's" (later "lifestyle") editor.

I was looking for a newspaper where I could learn everything about the craft, doing pretty much everything related to reporting, writing, editing, and photography. I couldn't have picked a better one than the *Sun & Booster.*

About a week after I was hired, the editor quit for greener pastures, and I was given her job. As this was my first real newspaper job, and since I had only been aboard long enough to know that I didn't know anything, I struggled to find a breath. In charge, huh? Right.

I found the OJT to be the best way to learn. As if I had a choice. It's amazing how motivational a deadline can be when you know the next edition will feature a lot of naked newsprint if you don't fill the news hole. So I started filling.

It didn't take long for things to start popping in Edmond.

Literally.

A couple weeks into the job, I was awakened about 3 a.m. by a phone call from my publisher who said I needed to get over to the local nightspot, the Kit Kat Klub immediately. It seems a disgruntled patron had returned and tossed a stick of dynamite through its window, sending bricks and brew spewing into the night sky. Fortunately, no one was inside at that hour. I always wondered about the name of this bar and still wonder whether it may have had a backroom where the *other* KKK met. I don't recall if the bomber was ever found, but his handiwork provided great photos for the newspaper.

Then, a few days later, a thief broke into a local Goodyear store and blew a hole in the safe where the payroll was kept. Before leaving, he had scrawled a "Thanks, and have a nice day," message in white chalk on that overturned safe.

These twin events caused me to wonder who was running around town with dynamite, and I did start to feel my job might just be a blast, after all. For a quiet suburb, crime seemed alive and well here.

Getting to the crime scene on time was not always easy. I had only the external sound of police, fire, and ambulance sirens to alert me to breaking news. If they were close enough to where I was, I'd just jump in my car and follow them to the scene; if not, I'd call police dispatch for the location. But those pesky sirens had a way of going off in the most inconvenient times, and I would leave more than one date standing on her doorstep at night as I chased off after the news.

The most memorable crime story occurred shortly after the town hired a new police chief, Harvey Westlake. I liked Harve a lot, partly because he always called me to let me know if something big was happening. One of those calls came a couple nights before Christmas. Harve said he and his men were throwing a "big party" at midnight at the station if I wanted to come along and report on it. The party turned out to be a huge drug raid that was targeted at about two dozen homes and apartments around town where suspected drug pushers and users lived. College towns always had more drug activity than other towns, and Edmond was no exception.

It turned out, though, that Harve had not only called me but also *all* the TV news crews from Oklahoma City and a reporter from the metro *Daily Oklahoman* newspaper.

Harve had something of a craving for the spotlight, but he was a good cop and a nice guy, nevertheless.

The party started around 1 a.m., when a dozen of Edmond's finest, along with a couple agents from the ATF and DEA (and of course a small cadre of reporters and cameramen) snaked their way through the night streets of Edmond, hitting their targeted spots, rousting unsuspecting suspects out of bed, searching their premises for drugs, and making busts.

Most of the stops went smoothly, but there were some snafus. One of those was a home-based pants store called *Chester's Drawers*. This was the first stop on what proved to be a nightlong learning curve for Harve and his troops. Including the news trucks, there were five vehicles in our little caravan heading for Chester's. Others were hitting their designated targets. Drivers were told to douse their lights a block from each targeted spot and to park a few doors away to keep from alerting the suspects.

But Harve forgot about the TV lights. As cops, reporters, and photogs walked stealthily to the front door of Chester's, a cascade of arc lights from two TV cameras split the night and bathed Chester's Drawers in simulated sunshine. Before Harve's foot hit the front door, you could hear the sound of two toilets flushing hard and fast inside the home. Once the police were inside, few if any drugs were found.

One other ill-fated stop occurred in the supposed home of a pusher. Embarrassingly, it turned out to be the Newman Center, which was the student union for Catholic Students at Central State University. After the police entered, they were confronted by the center's startled priest, clad in his bathrobe, who told them the house they were looking for was next door. I could swear I heard more toilets flushing over there.

The raid went on through the night and, as dawn broke over Edmond, some 30 arrests had been made. Harve pronounced it an overall success. Even so, in later court appearances for the suspects, only about half the charges would stick past arraignment. Still, it was the biggest crime news this town had seen in many years, and the stories and photos I shot covered two pages of the newspaper.

Eventually I got the hang of it all, and the *Sun & Booster* editions just kept coming off the press every Tuesday and Thursday. I felt a sense of pride in what I was doing, keeping the townspeople informed, and I always liked seeing the lines form at our newspaper box out front as the latest edition hit the stands. The lines were always longer on Thursdays than Mondays, but my pride took a hit when I learned most of those patrons were buying papers to get the grocery ads.

So I learned about the blending of the news and business sides of newspapers. Some of the lessons were fun, and some were not. In the former category was the paper's participation in the annual summer Krazy Daze sales in downtown Edmond where much of the retail business moved to the sidewalks, and retailers would dress up in wacky styles to hawk business. The *Sun & Booster* was right in the middle of it, and I presented myself as – who else – Superman. Somewhere I still have a copy of the paper featuring its star editor decked out in red cape, blue tights, and the iconic red "S" in a yellow triangle on my chest. I was standing atop our news box outside the newsroom ready to launch into a life-saving flight.

The times that made me cringe were when advertising pressure was brought to bear on the publisher and me to cover pseudo-news that would benefit businesses owned by advertisers, but do little to inform the public about legitimate news. That didn't happen often but, when it did, we always tried to fight it. Actually, the most memorable such conflict took place on the *Dallas Morning News* a couple years later when grocery chains pressured the publisher into scrapping the front page of the food section featuring a big story about the popularity of alternative food co-ops. The publisher caved, and a canned page on National Sauerkraut Week replaced the food co-op story.

My tenure in Edmond lasted less than two years, when I decided to move on to metro dailies in Oklahoma City and then Dallas. Even after I left newspapering to return to college for graduate degrees and a second career teaching journalism at universities, I still loved freelancing for newspapers and magazines.

Over my career I saw the news industry move largely away from print to online, and I wept over the shuttering of so many newspapers. But I came to realize that the focus should always be on the news itself and not on its delivery system. The goal is to inform and to do it in an engaging way so people will read and heed it.

I was proud of my service to journalism, and I had no inkling that my biggest stories were yet to come. The biggest of them was just about to happen on this very homecoming visit.

9

A Separate Peace

My four years as a student at the University of Oklahoma had always been a pleasant bundle of memories, so I decided to return to that environment for a while. I extended my leave of absence from Boston College and rented a furnished apartment in Norman next to the OU campus, only 40 minutes away from Midwest City. Beyond that decision, I had no plans other than to reconnect with some old friends and tread water emotionally until I felt stronger about moving on.

By now it was April, and I was enjoying the new routine of settling into my own space in a new apartment complex that was only a 10-minute walk to the OU campus. My thought was to lengthen my Oklahoma stay for a few months more, soak up the sweet vibes on campus, and then see what developed for me, career-wise. Boston College was gracious enough to give me the time I needed and even kept me on the payroll while on leave. I suppose the dean felt the work I was doing as a reporter was beneficial to my teaching of journalism. I was very grateful, but I continued to feel like I wanted to start life fresh somewhere else.

Spring was moving in sooner than it does in some Oklahoma years, and I would start each day with an early morning run through the sprawling south campus lawns of OU. While living in the university's shadow, more memories began flooding back, but these were of my time there as an undergraduate nearly three decades earlier. As I let those settle in, reinforced by the campus where they had been born and raised, I felt the same centering that I did in reliving growing-up experiences in Midwest City. I discovered it was a tremendous asset to have time to rediscover who I was, and that part of this process was working.

I was reminded of something else, also. Something I had been telling young people contemplating college: If you can afford it, live on campus and immerse yourself in that experience. College isn't a place just for studying; it's a field of dreams that you embrace over four years. The experience will help form you as a person, and the memories will stay with you forever.

It was certainly that way for me. As I was doing one of my morning runs through campus, I thought about all that happened to me as a student there. No small part of my education was that OU had introduced me to racial diversity. I graduated from an all-white high school and, for the most part, lived in an all-white town growing up. At OU, I regularly crossed paths with black students on a daily basis, and lived with some of them in my own dorm complex. I became friends with some of them and realized how monochrome my world had been up to then. It was an important broadening experience for me personally, and I'll always be grateful for it.

I reveled in the memories of the zany freshman dorm experiences that most college students collect along the way. I was assigned to the Cross Center, a large multi-building complex on the south campus that had been built in the 1950s. Each building was divided into "houses" and mine was Ditmars House. It's one of the many ways that the university advancement people make money for the school. The individual houses are named for big donors, and the more houses you have in any one of the buildings, the more chance the university has for getting more money.

I had taken potluck with roommates, and OU assigned me a real question mark: the kind of nut you could talk about the rest of your life if you weren't so busy trying to erase him from your memory. I sometimes reflect on how risky a potluck roomie could be (how do you know you're not getting a serial killer?) But then I realize how naïve, yet resilient, a college freshman can be.

My roommate was a guy named Tommy from Oklahoma City and, aside from being one of the quirkiest guys I've ever met, we got alone okay. It helps that I find it easy to be around guys who seem a step or two removed from the rest of society, and Tommy certainly was that. He had arrived early on campus to go through the fraternity rush week, hoping to be invited to pledge one of the Greek houses. His efforts were rewarded when he received an offer to pledge Pi Kappa Alpha, known on campus as "the Pikes."

Three things stand out in my mind to this day about Tommy. First was his questionable personal hygiene. Tommy didn't take that many showers, and I could never tell if the odor in the room was coming from his body or from his bed sheets. He had put sheets on his bed in late August, and he slept on those same unwashed sheets until Christmas break.

Second was his undying loyalty to Sen. Barry Goldwater, Republican from Arizona, who was running for president that fall against Lyndon Johnson. Tommy volunteered as part of Goldwater's Oklahoma campaign staff, and he bored me endlessly at night about what a great visionary Goldwater was. He was the only guy I knew who thought Goldwater ever had a new thought since puberty. Tommy saw himself as an up-and-comer in GOP politics, which I perceived as total fantasy, and he felt graduating from OU would solidify his chances. After all, Oklahoma is one of the reddest states in the country.

The third thing about Tommy was his craving to become an OU "Ruf/Nek," the oldest collegiate all-male spirit squad in the country that was founded in 1915. The group still exists today and has allowed women to join through its "Ruf/Nek 'Lil Sis" auxiliary.

To detractors, the double-misspelling of "roughnecks" is an indication of the misfit nature of the squad at an educational institution. To others, these are just guys who want to have a lot of fun, support the Sooner football team, and let off a lot of steam in the process.

Each year, about 100 students apply for membership in the Ruf/Neks and only a dozen are selected. Their on-field presence is highlighted by their driving the red and white Sooner Schooner, powered by two white horses, onto the field after OU scoring drives. The wagon is a scaled-down replica of the Studebaker Conestoga wagon used by settlers who participated in the Oklahoma Land Run of 1889.

Several embarrassing gaffs involving the Ruf/Neks and the Schooner have occurred over the years. Most have occurred in driving the Schooner at a breakneck pace onto the football field. One came in the 1985 Orange Bowl featuring OU and the University of Washington. When the Schooner came out a little early onto the playing field to celebrate an OU field goal, it received a penalty flag from the referee for unsportsmanlike conduct. After the loss of 15 yards resulting from the penalty, the second Sooner field goal attempt was blocked, and the Sooners went on to lose the game to the Huskies.

Years later, in a 2019 home game against West Virginia, the Schooner raced onto the field after an OU touchdown, made a tight turn and flipped over, separating the wagon from its frame. The wagon was carrying several Ruf/Neks who were all spilled across the field. Three were treated and released at the local hospital. The Schooner went into the shop for repairs, and new safety precautions were put into place by the OU Athletic Department, which today oversees the Ruf/Neks as one of its programs.

In addition to his vision of being a Republican politician, being a Ruf/Nek was Tommy's second dream, and he nurtured it throughout the fall term. The group's initiation ceremonies were legendary on campus, and one week, as he was undressing for a shower, I noticed Tommy had a raw egg, still encased in its shell, tied to, and dangling from, his penis. Since that's not the sort of thing you recall seeing before, I asked him about it.

"Er ... Tommy, what is *that*?!" I asked.

"Oh, this?" he responded. "It's part of my Ruf/Nek initiation. I have to carry it around like this for three days without breaking it. I guess it must look kinda weird."

"Kinda," I said, and let the matter drop.

I guess the egg came through the week unbroken, because Tommy was accepted into the Ruf/Neks, and he was ecstatic. To me, he and the Ruf/Neks were a good match.

In truth, I actively tried to blot the whole scene – and the Ruf/Neks – from memory. Alas, being a die-hard Sooner fan who watches every game on TV, I'm reminded of both the Ruf/Neks and Tommy every time the Sooners score points on the field.

As for Tommy joining Pi Kappa Alpha, I do remember his dejection over his rejection when the Pikes blackballed him from membership. I didn't ask why. With Tommy, there could have been several reasons.

With the start of my sophomore year, I wound up in the newly constructed Towers dorm, and I also wound up with a room all to myself. Something unheard of in those days. It happened when the roommate who had been assigned to me decided college wasn't for him. Kenny was a nice guy and he had a great Gretsch hollow-body electric guitar which I coveted. I had my own guitar with me, and we would jam into the night hours of the first two weeks of the fall term. It was then that Tommy let me in a plan he had hatched.

"Jim, I really don't think I'm going to stay in school," Kenny told me early in the term. "But I'm not ready to tell my parents I'm quitting. They've already paid the whole semester for the room, but I'm leaving."

"So what do I do when they call asking for you?" I queried.

"Can you just tell them I'm out and then let me know they've called. I've got another phone number I can give you. Then I'll call them back from where I'm staying with my girlfriend."

Assessing the possibility of having a whole suite to myself for the semester, I responded, "Sure. Any chance you're leaving that Gretsch behind?

"No chance in hell," he said.

And that was the last I saw of Kenny.

The most indelible memory of my college experience, however, came courtesy of the United States Navy after I joined the Navy ROTC unit at OU in my freshman year. In telling this story, however, I need to return to my dad because this part of my life has reminded me of how similar he and I are. As I mentioned earlier, it has taken me years of reflection to realize that.

I cannot think of Dad without also thinking of the Navy, because Dad had been commissioned as an officer in the Navy sometime after WWII began. I say "sometime," because Dad's time in the Navy was always cloaked in mystery for me. It just wasn't spoken of around our home, and Dad rarely said anything about it.

It is odd not only in and of itself, but also because such has been the case with my own naval experience, although Selena often asked me about it. My response has almost always been silence on my part, and a fairly long one at that, as I would sit with a fixed gaze.

Just like my dad did, I have chosen to defer talking about the Navy until, well … now, I suppose. That has been because of the tangled feelings I have that are wrapped up in that time of life and, more importantly, the emotional impact of it on my life ever since. As I write this, I'm picturing two cats, climbing into a bag of yarn and turning it into a twisted and tangled mess on the floor. It would be so time-consuming to straighten it all out that, out of frustration you just gather up the whole mess, toss it back into the bag, and shove it to the back corner of the closet.

As for my dad, I have two pictures of him in his Navy year or years (I don't know how long he was in). One is of him in his dress blue officer uniform (he left the Navy as a lieutenant junior-grade, the equivalent of a full lieutenant in the Army). The other is of him in his khaki uniform and garrison cap, sitting in the rear open cockpit of a Navy trainer, his hands on the trigger of a machine gun, and his eyes drawing a bead on a target.

Sometime in Dad's mid-50s, he was rummaging through a chest of drawers in our den, and he pulled out his few military artifacts, in the form of his shoulder boards, collar rank pins and aviator wings. He took them out to his garage studio where he painted pastels and oils, and he framed them. The next day, he brought them back and hung them in the den. No words were spoken about them; one day they weren't there, and the next day they were. I know he was a naval aviator, although I believe he was a gunner instead of a pilot.

How can a son go through life not knowing more than that about his dad's military experience? Because Dad emitted all kind of hints that he didn't want to talk about it. That being the case, I don't recall pressing the point, although I may well have done so as a child or young teen. I just don't remember. Three things I think I do know, though, and one of those I don't know for sure:

First, Dad served at the Naval Air Station in Jacksonville Florida, because that's the city where my sister Elaine was born in 1944. So far as I know, Dad was never deployed in Europe or the Pacific, but I could be wrong. He never once mentioned it if he was.

Second, Dad often seemed nervous around water, and I don't remember ever seeing him go swimming. In retirement, he did have a fishing boat that he liked going out on, but I never actually saw him in the water. I always thought an apparent fear of swimming was curious for a Navy vet.

Third, Mom mentioned to me once (possibly in a question I asked her, about Dad's Navy time) that he had suffered an "anxiety breakdown" once. She hinted that this was the reason his Navy time was cut short.

Despite not knowing the nature of Dad's military experience, I knew I wanted to follow in his footsteps and join the Navy. The fact that I was also a dedicated swimmer, lifeguard, and SCUBA diver would have probably steered me toward the Navy anyway, but following in Dad's footsteps was a definite motivation. In fact, I wanted to join the Navy right after high school instead of going to college. But, with my sister's encouragement to continue with school, I chose college instead.

Still, in choosing the University of Oklahoma, I did also choose the Navy because when I enrolled at OU, I applied to join the elite Naval ROTC program there, was interviewed about my knowledge of world affairs, and was accepted. I was surprised, because I was not tuned in to world news that much, and several of the questions concerned that, most notably what was going on in Vietnam.

The year was 1964 and, as any OU student at the time knew, ROTC was a compulsory course for male students (this was early in the Vietnam War), although you could get exempted by taking four semesters of physical education courses instead. Since the military draft was still in place, though, and since guys knew they were probably going to have to serve anyway, a lot of us thought that going into the military as an officer would be better than as an enlisted man. So, the ROTC ranks were at full capacity. At least that was the case in the Army and Air Force. The Navy was a harder unit to get into, and we were the leanest branch of all ROTC units as a result. Still, there were a couple hundred of us.

I was proud to be a part of it, and Mom and Dad were even prouder. It turned out to be the most consistently demanding part of my college experience, but it also offered some needed structure throughout those years and, in the end, had become my fraternity. Although I did pledge a social fraternity in my second semester – Delta Upsilon – I found myself drawn more to the Navy ROTC guys and ultimately backed away from the DU's.

The way it worked was that all four years were spent taking one NROTC course per semester and participating in weekly drills, held outside each Tuesday from 4-6 p.m. These were mostly marching drills and, because it was the time of Vietnam, we had plenty of war protesters taunting us on the way to the drill fields each week.

My favorite drills were those spent in the OU field house swimming pool where we were honed into fast swimmers. I already had a head start on swimming, having been on the high school swim team, and worked as a lifeguard during high school summers, earning senior swimmer and lifesaver certifications along the way. I also went through SCUBA diving classes and earned certification as an open-water diver. I loved being in the water, and that was another allure the Navy had for me. As it would turn out, I would be called upon to use those diving skills.

During the first two years of NROTC program, the midshipmen had not officially *joined* the Navy yet. These years were more of a straight educational experience for both mind and body, and the courses were regular university courses focused on leadership, Naval history, and some physics related to the operation and navigation of naval vessels. Along with those were the physical activity of the weekly drills.

If you passed your first two years successfully, however, you were allowed to sign a contract with the Navy for your junior and senior years, and you would be paid while finishing your training. But, if you signed the contract, it meant you were now officially in the Navy and were committed to finish the NROTC program, be commissioned an ensign, and serve for at least three years as a Naval officer. Some midshipmen chose to join as "regulars" while some chose to join as active-duty reservists. If you were a reserve officer, you were committing to serve for three years; if a regular officer, you signed on for a longer hitch of at least four years. I had not planned on making the Navy my career, but I wanted to do my part. I joined as a reserve officer.

When my time came, I signed the contract and couldn't wait for the next two years to pass. I wanted to get to sea. It is impossible to understate how much I looked forward to serving in the Navy, and that's what made future events so hard to accept when they happened.

My junior year did pass quickly and, before I knew it, I was a midshipman first class and was, at last, headed to sea in June for the biggest event of any midshipman's life: about three months aboard a ship of war for the First Class Cruise. In my case, I would spend it aboard a Fletcher Class destroyer, the U.S.S. Benner (DD807). The Benner was a survivor of WWII, still in good shape and just back from Subic Bay in the Philippines, not far from the coast of Vietnam where it had been continuing to do its part in the war there.

This was the real Navy, and I was eager to get going but also more than a little intimidated by the task ahead. Nevertheless, I will always remember my first few nights on board the Benner, and especially the evening hours in the officers ward room, dining on an elegantly prepared dining table, being served by Filipino waiters in white uni-forms. It seemed ironic to find such a setting on a U.S. war ship.

The after-dinner conversations were enjoyable as we all got to know each other, and then off to bed to catch a few hours' sleep, before stand-ing the next watch. I was usually standing a midnight-4 a.m. watch on the bridge as junior officer on deck, helping ensure the Benner was staying on course. That watch is called either the Blue Watch or the Mid Watch, and you need to get your sleep before standing it. Otherwise, drowsiness becomes a big problem.

When you're onboard a naval ship, your shifts are usually broken up into four-hour watches in various stations of the ship. That means your sleeping hours are shorter and are themselves broken up into shifts. The Navy realizes that life at sea is arduous for the personnel, and the idea is to keep sailors as busy as possible, hopefully distracting them from the loneliness and isolation they are feeling.

The average sailor spends about eight hours a day standing watch and one of several stations on ship, and then often has a regular job related to their specialty for maybe another six to eight hours. Such strategy has no doubt prevented many more suicides at sea than have occurred. When you're working you're not sitting idly thinking about being so far away from home in the middle of a huge ocean.

The main thing that distinguishes the First Class Cruise from the Second Class Cruise, which the regular second class midshipmen take between their sophomore and junior years of college, is that first-class middies are treated as junior officers on ship and do the jobs that the officers do, working through all the different ship stations over the course of the summer. The second-class middies work alongside the enlisted men and do not live in the mid-ship staterooms known as "officer country." There were even cases where midshipmen wound up in hot war zones if that's where their ships were patrolling.

At sea, I would stand watch at various stations alongside officers, practice leadership skills, and partake in drills and activities for which I had been trained in my NROTC classes at OU.

Life that summer at sea was as real as it gets in the Navy for us middies on the Benner, right up to and including assisting in a search for a sailor who went overboard one night in the Pacific, while walking from his bunk to the head (bathroom). Some said he did it on purpose; just tired of so much time at seas; others said it was an accident. We never found out, because we never found the sailor, despite spending a day circling back and looking for him in the waters.

Most weeks were spent in gunnery drills, simulated attack and damage control exercises, gunnery drills, anti-submarine warfare (ASW) drills in CIC (Combat Information Center), and the like. But there was one ten-day stretch that was not ordinary, and it would affect me inside for many years to come. It's a story I never told my family about when I returned, partly because the mission was classified, but partly because I was just trying to bury it in my subconscious. Combatants were killed, and I was nearly one of them.

Briefly, however, I had the opportunity to volunteer for a team that was to be inserted into Vietnam waters to carry out a reconnaissance assignment that was deemed important by the Navy. My dual certifications as a SCUBA diver and rifle marksman helped me fit the profile needed for the position. I was accepted and was gone from the Benner for 10 days.

Even though it has been nearly 60 years since then, this is all I feel comfortable saying about this episode, except to say I felt very different inside – older and sadder -- when I returned to the ship, and I was carrying the baggage of survivor's guilt.

Nevertheless, the whole sideshow had taken only ten days, and I rejoined the Benner -- now in Pearl Harbor -- and resumed my cruise. My life had gone from total routine to a surreal experience and back again within less than two weeks' time.

People find it hard to fathom that I would keep this all from my loved ones and friends, but it's not unusual for returning veterans to omit the most traumatic of their experiences. When you come home – if you come home – from a battlefield, the world you return to is so vastly different from the one you left, and the things you did then would rightly be seen as uncivilized, if not monstrous, back in your hometown.

A month later, I was back on the OU campus as a senior. To others who knew me, nothing much had changed. To me, a lot had. For one thing, I was more committed now than ever to finish my senior year, take my commission, and serve for at least the next three years with the Navy.

That senior year passed quickly and, before I knew it, I had orders to join a cruiser, the Newport News, on the East Coast after obtaining training in shipboard communications. I was to be a communications officer on the ship, and I was looking forward to it. The very next week, however, everything changed for me. It was the day the doctors were at the campus armory to give pre-commissioning physicals to those of us who had completed the NROTC program and were about to become commissioned officers in the Navy.

The last medical station was a hearing test, and it never occurred to me that my hearing would be evaluated. After all, I had been in the NROTC program for four years, undergone other physicals, and no one had ever checked or even asked about my hearing. Yet there it was, and I had to make a snap decision that would alter my post-graduation plans and – in some ways – change the trajectory of my life altogether.

The test was a simple one, or so it would seem if you knew you had good hearing. I did not, at least in my right ear. I have thought about that moment hundreds of time since April, 1968, when the doctor simply held his wrist watch up to my right ear and asked, "Can you hear that okay?"

To this day I am unsure why I said it, but in that moment, I decided to respond honestly.

"Actually, not really," I said.

The doctor tried the left ear, and I said, "Yes, fine."

Maybe I thought the fact I could hear so well out of my left ear would negate the marginal hearing in my right ear, and I was heartened when the doctor just thanked me and told me the test was finished. So

I moved on and didn't think much about it the rest of the day. A few days later, however, I was asked to drop into my instructor's office.

"Luke," the lieutenant began, "I've got some bad news for you: Your hearing doesn't meet the standards of the Navy, and we're going to have to assign you to an inactive reserve unit. You have completed the officer training program and received high marks for the work you did on your cruise, but the Navy won't let us put you on active duty with your hearing the way it is. We asked if you could serve as a supply officer instead of a line officer, but they said no. Rules are rules. I'm sorry."

I was stunned but thanked him for going the extra mile in trying to get me onto active duty. I walked out of the armory and onto campus, realizing that I had no plan for what to do after a commencement exercise that was now only a couple weeks away. All through my college career, I had assumed I would spending at least my first three years after college serving on active duty in the Navy. Now that was not to be the case. I would be *in* the Navy, but I wouldn't actually be *doing* anything in it.

My parents lived only 40 minutes away from campus, so I remember driving home and telling them the news. They put on a good front, but I knew they were disappointed for me, because they knew how much I was looking forward to my serving in the Navy. After talking for awhile, though, Dad asked if it might not be possible for me to have my hearing fixed through surgery. He had heard about an ENT in Oklahoma City who had innovated a procedure that restored hearing to some of his patients. The next day I asked the head of my NROTC unit if the Navy would reconsider if I could get my hearing fixed.

"Absolutely," he said. "We know how hard you've worked for this and what a good contribution you would make to the Navy."

Over the next few weeks, I met with the ENT in Oklahoma City who evaluated my hearing and said I was a candidate for his ear reconstruction procedure. We set a date for the surgery in July. The day came, and I was admitted to Baptist Hospital in Oklahoma City. The surgery took place, and the surgeon was cautiously optimistic it was a success. It would take at least two weeks to know if my hearing would improve enough to meet Navy standards, however, and I was instructed to avoid any quick movements with my head, for fear of shaking loose the reconstructed bones in my right ear.

The two weeks passed, and I was administered another hearing test.

No noticeable difference in my hearing was detected. The plan that would enable me to serve on active duty had failed.

It is important to remember the national context in which my individual story was unfolding. This was 1968, and America was heavily involved in Vietnam. Thousands of young men were being sent to fight in this jungle war every month and many of them would never come home again. I lost track of the number of friends I had at OU who had been drafted to go to Vietnam or who had finished one of the ROTC programs and shipped out after graduation to join the fighting. Before it was all over, 21 men from my own high school would lose their lives in that country. Young men of my generation felt a unity then that has not been felt since then, and we were unified by the surreal feeling that any of us could wind up in a war none of us really understood, and stand a good chance of not coming home.

The reason this background is important is because it produced in me a survivor's guilt that I will never fully get out of my system. In being assigned to inactive status in the Navy, I had been given a pass from the danger and horror that so many of my friends were facing. My briefest of moments in a jungle fight during the summer of 1967 were nothing compared to the year's deployment time that so many other men my age had faced or would face in Vietnam.

The guilt became a silent, personal weight inside me. On the surface, I carried on after graduation by going to a graduate seminary to study theology, but one day I found myself applying to the United States Army to be commissioned an Army officer. I ran into the same obstacle there, however, with my hearing loss.

So that was that. I kept thinking maybe the Navy would change its mind, and I did get one letter from them a year later, asking if I knew of any reason why I shouldn't be called up. I said no reason that they don't already know about, without mentioning my hearing per se. It didn't matter. I never heard back from the Navy again. It was about that time that I read about a huge fire at the combined military personnel facility in St. Louis where many of the personnel files were stored. This was in the 1970s, in pre-digital days when all records were on paper. The fire consumed most of them, and I was especially interested to read that many records of inactive personnel in all branches were burned up. When I checked on this, I was told it was likely my records were among those destroyed, for which there were no backup records.

And so it is that whenever I am asked about my experience in the military, I usually try to skirt the answer or say I don't talk about that very much, or I sometimes just change the subject. In truth, there is no easy answer for me to give. I mean, how many pages has it taken for me to even summarize that experience here.

And there is this: it was not time spent in combat or what I experienced when I was on my summer cruise in 1967 that has given me so much trouble. Instead, it is the remains of that survivor guilt; the feeling I still have that I was given an undeserved pass from the earth-shattering experience that so many other men my age had to encounter, month after month after month in the jungles and highlands of Vietnam. And there is the related question of how I myself would have reacted in such a protracted experience, whether I was on a ship of war or back with a ground team. Might I have had a similar breakdown experience like the one I believe my dad had during his time in the Navy? Because of what happened ... because of being consigned to inactive status ... I never had the chance to answer that question.

It's like I skipped a step on the climb to manhood. There is also some frustration associated with putting four years of my life into training for service that I never got to perform. I feel somewhat cheated by that; I feel all of that knowledge that could have been put to good use for my country, was never used at all. And the dreams of serving on a ship at sea were reduced to a three-month cruise while I was still a midshipman.

In the end, I find some consolation in the fact that this was all so long ago, and in the fact that I did all that was asked of me by the

United States Navy and nothing less. Also, beginning in the mid-1990s, I was called upon to do contract work for the U.S. State Department as a guest lecturer in media communications in Germany, Spain, and Latvia. I even spent 10 days in Russia doing a series of Master lectures for an international exchange program. All this was under the aegis of international diplomacy, and I believe it was -- and is -- extremely important work for America in maintaining allies around the world.

All of these memories and more returned during my time spent near the OU campus. Once these floodgates opened, these memories came swirling back as I jogged through the campus in the early spring of 1995. You might say I became reacquainted with myself which, once again, was the main reason I had returned to Oklahoma in the first place.

As for my university, it was now poised to start its massive growth spurt under its new president, David Boren, a former U.S. senator from Oklahoma. Over the next several years, the University of Oklahoma would undergo renovation and expansion and morph into one of the most beautiful and well-planned college campuses in America. On the academic side, this school that was once known nationally for only its football team would rise to become ranked 9th in the nation for the freshman recruitment of the most National Merit Scholarship Finalists. There was a new spirit at OU, and it was felt by the students and alumni of the school.

A part of me was glad to be running free, both literally and figuratively, in a place I still loved. If those moments could overtake my hours of sadness, this return to my roots would be validated.

I had some money in the bank and, being the impulsive guy I am and having no one to answer to about what I did with my money, I decided to spend some of it. I was driving a two-year-old black Mustang GT at the time, and I loved the car dearly. But I was getting into the swing of being back in Oklahoma with its cowboy roots, so I looked up an old friend who owned an auto dealership and bought a fully decked-out red pick-up truck with an extended bed and cab. It was a red Chevy Silverado, and I loved driving it around the surrounding hills and plains listening to country singer Joe Diffee belt out his upbeat song, *Pickup Man.*

There I was, as far removed from the Brahmin culture of Boston as possible, driving through the Oklahoma wheat fields and singing, *"I met all my wives in traffic jams, you know there's something women like about a pickup man."*

Well, I reasoned, if you can call it that, if I'm going to escape a grim reality by living a fantasy, why not go all the way?

I noticed my cousin Bob, who was hanging out with me these days and trying hard to perk me up, doing his share of eye-rolls over my quirky behavior these April days. But Bob was a smart guy and knew I just trying to get through the pain. Just having him around helped a great deal.

It was on one of these April mornings that I deviated from my new-found jogging routine as I agreed to have breakfast with my brother-in-law Ben at a Norman Diner called *Jimmy's Egg.*

It would become a day I would be hatched into a new world.

Part Two

PAIN MEETS TRAGEDY

10

The Earth Moves

A folk music group from the 1990s who called themselves "Cry, Cry, Cry," released a ballad called *Shades of Gray*, in 1998 written by one of the vocal trio, Dar Williams. She was joined in singing it by Lucy Kaplansky and Richard Shindell. The lyrics follow three young men from Arkansas on their misguided road trip, full of mischief and entry-level crime, through the backroads of Arkansas, Kansas, and Oklahoma.

It seems a straightforward folk tale until the three guys – barely out of their teens -- cross the Oklahoma line. But it turns darker, flashing a stunning revelation, late in the song. The date of their arrest was late April, 1995, and the crime they were stopped for, mistakenly, was the Oklahoma City bombing.

I remember when I first heard *Shades of Gray* in the year of its release, 1998. because it took me back to 1995, and the time when I hit my career clutch and downshifted into low gear to take the exit ramp from teaching and recenter myself emotionally from losing Selena. I was in Memphis, but the song immediately took me back to my 1995 spring in Oklahoma. For not only was I then on my own road trip – destination uncertain – but it brought back with shocking clarity how stunned I was when I heard the news of what happened on the Wednesday morning of April 19.

The Jimmy's Egg diner in Norman, Oklahoma, was full of breakfast patrons, and Ben and I were at a corner table chatting away over our omelets and grits. All of a sudden, the tile floor beneath our feet jolted, the walls around us jerked for a split second, and we heard a distant and muffled *boom!* A couple possible images shot across my mind.

First, I had grown up just a few miles away, near Tinker Air Force Base, during the time when the Air Force was running sonic boom tests overhead with their new jets. We residents would receive advance notice of when those tests would be run so we could secure valuable items that might otherwise fall off the shelves at home. When the booms came, they were jolting and carried an audible shockwave, and then they were gone.

The second possibility for this breakfast jolt was an earthquake, although you don't hear an audible boom with them unless something has fallen or exploded in the eruption. Oklahoma gets more quakes than people think, and some tie it to the way oil is urged out of the ground: a process called *fracking.*

We didn't have long to ponder, though, because a moment later a cook came out of the kitchen and announced that a TV news bulletin had flashed across the screen saying there had been an explosion at the Alfred P. Murrah Federal Building in Oklahoma City.

The building was located just north of downtown OKC between Northwest 4th and 5th streets and between Harvey and Robinson Avenues. The immediate news media speculation was an exploded natural gas line. It happened just after most of the offices opened for business at 9 a.m., and there may be injuries involved. This would be the first of an endless string of news updates over the next several days but, at this point, the cause and damage were unknown.

The cook brought the TV out of the kitchen and put it in the dining room for all of us to watch news reports. Within a few minutes, videocams were on the scene at the Federal Building, and the scene was devastating. The foreground was littered with dozens of charred, burned-out cars, some still on fire and others smoldering.

Running, staggering, and hobbling through this carnage were an untold number of people trying to escape the burning building, while firefighters in full gear were dragging hoses and pick axes toward the rubble, police officers were trying to set up barriers and string yellow caution tape around the area, and nurses and doctors trying to tend to victims on the spot, whether that be the middle of the parking lot or on the grassy lawns away from the building.

But what caught my attention even more was the still-standing, yet mortally wounded hulk of this 9-story concrete, steel and glass Federal Building, with most of its façade gone along with a mammoth, semi-circular crevice from the front side of the building. You could stare straight into the bowels of this carcass and see what was left of the upper floors and then, as your eyes scanned down to earth, the flattened, pancakes stack of concrete floors piled on top of each other. It was as if Godzilla had stomped into downtown Oklahoma City, reached down and taken a huge bite out of a 9-layer wafer cookie and spit the pieces out into the surrounding streets.

As the news cameras panned around to the surrounding streets, you could see that neighboring buildings failed to escape the wrath of the Murrah Building explosion.

Taking much of the punch were the Athenian Building, the Water Resources Board Building, the Journal-Record Building, and the Downtown YMCA, all lined up on Northwest 5th Street facing the Federal Building just across the street to the south. Watching the TV screen, my gaze hung on the YMCA for a moment, realizing that was where I had spent so many hours swimming with the Boy Scouts when I was young and earning all the Red Cross lifesaving badges plus – in later years – my SCUBA diving certification. The building was ripped apart and would undoubtedly have to be imploded.

Ten minutes later, the newscasters were revising their earlier speculation about a gas line explosion, and were calling this the result of a bombing by persons unknown. Also amended was the conservative estimate of a few people injured; now the reality had set in that many people were not only injured, but also killed.

Some were still trapped inside the rubble, and rescue efforts had begun. Then the sobering announcement was made that that second floor of the Federal Building housed not only offices, but a working day care center that had been fully populated with children and toddlers.

Newscasters soon began issuing pleas for viewers to give blood at their local Red Cross donor sites, and to buy and drop off needed emergency supplies. Everything was needed downtown, from bottled water, to first-aid supplies, to batteries, to blankets ... to diapers. Numerous drop-off locations were available for these volunteered items. It was then that Ben and I decided to leave the diner and start doing what we could to help.

We went our separate ways, as he headed toward Walmart and I went to find the Red Cross Blood Donation Center in Norman. When I arrived, there was already a long line forming. On this day, if you were in or near Oklahoma City, you wanted desperately to do even your small bit to help. While in line I filled out the necessary paperwork to donate my blood. Since all Red Cross workers had been called in to help, the line moved at a good pace.

Twenty minutes later, I was in the donor room, having my blood typed and tested. Ten minutes later, I was given the bad news that my blood could not be used because a trace of Hepatitis had been discovered in it. I explained that was because I had received the Hepatitis B vaccine as protection against the virus. Since the vaccine contained a weakened form of the virus itself, that was the trace that was showing. No dice. The Red Cross still wouldn't take my blood, but thanked me anyway for trying.

I was disappointed because I knew there was a great need for blood for the bombing victims, and I was feeling helpless in trying to do my part to ease the suffering in Oklahoma City. So, I pivoted and headed toward Walmart, finding many of the shelves already empty, but picking up some items I thought could be useful at the bombing site.

Throughout the day the news reports, which were now running

wall-to-wall, showed that the gravity of the situation downtown was much worse than originally expected. The casualty count was climbing, hour by hour, and estimates were it could reach as high as 100 or more dead and upwards to 1,000 injured.

Not all those casualties were inside the Murrah Building itself. Many of the injured were from those either outside on surrounding sidewalks and streets, or they were from the buildings that ringed the Federal Building. Flying glass, along with the debris blasting through those windows, found their mark on those going about their Wednesday morning's work.

Today, if you tour the museum portion of the Oklahoma City National Memorial and Museum, you will first find yourself in a darkened anteroom when the curtain on a large window rises and you are looking at a replica of the Oklahoma City Water Board conference room.

Then the lights in the room go out as an explosion is heard simultaneously outside. You realize what you have just seen and heard was what the moment of 9:02 a.m. sounded and looked like for everyone in the buildings across from the front of the Murrah Federal Building on Northwest 5th street on Wednesday, April 19, 1995. It was like that in the adjacent Journal-Record Building; it was like that in the Downtown YMCA. It was like that on the streets and sidewalks outside. And it must have been like hell.

Throughout the day, nearly everyone in the Oklahoma City area was multi-tasking: doing their day jobs while also listening to news updates on radio or TV. The picture was starting to become a little clearer as the day went on.

At 9:02 a.m. a person or persons had exploded what looked like a huge homemade bomb at the Murrah Building. The first day's investigation showed it had been placed in a Ryder rental truck, parked at the front entrance of the building.

The initial thought crossing many minds was that it was a terrorism act probably committed by Middle Easterners. The memory of the 1993 attack on the World Trade Center in New York City was still on the country's mind. That attack happened shortly after noon on February

26 when a blast erupted from the parking garage beneath the trade center and carved out a crater almost 100 feet across. Six people died immediately in the blast, while the injury count shot past a thousand. More than 700 FBI agents launched a huge investigation that ended in the arrest and conviction of four Middle Eastern terrorists, all of whom were sentenced to life in prison.

The initial similarities of the vehicle bombs were enough to send speculation in the direction of international terrorism. The spin on some media sites was that this was the work of foreign terrorists, probably Middle Easterners.

The Washington Post reported that the annual Muslim-Arab Youth Association Conference had been held in Oklahoma City in 1992 and that, "The FBI has been aware of the activity of Islamic student groups meeting recently in Oklahoma City, Dallas, and Kansas City." *The New York Times* noted, "Some Middle Eastern groups have held meetings in Oklahoma City, and the city is home to at least three mosques.

Another journalist said on a national news program, "This was done with the intent of inflicting as many casualties as possible. That is a Middle Eastern trait." As it turns out, the reporter was right about the first half of his statement, but wrong about the inference in the second half: this was not the job of Middle Eastern terrorists but a home-grown pair of disgruntled Americans who resorted to terrorism out of revenge.

As the sun set on April 19, I was exhausted emotionally but I still felt a driving need to pitch in and help in what would be a long recovery for Oklahoma City. Given my background and talents, the obvious way of doing that was lying right in front of me. It just took me the rest of the day to realize it.

11

Oklahoma's Longest Day

As emotionally draining as April 19 had been for all of us who witnessed daylong news coverage of this bombing, it was nothing compared to what those felt who went through it, in and around the Murrah Building. What had started out as a normal, quiet workday in spring turned, at 9:02 a.m., into a morning of mass killings in Oklahoma City. At 9:01 scores of everyday people who were in and around that building, had less than one minute to live. Hundreds of others would be hospitalized for injuries.

As later evidence would show, the original scheme of the bombers had been to detonate the bomb at 11 a.m. The trigger man was also the man behind the plot. His name, then unknown, was Timothy McVeigh, and he was to drive the rented Ryder truck containing the homemade explosives to the front door of the Alfred P. Murrah Federal Building, light the fuse, then escape to a nearby getaway car before the bomb went off.

On his way into Oklahoma City, however, he thought 9 a.m. might be better. The workday would have just started, and the building would be more occupied with workers and visitors than at 11, when some might be leaving for an early lunch. And a high body count was foremost on the mind of this small band of saboteurs. Doesn't all terrorism work that way? Produce the greatest fear by killing the most people?

As this designated driver headed toward the Murrah Building, located in the busy center of the state's capital city, he carried with him an envelope containing pages from *The Turner Diaries*, a fictional story of white supremacists who start a revolution by blowing up the FBI headquartered at 9:15 a.m. one day with a truck bomb. McVeigh was wearing a T-shirt printed with the phrase, *Sic semper tyrannis* ("Thus always to tyrants"). It was also alleged to have been the phrase shouted by John Wilkes Booth when he assassinated Abraham Lincoln in the Ford Theater.

This soon-to-be mass murderer entered Oklahoma City at 8:50 a.m. and headed his truck to the Murrah Building, located at 620 N. Harvey Avenue. Authorities would later say he lit his first fuse, a 5-minute one, while still driving toward the building. When he got to within a block of the building, he lit a second, 2-minute fuse. His escape window was a short one, he knew. He swung the truck to the curb in the building's drop-off zone. That zone was located next to the day care center in the federal building. He parked the truck, got out, locked it, and headed quickly on foot toward his escape car, parked a couple blocks away.

The lit fuse reached the explosives in the back of the truck and, at 9:02 a.m., more than 4,800 pounds of ammonium nitrate fertilizer, nitromethane, and diesel fuel mixture erupted upwards and outwards into the north side of the nine-story Murrah Federal Building. The explosion was heard all over Oklahoma City and many of its suburbs, including Norman, where I was having breakfast at the time. The truck bomb was equal to more than 5,000 pounds of TNT. It immediately destroyed one-third of the building and blasted a 39-foot-wide, 8-foot-deep crater on Northwest 5th Street, next to the building. The explosion measured approximately 3.0 on the Richter magnitude scale.

The building was destroyed by the explosion, which created a 30-foot-wide (9.1 m), 8-foot-deep (2.4 m) crater on NW 5th Street next to the building. Only a semi-circular, outlying carcass of the building remained.

The northern half of the Alfred P. Murrah Federal Building was rubble in the streets in just seven seconds. As the Ryder Truck exploded, it wiped out a key column of the building next to it, and it burst the entire glass facade of the building outward into the streets and adjacent buildings. The building's first three floors were thrust upwards until the fourth and fifth floors caved in onto the floors below. That weight destroyed a transfer beam that extended through the length of the whole building and which was supporting all the floors above it. In short, every floor above pancaked onto the floors beneath.

Some 645 people were in the Murrah Building at the time. One fourth of them would not survive the day. Hundreds of others were injured. In addition to the Murrah Building itself, some 300 other buildings in downtown Oklahoma City sustained damage from the bombing; some had to be razed.

There was nothing particularly special about this day when these people all arrived at the Murrah Building early in the morning. Many were full-time employees there, but many were also just transacting personal business at the Social Security office, or the myriad of other federal agencies located in the building. The Murrah Building had been constructed as the central location for all federal government offices in the city, an idea which would change dramatically after this day's events. Federal offices would be dispersed into different sites after today.

Some of the people in the building were not even from Oklahoma and had different business reasons for being there. One such man was Bev Allen who was from Hot Springs, Arkansas, and worked for the U.S. Forestry Service there. He was part of a group eight people who were scheduled for a 9 a.m. meeting with members of the Federal Highway Administration in a fourth-floor corner office.

Allen, who had never been to Oklahoma City before, was a University of Kentucky graduate in civil engineering. He and the members of his forestry team arrived at the building at 8:20 a.m.

Years later, Allen would tell me the story of that morning this way:

"By 9 a.m., all parties for the meeting had arrived, and we were seated in the Assistant Director's office located near the southeast corner of the building.

The director had considered using the conference room, but decided it was too cluttered with computers and materials left from a training session. Then, immediately before the meeting began, one of the group asked if anyone wanted to get a fresh cup of coffee from the conference room. No one did.

"Those two decisions, to use the office instead of the conference room and to not walk over to the coffee pot, proved to be monumental regarding our survival. Half of the conference room would soon be destroyed, and the coffee pot was located directly above where the truck bomb was then parked. Had we gone ahead and met in that room, we would probably all have died.

"I was sitting at the table next to the assistant director. There were four others seated around the office. In addition to the six of us in that office, there was a lady sitting directly across the hall from that office door and one other fellow in the adjacent office to the east. These are the eight that survived in that part of the building. Eleven other employees of the Highway Administration in offices near us, died that morning.

"I didn't hear the blast when it came at 9:02 a.m. I felt it, was thrown out of my chair and into shock. The main thing I remember seeing was there was dust and debris everywhere the whole room was full of it and smoke. When I turned to look north, I was staring straight at the plaza outside. There was no wall left. In fact, there were no interior office walls left either.

"Again, I did not hear the bomb explode. I was aware of tremendous turbulence. I remember brining my arms up to protect my face from flying debris. I don't know how long it was from the initial explosion until the building had finished its collapse. We have been told it was a matter of several seconds. What little I could see during that time had a strobe light effect – like a flashing light. Others later commented that it was like things went into slow motion.

"Questions of 'What was that?' and "What happened?" were common. Someone wondered if a plane had hit the building. One said, 'That had to be a bomb!' One lady, covered in debris, said she was okay but was afraid to move. She was lying on the floor, positioned no more than 3 feet from the edge of what remained of the fourth floor."

Later reports would show that the building's first three floors were thrust upwards until the fourth and fifth floors caved in onto the floors below. That weight destroyed a transfer beam that extended through the length of the whole building and which was supporting all the floors above it. In short, every floor above pancaked onto the floors beneath. Only the spaces around the outer perimeter of the crater were still standing.

Bev Allen and his group were lucky to be meeting in one of those spaces.

"The eight of us at that point were helpless," Allen continued. *"There was nothing more we could do to physically gain our escape. Thankfully, the floor remained stable, and a ladder soon showed up just outside our floor. The ladder was just long enough and had to be placed almost vertically against the building. That, plus the sloping ledge outside the window, proved to be a real challenge, especially for the women, when it came time to make it town.*

"After the ladder was in place, the first man up was a large guy in a white shirt and blue pants. I don't remember him saying anything. He climbed into the building, wrapped his arm through and around the window frame and stood there holding the ladder firmly against the building. My friend from Atlanta and I were the last ones out, and this large man was still standing there when we left. Until someone presents evidence to the contrary, I am content to believe he was an angel.

Workers shoring up the remains of the Murrah Building so searchers could pull bodies from its carcass before its remains collapsed entirely.
Photo by Jim Willis

"*When we were on the ground outside, a primitive triage system was set up by medical staffers and volunteers. I didn't realize I needed medical care, but it turns out my body was punctured with small shards of glass, and the medics had to remove those. Then we were pretty much on our own to leave. No one that I saw was taking names of the survivors.*

"*My car was heavily damaged, and I couldn't get to it, anyway, so a friend drove a few of us to his place, and we called our families, cleaned up, and made airline reservations over his phone.*

"*My wife knew I was in Oklahoma City, but she didn't know I was in the bombing. She had her fears, though, and she was very relieved.*

"*I got home the next day (Thursday), and I was back at my Hot Springs office right on time Friday morning, just like clockwork. That was about it, except for this: Three weeks later, I came home and found my suitcase in a delivery box on the front porch. Someone had found it in the Murrah parking facility and sent it to me.*

"*The contents were intact, but the whole suitcase, as well as the box it was put in, were wet. Probably because of all the water from fire hoses that day. As I looked through the suitcase, I noticed that everything was wet except for one thing: my Bible was not even damp.*

"*God had a reason for me being in Oklahoma City that day, and part of it I believe was to share the story of what it was like for people in the Murrah Building. So that is something I have done many, many times since then.*"

Another eyewitness account of that morning of April 19, 1995, comes from Richard H. Dean, who was a claims representative for the Social Security Administration. That agency, like so many other federal agencies, was located in the Murrah Building. It had a normal staff of 62 employees, of which 50 were on duty at 9:02 a.m. that day.

Of that morning, Dean said, "*Within minutes, nearly one third of our staff (16) and 24 visitors in our reception area had been murdered. Twenty-six of the remaining 34 employees required medical treatment. Four had to be hospitalized; the last, Sharon Littlejohn, being released May 22, 1995.*

"*I was sitting at my desk located against the north wall (NW 5th street) 10 feet east of the large glass windows which exposed the front half of our office* and determined the portion of our office located under the additional 8 floors of the Alfred P. Murrah Federal Building. I had just finished my first cup of coffee and paperwork started the day before.

"I remember seeing a brilliant flash of light, simultaneous with the sensation of an invisible force pressing me out of my chair to my knees and hearing a huge explosion before everything turned pitch black. I found myself covered with bulky 5-foot square ceiling tiles, shattered glass from light fixtures, modular furniture panels, and overhead doors from my modular credenza unit which had sheared off hitting me in the back.

"My immediate concern was my ability to see. I thought my eyes were wide open but they were not adjusting to the darkness. Breathing also became difficult due to dust and debris floating in the air. While groping for anything familiar I could hear the cries of individuals trying to free themselves over the roar of what sounded like sliding gravel being dumped from a truck.

"The cries for help from the front of the office and the sound of the collapsing upper floors stopped simultaneously. As my eyes adjusted to the darkness, I responded to the cries for help from Claims Representative Sharon Paulsen and Operations Supervisor LaQuita Cowan. They were both covered with 2 to 3 foot piles of rubble and debris.

"I led them out the emergency exit located in the breakroom at the rear of the office (east end of building). The interior walls surrounding the breakroom had collapsed and the exit door had been blown open providing the only light source for the back half of the office.

"I immediately returned, working my way to the center of the office. Aisles and reference points had all but disappeared, debris and rubble was a minimum of 2 to 3 feet deep. Some employees who had been initially knocked unconscious at their workstations were regaining consciousness and slowly making their way to the rear exit.

"The only light source at the front of the office was the skylight located in the stockroom whose interior walls had also been knocked down. From out of the darkness, Claims Representative Laura Bode grabbed me from the front with both arms around my neck. She was obviously hysterical and disoriented. She had to be carried to the rear exit before she thought about letting go.

"During my third trip back into the office my concern turned toward the

8 inch pressurized pipe located above what used to be the office ceiling. The pipe, which provided 'chiller water' for the building's entire air conditioning system, had severed and was pouring 42 degree water into the work area. It was apparent anyone trapped on the floor could possibly have drowned.

"An Oklahoma City firefighter appeared and made his way to my location in the center of the office. After indicating my concern for the rising water in the work area, he attempted to radio out but encountered too much interference and had to exit the building. Approximately 20 minutes later the water was finally shut off.

"During this third trip I located Sharon Littlejohn, Service Representation, who had been standing in the front of the office. The force of the explosion had blown her 40 feet back from the reception area. She was under 3 to 4 feet of debris and rubble.

"Her outer clothing had been blown off and she was completely soaked with blood and water. I had to ask her name because she was not recognizable due to significant blood loss in the scalp and facial areas. She also complained she was not able to breathe and requested CPR. It was apparent I could not get her out by myself due to her extensive multiple injuries, blood loss, and shock.

"I explained to her I needed additional help to get her out and went to the rear of the office where I found Sgt. Richard Williams and Sgt. Keith Simmons of the Oklahoma City Police Department. It took the three of us to carry her out due to the debris we had to climb over and through.

"The scene outside the rear exit on Robinson Avenue was frantic. The area surrounding the north, south, and east of the building was saturated with rescue workers, firefighters, police, and ambulance personnel. The streets were congested with the walking wounded. Temporary first aid stations shared opposite corners with burned vehicles.

"Later, charter buses were brought in to transfer the walking wounded to area hospitals.

After borrowing a flashlight from an Oklahoma City firefighter I reentered the building concentrating my search on the front part of the office. Accompanied by firefighters, I pointed out areas where employees should have been sitting at the time of the explosion. We found an office visitor partially buried in the rubble. Unfortunately, there was no pulse. Moments later, I discovered *my supervisor, Carol Bowers, a dear friend of over 20 years, who had taken a fatal blow to the back of the head."*

"Unfortunately, I was not able to find any more survivors among the debris and I exited the building."

Nine months later, on January 26, 1996, Dean represented the federal workforce as the President's special guest in the gallery of the House of Representatives. The occasion by the State of the Union Address by President Bill Clinton, who gallery. cited the 49-year old Vietnam veteran as an example of one of the 'hard-working Americans who are now working harder and smarter than ever before to make sure that the quality of our services does not decline.' as the federal workforce shrinks.

He noted that Dean, after digging himself free from the rubble after the Murrah bombing, helped rescue crews locate and rescue his colleagues from the savaged building. He saved the lives of at least three people.

Included among the many killed in the attack were two airmen from nearby Tinker Air Force Base in Midwest City. They were Airman 1st Class Cartney Jean McRaven of the 32nd combat Communications Squadron, and Airman 1st Class Lakesha Richardson Levy of the 72nd Medical Group. Those who knew McRaven called her exemplary in her work. She was off-duty Wednesday morning, picking up a new Social Security card at the federal building. She had just recently returned from a six-month deployment to Haiti as part of Operation Uphold Democracy.

Levy's reason for being at the Murrah Building was the same as McRaven's: to get a new Social Security card. She was only 21 when she died, was a native of New Orleans, and had just moved to Oklahoma a few months earlier. Her mother would later say her daughter was hugely proud of her dedication to and work for the Air Force. Levy had a wonderful sense of humor and hoped to one day become a standup comedian.

She would never get that chance.

The Murrah remains at night, April 24, 1995
Photo by Jim Willis

As was the case with me and others I knew in and around Oklahoma City, the Wednesday morning bombing turned our day around dramatically, and whatever our agenda had been for the day was blown out just as the glass had exploded from the Murrah Federal Building that morning. While we were all scrambling to find ways to help the search-and-rescue mission under way downtown, first-responders from across the state and around the country (called into action by FEMA) headed to 620 N. Harvey to help save as many victims as possible and prevent further deaths.

Locally, in fact, some 1,000 military and civilian workers at Tinker AFB were on-site quickly to provide support and work as a focal point for incoming relief teams engaged in the recovery process. They joined responders already at work from units of the Oklahoma City Police Department, Fire Department, Sheriff's Department, National Guard, Red Cross, FBI, ATF, and many other local fire, police, and sheriff's departments in the state, and numerous fire departments around the country who were part of the Federal Emergency Management Agency (FEMA) network of first responders for disasters.

It was a very long day for all involved, and it would be followed by many more until all bodies were found, and the Murrah Building was imploded. I felt privileged to be able to provide one service in the midst of this horror: informing the hundreds of thousands of Oklahomans eager to know what was happening in Oklahoma City.

12

A Reporter Again

As the hours of April 19 ticked toward evening, I was feeling the sadness and shock experienced by the bombing victims and survivors a few short miles away in Oklahoma City, and I wanted to help in any way I could. The realization grew inside that this *was* my home state and that I grew up in the shadow of this Oklahoma City skyline that had just suffered a serious and unwarranted attack.

It's true that as that young person, I had wanted to put distance between me and Oklahoma; to look for more adventure and find it in places like Dallas, Boston, and L.A. I had taken for granted what Oklahoma had offered me while growing up: a home, family, a safe community, and a lot of friends.

Now that I was back and the city was facing a crisis, I suddenly felt reconnected to this place; this state; these people.

I wanted to help.

Why it took me most of the day to figure out how I could best help, I don't know. But sometime in the afternoon hours of April 19, the realization hit me: Even though I'd been in the classroom teaching journalism instead of practicing it the past two decades, that I still knew how to report and write a news story. And if everyone else was as hungry as I was for answers about what happened, how, and who was responsible, why couldn't I put my journalistic skills to use in helping find those answers for them?

It shouldn't be that hard to slide into that role. After all, I had once worked as a reporter and editor for both *The Oklahoman,* as well as *The Edmond Evening Sun,* the metro daily for Oklahoma City and the respected daily serving the northern suburb of Edmond that housed the University of Central Oklahoma. I had also reported and edited for two Dallas dailies before venturing to Missouri to get my PhD in Journalism. Surely someone could use my services downtown or in Edmond. I knew that in times of mass tragedies like this, newsrooms were bringing in all hands to help out.

My first call went to the publisher of *The Edmond Evening Sun,* Ed Livermore, who I had worked for back when I was starting out in 1970. We hadn't seen each other since then. Ed was only two years my senior and we had both been journalism majors at OU in the 1960s. The conversation went something like this:

"Hi Ed, this is Luke Jarrett, your old managing editor at the *Sun.* I'm back in Norman for a while, and I was wondering if you guys could use some help covering the bombing and its aftermath?"

Ed's response was a welcome one and got right to the point.

"Hey, Luke, great to hear from you. Can you be down here tomorrow morning at 8? We can definitely use you. I have a very young staff, and I'd like to put you downtown at Ground Zero to lead our coverage there. It's going to be an ongoing story for quite a while."

My response came tumbling out of my mouth.

"See you tomorrow morning at 8, Ed. And thanks."

Immediately I felt a sense of gratitude, and my perplexing question of how I could help was answered. The old familiar feeling of an adrenalin rush, one I used to feel when covering breaking news, was there again. So here I was, offering my services again as a special correspondent for what was now the *Edmond Evening Sun.*

What a privilege it was to be able to return to that newspaper and channel what I had learned over the years into serving my fellow

Oklahomans as they awaited any tidbit of news updates from the site of this tragedy. I realized there were still a lot of people who didn't know whether any of their loved ones or friends were among those killed; bodies still unearthed from the rubble of the Alfred P. Murrah Federal Building in downtown Oklahoma City. I empathized with them because I knew what it felt like to lose the love of your life.

My first day on the job came quickly, and I was on my way north to Edmond, about 25 miles up Interstate 35 and the Broadway Extension that ran north through Oklahoma City. When I got to the newsroom, I saw what Ed was talking about the day before: the staff was indeed young, most of them still in their 20s and – for some – this was their first news job. I was greeted by Carol Hartzog, the managing editor who impressed me immediately as a competent, poised, and dedicated journalist. In her late 30s, Carol was the most experienced journalist in the newsroom, by far.

As I got to know her over the next few weeks, it was obvious she was a fine teaching editor as well, working with her reporters to show them how they could make their stories even better and more accurate. She certainly helped me clear out any remaining cobwebs hanging from my years of inactive status as a reporter.

She would also allow me the freedom to compose my stories in somewhat unique ways. The days and weeks ahead would see me moving beyond my traditional inverted pyramid structure (most important to least important facts) and creating new ways of telling stories that begged to be told differently. More on this later.

But that was in the days to come; today was my re-entry day into daily journalism, and it would be a baptism by fire as I readied myself to drive south to the bomb site in Oklahoma City, the morning after the worst incident of domestic terrorism on American soil. It was 9:30 a.m., and my deadline for the afternoon Sun was noon. I had not worked the streets as a reporter for more than a decade, here I was about to walk into the biggest story of my life, and I had 150 minutes to make final preparations, get to the scene, come up with some interviews, shoot some photos, drive back to the paper, write the story, and file it with the managing editor. The pressure was rising as the minutes ticked away.

First on my readiness agenda was obtaining a press pass that would get me past the police tape and guards surrounding the Murrah Building. The Sun reporters didn't use them at the time, but I knew one would come in handy for this story because security would be tight around the Murrah Building. So for that, I drove a couple miles to the Oklahoma Press Association Building to pick up a generic Oklahoma press pass, then typed in the name of the Edmond Evening Sun, then went to Kinkos, had my mug shot taken and inserted onto the card, then had the whole thing laminated. I threaded a lanyard through it, slung it around my neck, and I looked pretty official.

I learned years ago that all you really need to get into a restricted area is a laminated card on a lanyard and a pencil stuck over your ear. Now to see if this would actually work at the police lines downtown.

It did, and the guard at the police tape waved me on through. It was then I got my first close-up view of the Murrah Building's carcass. Reporters were kept at arm's length, a block away at Northwest 6th and Harvey, because the ground on which the Federal Building stood was an active crime scene as well as the ongoing search-and-rescue site. But I was close enough to have the Murrah Building fill the frame of my vision, and it was a severe sight.

At least one-third of the 9-story building was gone, hollowed out in a semi-circle from the front, with the missing concrete, steel and glass all piled on top of each other below in a massive hole in the ground. Huge cranes were in place adjacent to the rubble, picking up large pieces of debris and depositing it elsewhere, or simply trying to hold pillars and remaining floors in place to prevent them from falling on the searchers and rescue dogs plowing through the pieces below.

At that time, there were still many bodies left under the rubble and now, over 24 hours after the explosion, hope was fading that anyone would be pulled out alive. It dawned on me that, whatever my own personal sadness over Selena was, it was small compared to the suffering going on among loved ones of the Murrah Building bombing victims.

That realization would revisit me many times over the next three weeks that I was at ground zero.

The longer you work at being a reporter, the more you get the sense of what to do at a disaster scene and who to interview. For me, I knew I wanted to talk with someone who had been among the searchers plowing through the rubble, looking for survivors. I felt it was important to know what that was like. I was surprised to find someone who fit that bill perfectly, and who actually looked like he was waiting to tell someone about it; just get it off his chest.

That person appeared in the form of a weary fireman in full gear, sitting on a curb along Harvey Street, breathing slowly and staring straight ahead. He seemed to be focused on something that was more an image in his memory than on anything physically in front of him at the moment. His legs were sprawled out and, in between them, sat one of the most beautiful Golden Retrievers I had ever seen in my life. I approached them both.

"Excuse me, Sir, but my name is Luke Jarrett, and I am a reporter for the Edmond Evening Sun," I began. "If you don't mind, I'd like to chat a few minutes with you, and your dog too, if you two don't mind."

The firefighter and his dog both turned their gaze toward me.

"Okay, I guess that'd be alright," he said. "But I'm pretty tired so don't make it too long please."

Pointing to the Murrah Building just south of us, he continued, "Aspen and I just came off of that rubble pile where we've been searching all night for survivors."

"I see," I replied. "Could I have your name please, and I believe 'Aspen' is that fine looking dog with you. Correct?"

"Yes," he said. "My name is Skip Fernandez, and this is Aspen. We're from the Miami Dade Fire Department in Florida and we're part of the FEMA team dispatched here yesterday to help out. There are units like us from several cities around the country."

Wow, I thought: all this information from this guy after just one question! This guy really does want to talk.

"How did your shift go?" I asked. "You look pretty worn out right now."

"It was tiring, but I didn't want to leave the pile. This is the most important job I've ever been on, and also the saddest. So many people were killed and injured here yesterday."

Skip Fernandez and Aspen
Photo by Jim Willis

He paused, then continued, "It's emotionally draining for those of us – including these great dogs like Aspen – to keep coming across dead bodies. But it's important for their loved ones that we dig them out so they can have proper funerals."

By this time, the count of those known dead stood at about 130, although only some 80 bodies had been found by then. But we were told that number would be rising over the next few days.

Skip was a fountain of information as we talked another 15 minutes. He told me about what it was like digging through the rubble, and how much help Aspen and the other search-and-rescue dogs were. Golden retrievers were used because they are such great "people dogs," and are trained to find those buried under rubble. Given their size and agility, they can also go into narrow and crooked spaces that humans can't.

As the interview came to a close, Skip allowed me to take pictures of both him and Aspen, and I swear that dog never took her big brown, sad eyes off me. It was then I realized what a long night this must have been for a dog that loves people so much. On this night, some of the people Aspen met were already dead.

To relieve the daily stress of these many rescue dogs, Oklahoma City had set up a large play area for them in the downtown convention center, which also housed their handlers and most other first responders from out of town as well. After the K9 teams finished their shift, they would go back to the convention center for rest and relaxation where the dogs, who had a strong play drive as well as a sense of mission, could unleash their natural instinct to run and chase tennis balls before bedding down for the night.

I thanked Skip for taking the time, and I don't think I've ever meant it more. His help was invaluable and gave me great insight into what it was like for these first-responders crawling through the mountain of debris that had been the Murrah Building. As I glanced at my watch, I saw it was only 10 a.m., and I already had what I came for.

I had plenty of time left to get back and write this story, so I decided to stay and pick up some more facts from the assistant chief for public affairs officer of the Oklahoma City Fire Department, Jon Hansen. This was the man who all of us reporters came to depend on so much during the weeks following the bombing. Hansen seemed tireless in carrying out his duties to hold regular briefings with the press, several times a day, right out in the midst of the parking lot where we were gathered. He was a committed firefighter and former fire marshal and believed in being as transparent as possible with the press corps.

Hansen has since passed away, and Fire Chief Gary Marrs noted in Hansen's obituary, "Jon Hansen was the voice of public safety and, for a long time, provided what the citizens needed to hear."

Former Oklahoma Gov. Mary Fallin said Hansen was "an instrumental figure in Oklahoma City's recovery from the 1995 bombing." She added, "His calm voice reassured everyone who was watching [and left them] with an implied promise that we could overcome the terror of that tragic morning. He personified the Oklahoma Standard before we had even put a name to it."

By the end of my first day hearing Hansen's reports, I agreed totally with both those descriptions of him.

So, my first day on the bombing site as a journalist was proving successful, and I was beginning to feel some self-confidence returning; probably for the first time since Selena died.

It would take me 20 minutes to get back to the paper, an hour to write the story and get the photos developed. I should have it all filed with Carol Hartzog a half-hour before deadline. And that's how it played out on this April morning. Here was the story I filed:

A 45,000-pound slab of concrete swayed dangerously above more than 220 rescue workers this morning. The rescuers are sorting through the rubble of the Alfred P. Murrah Federal Building for more bodies from Wednesday's bombing.

The 1,000-square-foot slab posed the primary danger and slowed rescue efforts even further.

"It's real big," said a grim-faced Skip Fernandez of the Metro Dade, Fla., Fire Department. Fernandez, who had just finished a 12-hour shift sorting through the rubble, added, "The engineers gotta work this problem out. It's in a key spot.

Fernandez, 39, is among the Miami firefighters who were called Sunday to the scene of the bomb blast. His 56-person unit works 12-hour shifts, and most of their search involves picking up by hand the 300 tons of pieces and slabs of debris.

"We're moving slowly, but there is still a lot of progress," Fernandez said.

He sits on a curb at Eighth and Harvey with another Miami rescuer named Aspen, a 2-year-old Golden Retriever. Aspen and the other dogs like her are working wonders, although she just started her career six months ago.

"She located two bodies just this morning," Fernandez said, stroking the fatigued dog as she sat panting in the shade of a small tree. "They were on the second floor, and she alerted us they were under the rubble."

Fernandez said workers had cleared most of the rubble out of the center of the building, but Capt. Gregory Gerlach, also of the Dade County team, estimated it would take another week to get to all of the bodies.

"You're dealing with people's lives, so you can't just go in and start swinging away," he said. "There is always an outside chance a person is still alive."

Gerlach said that, officially, the workers are still in a rescue-type operation. He acknowledged, however, that the chances of finding survivors alive is remote because of the amount of debris on top of them and the risk of hypothermia from the cold temperatures the past few days. Even if workers were to assume the status of simple body locators, Gerlach said the progress would be slow because of the peril that workers operate under.

"If you rush in, sometimes you create more of a problem than you're solving," the 46-year-old Gerlach said. "We have to be careful for the rescuers' sake if nothing else.

Gerlach, a 23-year firefighting veteran, said some additional children had been located early today, although none of them was found alive.

"We've located some children, but we haven't gotten them out yet. We've just seen their bodies in the voids."

In the search for bodies, the dogs and small cameras are proving invaluable.

"When we believe we've found a void behind a pile of rubble, we send in the dogs first so they can alert us if there is anyone in there," he said. "If so, then we send in the search cameras, which operate on fiber-optic cables and can transmit pictures back to us on the other side."

Gerlach and Fernandez agreed they take no major initiatives without first notifying the Oklahoma City firefighters. Altogether, there are four teams of 56 rescuers each, operating at any time in the building. At least a dozen of each team is made up of Oklahoma City firefighters. The two Miami firemen said they like to think they are "repaying a debt" to all the outside rescue teams who helped them out in the aftermath of Hurricane Andrew.

Still, Fernandez said he has never seen anything like this tragedy and the support from Oklahoma City at large in assisting the rescuers.

"I'm more impressed than I was with the cooperation I saw in Operation Desert Storm," he said. The former Marine, who still serves in the Reserves, added, "The people of Oklahoma City are one hell of a morale-booster."

Gerlach agreed. "We are used to eating regulation rations on these work sites, but these people have been feeding us calamari." He paused a moment to choke back tears. "Even my underwear came from these people."

It felt good to get this first story under my belt, and I left the newsroom shortly after filing it and drove back down to Oklahoma City to get more updates from officials and think about my next day's story. Then, worn out by the day's unrelenting pace, mixed with the sadness of what I had seen and heard that day, I got in my Isuzu and headed south on I-35 to Norman and my apartment.

As I drove, I sensed a familiar mood: the feeling of what it was like to be a street reporter again. It had been a long time since those days, and it reminded me of who I was *before* I met Selena. Strangely, that feeling reintroduced myself to me. It hit me that this was the first time since losing her that I realized I did have a true individual identity, apart from her. I was, in fact, an *I and not a We* anymore, and I hoped this could be my first real step in moving forward. Had it taken a tragedy like the Murrah Building bombing to open my eyes to that? If so, that was a feeling tinged with guilt.

13

An Ongoing Danger

Day 2 of my coverage began in the Edmond newsroom, reading through *The Daily Oklahoman*, which hit the streets at 6 a.m., and visiting briefly with my young colleagues about how the search had gone through the night at the Murrah Building remains.

Although most of the staff was inexperienced, they were all eager to learn and do well as reporters and editors. *The Edmond Evening Sun* had a long history of producing good reporters that went on to bigger things, and they contributed to a good collection of state press association awards for the newspaper while they were there.

I departed the paper about 8:30 a.m. and headed back downtown to Oklahoma City to catch the first news conferences of the day from Police Chief Gary Marrs and Assistant Fire Chief Jon Hansen. A key topic of discussion was the danger faced by the search-and-rescue teams – although by this time there was little hope of finding survivors.

The danger was posed by the extremely unstable nature of the rubble the searchers were trodding every minute of every hour of the day. There were reports of searchers falling through cracks and being injured, and others who were hit by falling debris that had broken loose from other pieces of steel and concrete above them. I had reported some of this danger in my first story, but I decided to go more in depth on this second-day story.

"We can't keep these people around here forever," said Oklahoma City Police Chief Gary Marrs, a week into the search process. He was referring to the many out-of-state units of firefighters, sent by FEMA (Federal Emergency Management Agency) to help the Oklahoma City firefighters in combing through the rubble. There were 56 from Dade County, Florida, alone, and they were each working 12-hour shifts.

Each day was dangerous for those searching through the bricks, mortar, steel and glass. The remaining portions of the 9-story carcass of the building towered above them, while the rubble they walked on could give way at any moment to added weight. That was especially the case in what was known as "the pit" or the massive hole in the ground in front the building where the bomb had gone off. Much of the cratered out portion of the Murrah Building wound up in that pit.

The unsteadiness of the remaining portion of the Murrah Building was dangerous enough. But Oklahoma winds in April blow hard and that created even more of a danger for searchers working beneath the twisted iron and steel carcass. High winds hampered workers most days as gusts would reach 40 mph at times. The wind would often come out of the north but, when it reached the hollowed-out building, it would swirl around and bounce back from the south.

"It is pretty scary in there," said Chief Marrs.

Structural engineers determined that when the building's pillars swayed past a certain angular degree, it was time to blow the horns and evacuate the site of workers. Large orange dots had been spray painted on the pillars and a drafter's compass was superimposed over the lenses of video cameras that was focused on these key pillars. When the pillars swayed too much, those horns went off loud and clear.

On one day, a mild shift in the rubble above – apparently caused by the winds -- caused a huge slab of concrete flooring to drop two floors before coming to rest on loose debris just above a busy work site. Some of the workers were below the falling slab, while others were standing on it when it fell. One of the rescuers threatened by the flab slide said it was a frightening moment.

"The slide occurred even before they could blow the evacuation signal," said Bill Lyons of the Metro Dade, Florida rescue task force. "It just happened so fast that we were running before the signal sounded."

But many could not run because of the tangle of debris they were already working in, he added. "There was also a body extraction going on in the pit when the slide came and it had to be stopped," Lyons said. "A couple of the firemen had to be dragged from the debris by others. The slab was just dangling above by a reinforcement bar in the floor. This was an aggressive work site. People were working with saws, backhoes, and there was a lot of teamwork going on."

Lyons said he thought the rescuers all escaped injury but the entire building had to be evacuated of workers as work was suspended for hours.

Coming out of the rubble with a search camera, one rescuer from Fairfax County, Va., compared the disaster to the 1988 earthquake in Armenia that killed 60,000 people.

"The worst I've seen before this was in Armenia," said Mike Regan of the FEMA Urban Search and Rescue Task Force. "The difference is that there we were trying to find people who were alive." By this stage in the search (three days after the bombing) rescue officials had given up nearly all hope of finding anyone else alive in the rubble.

There are a lot of things reporters should consider when reporting on disasters, especially those that take human tolls. I had taught these lessons for several years before covering the Oklahoma City bombing as a reporter, and my list of do's and don'ts expanded after the first few days of telling this story.

Although I had covered events (mostly natural ones like tornados and man-made ones like fatal traffic accidents) that cost a few people their lives, I had obviously never encountered any tragedy of this magnitude. It wasn't until a couple days in that the enormity of human lives lost, multiplied some four times by those people injured, sank in.

One of the lessons reporters learn about disaster reporting, especially in the immediate aftermath of the event: be careful not to either over-inflate the casualty count while, at the same time, not minimizing it. You don't want to be accused of either hyping a story beyond what actually happened, nor underplaying the magnitude of it. You don't want to panic readers and viewers, nor do you want them to think this was just another day at the office for violent offenders.

The years beyond 1995 would only make this balancing act harder for journalists covering mass acts of violence and terrorism and one – the 9/11 disaster – would even make Oklahoma City's day of violence pale in comparison; except for the citizens of Oklahoma.

14

The Human Element

American news stories *personify* tragedies and issues more than other countries of the world. So, focusing on the *human element* in disaster stories is another lesson journalists quickly learn. That approach zeroes in on the humans caught up in the suffering as a way of showing the depth of the broader disaster. It's like stopping a passing parade of disabled veterans to focus on how one trombone player is struggling with his prosthetic arm.

Writing about the Oklahoma City bombing and how it affected so many lives, I found myself at home in this role of telling individual stories about everyday people caught in this extraordinary tragedy.

It was an easy fit for this kind of story, albeit a departure from my traditional way of writing news.

I this this personalized focus resonates well because of our American nature of attaching so much importance to the *individual* rather than the group at large. Social scientists tell us that America is much more of an *individualist* culture than a *collectivist* one, prioritizing individual rights over collective ones and identifying more with their individual plights. Countries like Japan and Mexico are examples of collectivist cultures, while the U.S. is one of the most individualistic nations in the world.

This personification approach also comes out of the American belief (or at least hope) that the individual exerts *control* over his or her destiny: that individuals can change the course of history. America has always been an optimistic nation. Taking the lead in nation-building and winning both world wars has helped fuel that optimism.

I realized that what I was witnessing in downtown Oklahoma City was a display of that optimism; a refusal by the survivors of this terrorist assault to buckle under and instead to rise up stronger and move on to a better tomorrow.

FEMA responders bow in a moment of silence on April 26, 1995, at 9:02 a.m.
Photo by Jim Willis

The American news consumer often comes to care about disasters and troublesome issues largely because they identify with the individuals caught up in those events. So, the focus of much American journalism is on the tragedy of human lives lost as well as the bravery of those individuals helping to save lives.

I've spent a lot of time working in Germany and watching as German journalists focus more on the macro event or issue rather than the story of the individuals involved. There is a deeper willingness on the part of German readers to pay attention to issues themselves, without needing the connective factor of how individuals are being impacted by them. Certainly, there are exceptions to this, but the norm is less personification than in American stories.

Focusing on the individual is deemed so important by American editors that the Poynter Institute for Journalism published a "Writing Tips Sheet" on how to do it. Written by the Poynter writing coach Don Fry, the tip sheet is called, *Getting Real People into Writing,*" and includes the following principles, among ten others:

1. *Remember that news is about people and not about data.*
2. *Let the reader see and hear people in the story in action on site.*
3. *Describe gestures and actions more than things.*
4. *Select details that reveal character, and develop that character with little touches.*
5. *Don't read minds, but don't hesitate to convey thought and emotion if you have the evidence.*

On the morning of Wednesday, April 26, exactly one week after the bombing, I saw a great example of that human face as first-responders and everyone assisting them stood with heads bowed for a moment of prayer at 9:02 a.m. That was the time the blast had erupted and it was marked by a broad display of sadness and respect for those who had lost their lives.

"It's a week after the bombing, and I still can't believe what I'm seeing," said Miami Dade Fireman Angel Machado, who was among those bowing their heads for the moment of silence. He thought of the children in the day care center and wasn't sure how he would hold his emotions together when the searchers' digging finally reached that second floor. He only hoped it would be soon.

"We keep finding things we think may belong to the day care center, and we often think we're close," he said. "But we really may not know we're there until we are right on top of it.

Machado, who is a member of the K-9 unit who searched alongside his golden retriever, said progress had been slow because firefighter unit had to work in a small group of workers, each of whom has a different function. Attached to each search unit is a safety officer who alerts them to pending danger from falling debris or unstable footing, an agent from the FBI and one from the ATF. The latter two are searching for clues and reminding the searchers that this is not just a search operation but also an active crime scene where clues need to be found and preserved for later trials.

There was no escaping the human element of the bombing story. The following account of one bombing survivor came from an interview by the FBI and not a journalist. It shows the kind of impact such human-focused stories can have and why they are such a big part of disaster reporting.

This first-person account comes on the 20th anniversary of the bombing, and it is from Florence Rogers who was CEO of the Federal Employees Credit Union that was located on the second floor of the 9-story Murrah Building. It has since been published on YouTube, and it shows how innocent civilians bore the brunt of this violence as they were going through their morning routine just after their offices opened for the day:

"We always had people. We didn't open until 9 o'clock and we were open 'til 5 o'clock every day. The credit union was a place where everybody could go in there. Or the snack bar, the credit union and the snack bar. We were constantly inundated with people just coming in to visit, or draw out a little money for their lunch, or apply for a loan, so everybody—everybody—visited the credit union.

I got there as early as I could that morning; I had my cruise pictures from my vacation the week before. I had them all put in there and I was going to share all those with these gals when we met that morning. So we didn't get started on this meeting until about 8:20 that morning. I would turn around and look at my computer screen, at the next item that we were to discuss. I'd rear back in my chair and let them chat about who's going to copy this, and who's going to do this. Get this ready for the banking department so they could hurry with their audit.

I had just turned around in my chair and kind of reared back and was getting ready to discuss the next item that I had mentioned when the bomb went off. It had to be longer but it felt like seconds. All the girls that were in the office with me disappeared. I thought they had ran out and left me alone. I started hollering, 'Where are you guys? Where are you guys?'

Then, realization set in somewhat, and I realized that I don't know where they are. They are gone. Eventually I found out, that when the bomb went up and everything started coming down, that the seven floors above us had taken them down into what was eventually known as the pit.

There was just an eerie silence that fell over that whole scene. The papers were still fluttering. When the glass and stuff stopped, you know, there was glass found on buildings blocks away, everywhere. But this eerie silence was something.

I had been thrown on the floor and packed into my spot with stuff packed around me. I found out later that there was only 18 inches of exterior wall that did not break away, which kind of helped me there. My desk was sitting at an angle ready to topple over into this hole that the bomb had made where all my employees had landed

The stories of the Oklahoma City bombing produced many examples of both of this kind of personalization, and I wrote several of them myself. The balancing act comes into play as a journalist tries to focus on the individual victims without *re-victimizing* those who survived and the families of those who didn't. And that can happen simply by invading their privacy by trying to interview them while they are still reeling from grief, or by their reading your graphic stories of the horror that violently killed their loved one.

In Oklahoma City, the First Christian Church (the locals know it as the "Dome" church because of its architecture) became the gathering place and safe haven for survivors of the bombing and for families of the victims. Located at N.W.36th Street and Walker, it is not far from where the Murrah Building stood and has large grounds and parking to accommodate all who came to find solace there after the bombing.

The church as staffed with counselors and pastors from around the city who consoled these individuals and families, and it allowed survivors and families who lost loved ones to intermingle, hug each other, and offer support. The press was kept at arms-length and journalists were not permitted inside the building. Outside was a different matter, however, as many of us reporters would take a seat on a bench or just sit on the grass or curb and see if any of the survivors or family members wanted to share their stories of grief. The general rule among these reporters was to not urge anyone into being interviewed, nor to bother them if they just wanted to be left alone in their grief.

I felt very uneasy about asking anyone for an interview, but I was wearing my press credentials on a lanyard around my neck and, if someone wanted to talk, I would oblige them in as sensitive way as I knew how. From what I witnessed, most of the other journalists at the scene did the same thing.

Some of my interviews were done with people who were in their downtown offices working in one of the many nearby buildings that felt the effect of the bombing. One of those interviews was with Bill North, who was executive vice president of C.R. Anthony, a large chain of Oklahoma clothing stores. North's office was at Sixth and Broadway, just a block north of where the bomb exploded in front of the Murrah Building. I spoke with North eight days after the bombing, on April 27, as he and his staff were being allowed to return to work after the two-building Anthony complex was deemed safe for occupancy.

"By and large, we are all happy to be back," he said. "Most of us are glad to have a connection and a mission. People's emotions are wide-ranging. Most are glad to be back at work, but some are feeling discomfort over returning to the scene of the tragedy."

Although the building housing North's office was deemed usable, the second building of the Anthony complex was damaged beyond repair by the Murrah bomb and would have to be razed. Evidence of the damage to both buildings was immediately evidenced in the form of huge plywood panels covered gaping holes where windows had been blasted out by the explosion. In fact, plywood windows could be seen on most buildings over a six-block radius of the bombing site.

To North and his employees, it had seemed on April 19 that the bomb had exploded in their own building instead of a block away.

"The blast came right through the wall and knocked me to the floor on my face," North said. "I didn't think about what had caused it at first. I just remember thinking, 'Explosion!' My thought was, 'Am I hurt?' and when I found I wasn't, then my thought was that we all needed to get out of this building. It was like a hailstorm of debris in here. Fortunately, our injured were few in number."

All told, seven Anthony employees were treated for cuts and lacerations at area hospitals, but all were released. Anthony management sent all employees home immediately, but senior managers like North were back in the building that afternoon, gathering needed files and items to move to the Anthony warehouse at Reno and MacArthur.

"It was there that we developed a battle plan to get through this crisis," North said.

Six days after the Murrah bombing, the Oklahoma City Building Inspection Department gave Anthony management the all-clear to move back into at least some of the main downtown offices. But the work of dealing with employees' emotions was just beginning for North and his fellow managers.

"We needed to give these people every reason to understand this is a safe building and environment for them to be in," he said.

To that end, management assembled all employees for a 90-minute session and covered a variety of issues with them pertaining to the bombing and the effect on the Anthony facility and on employee emotions. Workers were told that experts in building safety had been through the facility and pronounced their portion as structurally safe. Cleanup crews had picked up all the debris and straightened the place up. Anthony also brought in four psychologists and made them available to employees – first by dispatching them to department assemblies which followed the main gathering – and then for employees to meet with individually if they wished.

While it may seem odd that an explosion directed at one building could cause so much collateral damage for so many other downtown buildings (300, according to the FBI), much of the answer is found in the kind of homemade bomb used to blow up the Murrah Building.

That was the focus of one of my stories about 10 days after the bombing where I interviewed members of the Oklahoma City bomb disposal unit who were still on site doing their job. On Day One, their job had been searching for any other bombs the terrorists might have planted in or around the Federal Building. There was also concern that, if there were other bombs, some might have had delayed fuses or could go off for some other reasons, days later. So, they were at the building site daily throughout the search and rescue process.

Their role had quickly expanded into trying to find enough parts of that bomb so that it could be identified, show why it had the effect it did, and be used as evidence when the bombers came to trial. By the time I interviewed bomb disposal officer Ron Keef, the unit knew exactly what kind of bomb it was and why its effect was so wide-ranging.

The Oklahoma City Police Bomb Disposal Unit is a volunteer force of (then) 13 officers, and it has never lacked for volunteers, Keef told me, ten days after the bombing, while on break from his 10-hour shift. He said there were at least four bomb unit officers were working on the site at any one time.

"We have had a large number of requests from police officers to join the team," Keef said. "And we haven't just been looking in the building itself, although that is where most of the bomb landed. Most people may not know it, but there are pieces of this bomb scattered over a 25-block area of downtown Oklahoma City."

Keef said nitrate-based explosives such as the one used April 19 have a unique kind of effect on its target and surrounding buildings.

"An aerial bomb has a cutting effect, but a nitrate-based bomb is more similar to dynamite and has a *heaving* effect," Keef explained. "It is designed to produce a massive shock wave, and this is what caused so much damage to area buildings."

Some of those damaged structures were declared unsafe for occupancy and actually collapsed over the week following the bombing.

Journalists covering the first days of the bombing carried with them another lesson learned from reporting on previous stories of mass violence. That lesson was to attend and report on the daily briefings held by the various fire, police, FEMA, and national guard units responding, but to realize that sometimes the presenters err in what they say. Sometimes that's intentional; sometimes not. Most agencies want to be as transparent as possible, but no presenter wants to make his unit look bad and will sometimes shade the truth to make them look good.

Happily, in the case of the Oklahoma City Fire and Police Departments, instances like this were few and far between. The briefings were usually very good and accurate, especially those done by Jon Hansen of the OKC Fire Department. He was tireless in making himself available to reporters, and we all appreciated that, and his candor.

My experience and training as a journalist were sufficient to keep my emotions from distorting the facts I gathered in Oklahoma City, but my feelings did influence the new ways in which I *wrote* my stories. Covering the aftermath of this tragedy had allowed me to find more appropriate ways to frame these facts.

For most of my professional life, I had usually written my news stories the *inverted pyramid* structure, but this destructive event I was covering caused me to present my work in different and more readable ways. I did that more from instinct than from conscious thought, especially as I saw how the bombing was affecting people.

For those who don't know, the inverted pyramid structure of news stories has its roots back to the Civil War days. When news correspondents were trying to send their war dispatches back to their home newspapers far away, they had to rely on the telegraph wires as their communication means. But those wires were always subject to sabotage by enemy troops and their allies; wires were often cut in efforts to shut down communication links that opposing forces were using.

Rather than building up to the most vital and interesting parts of their stories and risk having the lines cut in mid-transmission, the correspondents began the new technique of *starting* the stories off with those key points, and saving the details for later. Those key points have come to be known in the profession as answers to the "5 w's and h" questions (who, what, when, where, why, and how). If the wires were cut later during transmission, then as least the main parts of the story would get through to the editors back home.

Following the Civil War, this inverted pyramid structure continued to be used as the main way of telling breaking news stories. The allusion to the inverted pyramid depicts the wide mouth of a funnel (the summary) at the top of the story, funneling down to the details of that summary. In the age of heavy newspaper competition, reporters were always scrambling to be the first to tell the latest elements of a news story, although readers' attention was always subject to diversions. So, it just made sense to spit the main elements of the story out first.

In more recent decades – in the age of television social media – the attention has turned to more conversational styles of writing. That is partly because it has become increasingly difficult for any news outlet to scoop the digital media and, sometimes, even the social media in breaking an important news story.

These conversational structures of storytelling come out of the worlds of television news and of literary journalism. The latter was founded on the styles of writers like Tom Wolfe and Hunter S Thompson from the 1960s and 1970s. They offer more leisurely ways of moving into the heart of a story, much like the structure of a *novel* would. In a way, the writer flips the inverted pyramid back to the standard pyramid, starting with a relevant anecdote or description that suggests the story's theme, then moves on into the main elements of the story, finishing off with a climax and conclusion.

In covering the Oklahoma City bombing, I began using this *narrative* structure, starting my stories in a more anecdotal way and trying to blend the human element into the events and news updates.

This was not simply creativity for creativity's sake, however. There was a practical reason to frame my stories differently. That reason was our chief news competitor which was *The Oklahoman*, the metro daily for the entire Oklahoma City metro area and most of the rest of the state. We would obviously be reporting on the same daily events related to the bombing and its aftermath, and I didn't want to write stories that would be mirror images of theirs. The *Oklahoman* was a morning newspaper that hit the doorsteps around 5 a.m. while *The Edmond Evening Sun* was an afternoon daily, hitting the streets at 1 p.m. Often my front-page stories were covering the same updates as *The Oklahoman's*, so I had to put that wine into new skins; that normally meant focusing on the human aspect of those events and telling the stories in more of a narrative structure. We did, however, get the breaking-news advantage on updates that broke during the morning hours, after The Oklahoman's edition had already been published.

I had not been on the job long in Oklahoma City before I experienced the question that so many other disaster reporters have faced as they reported tragedies. That question is how to gather and deliver those facts as an objective journalist, yet also behave as a compassionate human being while in the midst of those tragedies.

Is it wrong to exhibit feelings of support for the victims? Is that somehow seen as taking sides? The most visible symbol of that debate became an innocent blue, white, and gold ribbon. Many mourners were wearing these as a symbol of grief and unity for those killed and injured in the blast. These ribbons were being handed out in Oklahoma City to wear on the shirts or jackets. They are the colors found in the Oklahoma state flag.

The question journalists faced – and I didn't even know it was an issue until I met a Texas journalist on the scene – was whether wearing such a symbol meant you were somehow taking sides in the conflict. Here's how that nighttime conversation took place with a young reporter from the *Fort Worth Star Telegram* as we were surveying the carnage a few nights after the bombing. She came up to me on the curb, and without introducing herself by name, challenged me for wearing the ribbon.

"You're a reporter, aren't you?" she asked.

"I am," I said. "I work for the Edmond Evening Sun."

"I notice you're wearing one of those ribbons."

"Yes. I feel it's the least I can do," I said.

"But don't you feel it shows you are taking sides here?" she responded.

"Taking sides? What are the sides in a disaster like this?"

"Well, there are a couple suspects who are charged with this crime," and you know they haven't been convicted of anything yet," she explained. "So the sides would be them and the victims."

"And you think that, by wearing these ribbons mean I'm saying they're guilty?" I asked. "All I'm doing is mourning the loss of so many innocent people here and showing support for their families. Is there another side to that?"

She paused and then said, "Well, as reporters we're not supposed to be emotionally involved in what we cover."

"You're not from Oklahoma, are you?" I asked.

"No, Texas. But it makes no difference. We're still supposed to be objective."

"You know," I said, "I get it, but have you asked yourself exactly what are we covering here at ground zero? Emotions are on display everywhere by just about everyone."

"So?" she asked.

"So, you think it helps you stay objective by not letting yourself feel what others, that you are reporting on, are feeling? And that distancing helps you understand the story – which is these people – better?"

"I just don't think it's right that we wear ribbons," she said, as she walked away.

I continued to wear the ribbon throughout my coverage of the Oklahoma City bombing, and I never once felt that it compromised my reporting in any way.

<h1 style="text-align:center">15</h1>

On-Site Surgery

We journalists wrote many stories of how survivors were rescued from the rubble of the building and the immediate medical treatment their injuries required. Not all of these surgeries could wait until these victims were taken to the hospital operating rooms. Some procedures had to be performed in the dangerous cavities of the Murrah Building where smoke will still rising from the blast and dangerous conditions prevailed on-site.

One such story, which is an exhibit in the Oklahoma City National Memorial Museum, was reported later by Sara Lentati of the BBC World Service.

It concerned the ordeal faced by Oklahoma City doctor, David Tuggle, who was busy at his hospital with surgical duties, instructing medical students as he went along. The morning of April 19 would dramatically interrupt his daily routine as word came in about the bombing at the Federal Building. There was no disaster drill for such an event as this, but Dr. Tuggle didn't have long to wait to realize what he had to do.

The Murrah bomb went off at 9:02 a.m., and within a half-hour the first children were ambulanced into his hospital's emergency room.

"The first three children that came in needed surgery," Tuggle told Lentati. "One had an exposed brain, one had an open leg fracture, and one had an injury to a blood vessel in the leg."

Those cases alone would have filled up his day, but he quickly realized these three were just the tip of the iceberg. After tending to these cases, Tuggle and his colleague Dr. Andy Sullivan asked one of the police officers to drive them to the explosion site to see if they could help with on-the-spot medical needs.

"It was a surreal experience," he said about arriving at the building 90 minutes after the explosion. "All of the ceilings were hanging down, we could see bodies that had not been evacuated, and they were still brining bodies out. I saw my dermatologist in scrubs and a gastroenterologist I knew in a three-piece suit walking inside the building without any protection [from falling debris] at all."

There were still people trapped under the rubble, and on the first floor Tuggle and Sullivan located a woman whose right arm and leg were trapped under a pile of concrete and steel. A rescue team was frantically trying to unpile the debris. Then they were escorted down to the basement level where another woman was trapped.

Her name was Daina Bradley, and she was in a small hole, wedged under a concrete column that had pinned her right leg to the floor. She couldn't get out, and there were worries about a pending second explosion in the building.

"Daina was conscious but she was cold, in a little pool of water, and there were a number of firefighters, rescue workers and paramedics who were down there with us, trying to figure out of there was a way we could left the cement pillar," Tuggle told Lentati.

But dislodging the pillar could lead to an even more serious problem: That column was supporting the remains of that portion of the building. Knocking it down could kill them all. One of the cadre of rescuers at that scene was a firefighter who was touching the pillar with his hands to see if he felt any vibrations. If he did, he was instructed to sound an alarm and clear the building immediately.

As if the situation wasn't serious enough, that evacuation alarm did sound after one of the bomb dogs got a whiff of explosives on the sixth floor above. Tuggle and Sullivan didn't want to leave Bradley but were pulled away by the firefighters to safety. Bradley was pleading for them to stay, and Tuggle told her he'd be back.

Sullivan returned to the hospital for medical supplies and sedatives. An hour after his forced evacuation, Tuggle was allowed to return to the building. He immediately went to the basement where Bradley was. He called Sullivan on the way using an early-version cell phone he had. The two doctors decided the only way to save Bradley from the debris was to take her leg off, and it would have to be done right there in the basement.

Bradley gave verbal permission for the amputation, and Tuggle injected her with a pain-blocker through a vein in her neck. He then applied a tourniquet above her knee. While that was happening, Sullivan crawled into the narrow space head-first and began severing her leg.

"He would work for a while and then he'd have to take a break, and I'd have to pull him out because he couldn't get out on his own," Tuggle said. "He'd come out and take a sip of water, pant a little bit, and then go back in."

Another problem, other than the cramped, dark hole Sullivan worked in, was the size of his amputation knife: it was too long to use in the hole, and his other shorter scalpels had been dulled by overuse.

"So," said Tuggle, "he pulled out his pocket knife and cut the last tendon with that."

With the amputation complete, the doctors were joined by some 20 firefighters who helped pull Bradley from the hole so they could clamp the blood vessels shut to prevent further bleeding. Then they removed the tourniquet, and the rescuers faced the daunting task of getting her out of the basement and then out of the twisted remains of the Murrah Building to safety and to the hospital. Easier said than done, as it turns out. When they arrived at the nearest available building exit, the ambulance they had called for was not there.

"We were standing there with our cold patient, with no ambulance," said Tuggle. "I was not happy."

Another ambulance was quickly summoned, however, and Tuggle rode with Bradley to the hospital.

Although she survived the ordeal, Daina Bradley's story still goes down as a personal tragedy. She had been in the Murrah Building that morning to pick up a Social Security card for her 3-month-old son Gabreon Bruce, whom she carried. Her 3-year-old daughter Peachlyn Bradley, along with her sister Felicity Bradley and grandmother Cheryl Hammons, had all gone along with her. Gabreon, Peachlyn, and Cheryl were all killed in the bombing. Only Daina and Felicity survived.

Looking back on that day 20 years later, Tuggle told Lentati he is unsure if the city will ever recover from that bombing.

"I think it will have a lasting memory for Oklahoma City," he said. "Probably for as long as there's an Oklahoma City."

As I heard stories like this and interviewed other rescuers and witnesses, I realized how utterly painful this bombing was for victims and survivors alike. I felt a sorrow and kinship arising in me with the people of Oklahoma City like I had never felt before, and I did my best to remain objective about all this even as I felt myself changing inside. Perhaps, after some fifteen years living in a privileged world of loving a beautiful female celebrity and was the envy of other men – a world where I wanted for nothing – I was now coming face to face with the sobering reality of life most people face in the real world. Now I was a part of that world. I felt, if I gave it a chance, this experience would cause me to grow in ways I had not done before, both personally and professionally.

16

Emotional Intelligence

During the rest of April and first part of May, I became not only professionally focused on the disaster I was reporting, but it was clear I had become personally affected by it. Going to ground zero each day and staring up at the remains of that building, with bodies still awaiting recovery below the rubble, sometimes made it difficult for me to be objective in my reporting. That is, if you define objectivity as staying personally *detached* from the tragedy. But I came to develop a different definition of objectivity during my weeks of covering this carnage, however.

I realized two things:

First, there was no way I *could not* feel for the victims and their families. And even though I was not one of them, I was still a native of this state and metro area. I was still a Sooner, and I hurt for what had happened to my state and its people.

Second, I kept reminding myself that my assigned part of this whole story was largely the *human* part: the part where you write about not only how the search for bodies is going, but how this whole mass killing was affecting everyone around here and how they were coming to grips with it.

A few years after this, I would read Sebastian Junger's book, *The Perfect Storm*, about the crew of the fishing boat Andrea Gail who was lost at sea in 1991. In interviewing relatives and friends of those fishermen, Junger said he had to stop several times and remind himself, *"Never forget these are real people, with real hurts, you are writing about."* When I read that in the year 2000, I thought immediately of how I felt covering the Oklahoma City bombing.

I had similar feelings of déjà vu over a decade later when I read Anderson Cooper's memoir, *Dispatches from the Edge.* In some ways, I felt the CNN journalist was telling *my* story, at least insofar as the impact that the tragedy I was covering had on me. Cooper was writing about his own pain of living through his brother's suicide and finding a way to vent that pain through the telling of the stories of *others'* tragedies like Hurricane Katrina. And, except for the fact my story was the Oklahoma City bombing, the impact on both Cooper and me seemed identical.

What I had stumbled into by returning to Oklahoma City was the kind of situation that Cooper *purposely* had sought out when he decided to pick up a camera and go cover the tragedies of the world. In hindsight, I'm not so sure my return to Oklahoma City *was* accidental.

I think of my longtime psychotherapist and muse, Dr. H.S. Sandhu, mentioning in one of our Boston visits, that word "accidental" in one of our sessions and applying it to things I'd done in my life that revealed my hidden needs. In the world of Freudian psychiatry, he said, the word "parapraxis" is often used in connection with those "accidental" events. A parapraxis can be a slip of the tongue or pen, forgetfulness, misplacement of objects, or other error thought to reveal unconscious wishes or attitudes. That, said Sandhu, can and does include decisions that we make that wind up meeting a repressed need we have.

I had come to Oklahoma to recenter myself and find a way to deal with my pain. Once there, I had run into a great tragedy that allowed me to release my pain by telling the story of those in greater pain. I still feel a little guilty about finding some healing in the midst of such a tragedy. Or maybe I just don't understand how that could happen, or why it should.

In his book, Cooper puts his experience this way and – again – it resonated in a startling way with me:

"I wanted to be someplace where emotions were palpable, where the pain outside matched the pain I was feeling inside. I needed balance, equilibrium, or as close to it as I could get. I also wanted to survive, and I thought I could learn from others who had. War seemed like my only option."

In a real sense, my reporting assignment was to cover not only the story of death but also the story of life and survival: the emotional trauma of the bombing. So, would it make sense to *distance oneself from feeling that emotion?* Wouldn't that make it harder to really understand and feel how all these people are feeling? No, I reasoned. So, whether by logic or just by virtue of having no real choice, I let myself feel for the victims and the families involved.

And that insight set me to crafting stories in ways that both honored the facts, but also honored how such emotionally gripping stories should be told.

I did not feel my reporting was sensational; it was fact-driven. To me, "sensationalism" is hyping a story that is already an emotional one; hyping it beyond the facts. In the case of the Oklahoma City bombing, emotions were essential facts; everyone was feeling them, and those emotions were driving their work to find those remaining bodies as fast as they could and to overcome the crime of McVeigh and Nichols and move forward, no matter how painful that was.

I discovered I was not the only reporter here that was feeling the trauma simply by talking with others who experienced it themselves. The Oklahoma City bombing was probably the first time a trauma center was set up *specifically for journalists* who were covering the event. Sponsored by *The Oklahoman,* the center was a suite in a downtown hotel where trained psychologists would sit and listen to any journalist who needed to vent their feelings about the personal impact of covering this tragedy, day after day.

About a week into my reporting, I ventured up to this trauma center out of curiosity. I would have gladly talked to one of the psychologists, but there were several other journalists in front of me, and my deadline was approaching.

I did notice, however, that some of the reporters seemed nervous about being there or, more probably, nervous about being *seen* there by other journalists. In the midst of their assignments, reporters like to present a stoic, even hardened, front to other journalists. The idea of showing off your emotionally vulnerable side – of showing that what you're witnessing is getting to you – is something many reporters guard against.

Nevertheless, there they were, awaiting their chance to talk out those emotions to a professional therapist.

In my teaching preparations, I discovered the work of psychologist Dr. Daniel Goleman, who authored a book that came out the same year of the Oklahoma City bombing called *Emotional Intelligence*. Goleman has uncommonly good insight into the role that our emotions play as we try to rationally evaluate what we are witnessing.

In the book, he stresses the importance of emotions in discovering the truth. He begins with a quote I like from Antoine De Saint-Exupery's *The Little Prince*: "*It is with the heart that one sees rightly, what is invisible to the eye.*" As Dr. Goleman talks about our emotional and rational minds, he notes:

"The emotional/rational dichotomy approximates the folk distinction between 'heart' and 'head.' Knowing something is right 'in your heart' is a different order of conviction – somehow a deeper kind of certainty – than thinking so with your rational mind ... These two minds, the emotional and the rational, operate in tight harmony for the most part ...

"Feelings are essential to thought, and thought to feeling. But when passions surge, the balance tips; it is the emotional mind that captures the upper hand, swamping the rational mind."

I would later write that it is the last paragraph in this quote that I feel is so important for journalists to understand: In times of increased passion, emotions do play a larger part in our thought processes. And perhaps this is not such a bad thing.

Emotional events might well call for an appropriate emotional expression to convey them accurately to the audience. And besides, unless a reporter is superhuman, he or she may not even have a choice in the matter. According to Goleman, they *will* be emotional, to one degree or another, in this setting.

So, in Oklahoma City I came to believe that journalists should not regard emotions as the enemy of good reporting. Most journalists know the positive role that an adrenaline rush plays in getting them to meet a deadline. Goleman explains the positive role of emotions in two of many examples:

1. "With fear, blood goes to the large skeletal muscles such as the legs, making it easier to flee. At the same time, the body freezes, if only for a moment, perhaps allowing time to gauge whether hiding might be a better reaction. Circuits in the brain's emotional centers trigger a flood of hormones that put the body on general alert, making it edgy and ready for action. And attention fixates on the threat at hand, the better to evaluate what response to make."

2. "An essential role of sadness is to help us adjust to a great loss. Sadness brings a reduction in energy and enthusiasm for life's activities, particularly diversions and pleasures, and – as it deepens and approaches depression – slows the body's metabolism. This introspective withdrawal creates the opportunity to mourn a loss or frustrated hope, grasp its consequences for one's life. As energy returns, it let us plan new beginnings. This loss of energy may well have kept saddened – and vulnerable – early humans close to home, where they were safer."

Perhaps it is not so important for us to try to divorce ourselves from our emotions as to try to follow the advice of Socrates who advised his students to, *"Know thyself."* If we can come to know and recognize our emotions and channel them into producing accurate and engaging stories, what is wrong with that?

As I would reflect on all this in the ensuing years, I recalled an instance from years before when I was managing editor of the *Garland Daily News* in the Dallas metro area. I was showing a new reporter the ropes and he was a different kind of recruit for us at the newspaper. He was a Dallas Cowboy cornerback named Aaron Kyle who had been a first-round draft pick from Wyoming. Unlike many of his teammates, Kyle was already thinking beyond football, and wanted to get experience in his chosen major of journalism.

So the paper brought him on as a summer intern, and I was taking him out to the breaking news site of a car-train accident to show him how reporting works, up close and personal. When we arrived, we saw the body of the mangled auto driver which was still behind the wheel of the twisted wreckage. I had seen this before, back in Oklahoma, covering a similar wreck. But for Aaron, the sight of violent death was brand new, and it hit him hard, I could tell.

I wasn't so much bothered by Aaron's reaction as I was for my own. He was feeling what any normal person would feel at seeing such a gruesome sight. I was the one with the abnormal reaction, because I wasn't feeling much of anything beyond how best to tell the story.

I wondered: Have I been in this business too long? Am I becoming so hardened that I can't experience a normal rush of emotions in witnessing tragedy? Or have I just become so good at burying those feelings so I can go about my daily routine of distancing myself from the life so I can report it accurately?

If that is what I'm doing, then I wondered if there weren't a paradox built into that thinking: Can I really report accurately on an event that I am distancing myself from? And even if I could, wouldn't the reader sense that I just don't care about what I'm witnessing? In that sense of sterility, would they find any humanity at all in my stories? Any caring at all?

Fast-forwarding to these April and May days in Oklahoma City, I felt more at ease with myself than I did back in 1978 with Aaron Kyle. The reason was I allowed myself to feel a great deal of sadness every time I showed up at the bombing site to do my day's reporting.

This is *my* city. I used to swim with the Boy Scouts in the Downtown Y just across the street from the Murrah Building and now a darkened, hollowed out shell of a building. There is a feeling I cannot shake that my city and the people I have known have been grimly attacked. I cannot distance myself from these emotions, but I wonder if they will warm up my reporting and distort its accuracy. Surprisingly, the opposite occurred.

My sadness helped me understand the relate much better to the people I interviewed like Miami firemen Angel Machado and Skip Fernandez, and many others. These searchers have seen things up close that I can only imagine, and I want to know what they know; to see what they've seen. Not for morbid curiosity. Just for accuracy and just because – like the readers hungering for information – I find myself caring deeply.

Again, I realized my part of this story was about emotions everyone was experiencing. How could I understand those emotions unless I allowed myself to *feel* them. And again I realized, I had no choice in the matter. I could not turn off the sadness.

Then there was this: In deciding to turn east off I-17 onto I-40 back in Flagstaff, Arizona, I had brought myself to another intersection where my own personal pain from losing Selena had collided with the collective pain felt by those in Oklahoma City who had lost their loved ones. It may sound strange to say I found a renewed energy and life force in the midst of such a tragedy, but I did.

In searching for a way to deal with my own pain, I found it in joining with others who were grieving something much more painful.

What a privilege it was to have the chance to articulate their grief, and what a catharsis it was to be able to release my own in the process.

17

❧

The Day Care Center

A key question in the early days after the bombing was how close the searchers were to finding the second floor and the daycare center located there. It took the teams a little over a week to unstack the seven floors of rubble that had crushed that floor and were lying on top of it. The missing children and infants were somewhere beneath.

At one of his press briefings, Chief Hansen picked up a toy fire truck recovered from the rubble and held it high for reporters to see.

"A broken toy is maybe a sign of broken hearts," he said, choking back emotions.

I don't believe there was another line I heard during my time in Oklahoma City that hit me as hard as Hansen's. One reason is there were so many toys, ribbons, dolls and teddy bears hanging on a make-shift fence near the Murrah Building. Surviving family members of young children had placed them there starting a couple days after the bombing. It was a constant visual reminder of the children whose lives had been snatched from them by the Oklahoma City bombers.

In the early days following the bombing, no one was sure how many bodies would be uncovered. A week into the process, some 99 bodies had been pulled from the rubble by searchers, but they knew there would be many more. Some officials feared the final count would be as high as 228. Searchers were stepping up the pace of their work in anticipation – or dread – of reaching the second floor and the day care nursery there. They expected to find fewer children's bodies than previously feared. The number of known missing children had stood at 10 to 15 the afternoon of April 26, when searchers were only one floor away from the second, but had been lowered to only 5 that night. What they would find among on that second floor would sadden them, however, as there were more bodies there than thought.

Hansen had told reporters that "rescuers were relieved to know there won't be so many kids in there." But, within a day, they would find 16 children's bodies – four of them infants – in that rubble.

Many interviews were held with surviving adults familiar with that day care center, and stories were published and aired about their accounts.

The center was called the America's Kids Day Care Center, and the 21 children – four of them infants less than a year-old -- had begun arriving as early at 7 a.m. the morning of the bombing as parents brought them in for the day, kissed them goodbye and told them they'd pick them up after work. But those planned pickups never occurred that day.

Melva Noakes was the owner of the center, but was not at the center on April 19. She phoned the manager just before 9 a.m. to make sure everything was okay and was told it was and that the four babies were all placed in their cribs by a window where they seemed to enjoy the sunlight streaming through. The 17 older children were eating their breakfast.

Satisfied, Ms. Noakes bid the center's manager good-bye and hung up the phone. A few minutes later, disaster struck in the form of 4,800 pounds of explosives just outside the walls of the Murrah Building. Within a minute, the walls of the day care center crumbled as seven floors of concrete, steel, and glass came crushing down on top of the second floor. Miraculously, a few of the children survived. But 16 others did not, nor did three other children who were killed in other parts of the building.

"It's been an awful experience on everyone," Ms. Noakes told reporters. She added she had just taken ownership of the day care center four weeks before. "It's a calling from God to work with kids, but I never anticipated anything like this," she said. "I have lost words. Their little bowls were in the street. I thought, "Why can't the children be there if their bowls are?"

Ms. Noakes and her husband have two sons and they were foster parents to 166 more by 1995. On the morning of April 19, however, she was working on a payroll at another of her day care centers. She had planned to go to America's Kids later to serve lunch. She told reporters she tries not to think about the randomness of why the children and her employees died, yet she was spared.

The person she had bought the center from was Kathy Cronemiller who had originally named it Uncle Sam's Kid Farm. She was also heartbroken over the tragedy.

"It's beyond my comprehension that somebody could deliberately blow up a day care center," she said. "It they did not, they're heartless; the most evil, horrible people in the world."

Reflecting on the day, Ms. Oakes said she drove from her Choctaw day care center to the Murrah Building as soon as she heard the news of the bombing.

"As we got down there, I couldn't believe it," she said. "I couldn't believe what I was seeing. I couldn't believe what I was hearing. Nothing prepares you for that. When I walked and finally turned the corner, it was like, there wasn't a building, and there was no landmark that I remembered."

She said the loss is unbearable. In addition to the children and a delivery man, three of her day care workers were also killed. Ms. Oakes said 9 a.m. was Bible time and that one of the workers was found with a Bible and child in her lap.

The day care center was installed in the building in 1988 and was designed to allow federal workers to have their children in the same building where they worked. The government had outfitted it with all needed equipment and even built a fenced-in playground area just outside. But the security features like an intercom system and doors that couldn't be opened from the outside did no good on April 19 when confronted with a ferocious bomb.

So many stories came out of the tragedy of April 19, and reporting on them would be my daily routine for the next four weeks until the remains of the Murrah Building were imploded on Tuesday, May 23. The Oklahoma winds didn't abate much that spring, and officials worried that a controlled implosion was much safer for all concerned than letting those winds do the trick, scattering the concrete, steel, and glass across several city blocks. Through those weeks, I produced some two dozen stories on the search for bodies and how everyone was reacting to this tragedy.

My own hometown of Midwest City, just 10 miles southeast of downtown Oklahoma City, was also directly affected by the bombing and lost both victims and first responders to the tragedy. Of the 168 dead from the bombing (ages 3 months to 73 years old), thirteen were from Midwest City. Four of them were my fellow high school graduates, and two were airmen stationed at Tinker Air Force Base. Of the 19 children who died in the bombing, three of them were from Midwest City, and all were infants and toddlers ranging from six to sixteen months.

One of the victims who typified the heroism displayed at the bombing site was a Midwest City woman killed trying to help others get out of the collapsed Murrah Building. She was Rebecca Needham Anderson, a nurse who saw the breaking news bulletin on TV in her home and drove immediately to the bomb site, 10 miles east, to help rescue victims.

She was especially concerned for the children who were trapped in the day care nursery.

Arriving at the site and identifying herself as a nurse to the police, she rushed into the building's remains and began digging through its rubble, pulling out victim after victim, taking each outside to safety, and returning for more. On one of her return trips into the building, a slab of debris fell from the jagged edge of a hole above her head in the ceiling. The piece hit her in the back of the head, but she managed to stagger outside to tell her fellow first responders she had been hit.

Refusing to take a moment to rest, she turned and went back into the building to rescue more victims, but she collapsed from a sudden seizure. A fellow rescuer saw her fall, picked her up and carried her out where she was rushed to the hospital. There she regained consciousness two times. Her husband was at her side, and she told him when she awoke the second time that she had no memory of what had happened. She then blacked out again, this time for the last time. She was pronounced dead four days later April 23. She was 37 years old.

Even though Anderson did not die in the blast *itself*, she was nevertheless listed as the 168th and final victim of the bombing. She was honored posthumously with several awards for heroism, and a *Time Life Special Edition* of the bombing referred to Rebecca Anderson as the "Fallen Angel of Mercy." (3)

The two Airmen 1st Class females from Tinker, Lakesha Richardson Levy, 21, and Cartney McRaven, 19, were typical of many of the fatal victims who were in the building taking care of personal business. Levy was there to get a new Social Security card, while McRaven was there to have her name changed on her card.

The most famous face of all the bombing victims was that of 1-year-old Baylee Almon, whose family lived on the eastern edge of Midwest City in the Choctaw area. Young Baylee was one of the children killed in the second floor day care center. The iconic photo of her being carried away by Oklahoma City Fire Capt. Chris Fields from the building, with her head bloodied and life already drained away, was featured in the news media around the world.

Shot by amateur photographer Charles Porter IV on his lunch break, who submitted his photo to the Associated Press, became the worldwide face of the Oklahoma City tragedy. The next year it won the 1996 Pulitzer Prize in spot photography. As was the case with so many other families of victims, as well as first-responders themselves, life would never be the same for Baylee's surviving family and for fireman Fields again who struggled with emotions of that day for years, while rising to the fire department rank of Major and getting some good professional counseling along the way.

One of the Midwest Cityans who saw first-hand the life saving work at downtown hospitals on April 19 was Carol Bolding Sykes, a graduate of MCHS and the University of Central Oklahoma.

A registered nurse in Oklahoma City at the time of the bombing, Sykes recalled, "I was on duty at Integris Southwest Medical Center. I had a patient in the room at the end of the hall nearest to the bombing site. She had a miscarriage and then a D&C. She was bleeding too much, and I went to call her doctor at the desk which is in the center building. After I talked to the doctor, I went back to check her, and her husband told me they felt the building shake and it was on TV that a bomb had gone off downtown.

"I hadn't felt anything at the desk. My patient's blood pressure dropped some more and bleeding somewhat increased. I knew she needed a D&C. I went to call her doctor and couldn't get through. All their phones were not working. I called his office and told them what was going on and so they could get the doctor to come in if he called them. Meanwhile I looked for any of our doctors, but none were there. Finally, one came up because he had a patient in labor. He prepared to take my patient to surgery. A few minutes later her doctor came rushing in. We got her to surgery, and she did fine."

Six children who were in the Murrah Building did miraculously survive the bombing. One was then-18-month-old PJ Allen, who today is an aviation technician at Tinker Air Force Base. On the morning of April 19, 1995, his grandmother, Deborah Watson, had dropped him off at the daycare center on her way to work up the street. A short time later, the Murrah Building exploded, and a first responder found Allen's body in the middle of the street outside the building. The child was rushed to the hospital where he was treated for serious injuries but survived. His family, first told Allen died in the bombing, learned a few days later that was wrong. Refusing to accept that news, Deborah

Watson began scouring hospitals in the area and found her grandson at the OU Children's Hospital.

Years later as an adult, he told Tinker colleagues his grandmother "saw a baby wrapped in bandages and the only thing that was exposed was my belly button," said Allen. "That was all she needed; she immediately knew it was me. Sure enough, it was me and luckily, I had been taken to the hospital and given care that I needed to survive."

Allen suffered from second- and third-degree burns over half of his body, a collapsed lung, a broken arm in multiple places and severe head injuries. At age 11, doctors were able to finally remove a tracheotomy that assisted his collapsed lung. He was left with injuries that would prevent him from serving in the military as a young man but he was able to realize his dream of becoming an aviation maintainer, working on KC-135 tankers, when he turned 30. He told Tinker colleagues then that he had been inspired to work for the Air Force out of appreciation of all the airmen who responded to the 1995 bombing and helped saved lives like his.

An Air Force news release would later say that, despite everything he has gone through and overcome, Allen says, it's so important to stay positive.

"A lot of people didn't make it that day," Allen said. "God chose me and others to carry out a mission for him," said Allen. "I still don't know what that is, but I just hope that eventually I can fulfill that. I'm going to be grateful for everyday that I'm given."

As it routinely does, when surrounding cities need emergency help, Tinker assigned personnel from across the base to provide search and rescue efforts at the bombing site and helped in other ways. Units pitching in were the 552nd Control Wing, Tinker Fire and Emergency Services, the 38th Engineering Installation Wing, the Navy, and the then-Oklahoma City Air Logistics Center. One of the many at Tinker volunteering his service was Air National Guardsman Ronald Brazer, who was a training manager with the 137th Security Forces Squadron.

Shortly after the bomb went off, Brazer reported to the site to help by transporting first responders to and from ground zero on a

48-passenger bus and helped in securing the perimeter of the bomb site. "When the explosion happened, it reverberated even though we were like 16 miles from ground zero," Brazer said. "Because we were at the [Will Rogers World] airport, we actually all were thinking that an airplane must have crashed at the airfield because that was the strength of the shockwave."

Hearing these stories of how my fellow Sooners responded to the bombing, helped recreate the emotional bond I had felt so strongly growing up there. I had wanted to get away from the state and see the world. I had done that, but now I felt drawn back to my home base and was proud of all the first responders who rushed toward what everyone else was running from that day in downtown Oklahoma City.

Over the course of covering these stories in April and early May, I often dropped in to see my folks in suburban Midwest City, and they always wanted to know the latest of what was happening with the search for bodies. One particular question that they and so many others had been asking over the previous three weeks was, "Have they recovered the children's bodies yet?"

They were referring to the bodies of the 19 missing children who had been in the building's day care center, which was located on the second floor of the 9-story building. It was not only the public who were awaiting word about the children, however, Every day as we reporters showed up at Ground Zero, that was often the first question was asked of fire department spokesman Jon Hansen: "Have the searchers gotten to the second floor yet?"

Searching through the rubble of the Murrah Building was a grueling exercise of digging from top down, one pancaked floor at a time, starting with the roof, then the 9th floor, then the 8th, etc. Since the children had been on the second floor, it took several days to reach the day care center. When they finally did, the sad – but expected – news was not one of the 19 missing infants and children had been found alive.

It was heartbreaking news for all of us in Oklahoma.

18

In Good Company

As I think about the work that reporters did in covering the Oklahoma City bombing, I realize that the challenges and the emotional struggles I encountered were multiplied many times over by the hundreds of journalists who had ascended on downtown Oklahoma City in the hours and days following the massive explosion.

This was home turf for the metro daily newspaper, the *Daily Oklahoman* (now *The Oklahoman*). Its managing editor was Ed Kelley, who became a friend and who is a fellow graduate of the University of Oklahoma School of Journalism and went on to become dean of that school. He had the able assistance of editors like Joe Hight, who was managing editor for features and who now holds an endowed chair of journalism at the University of Central Oklahoma.

Ed and Joe have always been dedicated journalists, and they led the newspaper's coverage of the bombing story from start to finish. They were on it through the trials of the two convicted bombers, Timothy McVeigh and Terry Nichols.

When I returned to university teaching after my Oklahoma months ended, I asked Ed to speak at a University of Memphis conference I organized called, "Covering the Disaster Scene." In his talk, he described

146

the massive effort *The Oklahoman* made in covering the Murrah Building bombing, which led it to receiving top honors from the Society of Professional Journalists and finalist status for the Pulitzer Prize.

"The crime took its toll on the city and the state," Kelley said. "Most of our readers and readers across the country were not familiar with terrorism. To give you a sense of just how powerful 5,000 pounds of oil fertilizer can be, at 9:02 a.m. we heard what could be called an old-fashioned sonic boom. Our building (eight miles away from the bomb site) shook so hard we thought *we* had been bombed. It was obvious we needed the help of every staff member. Everyone got a piece of the story including retirees, some of whom volunteered to work for free."

As I conveyed a couple years later in my book, *Reporting on Risks*, Kelley said the newspaper immediately dispatched as many people as possible to the crime scene on April 19 and the days following. The staff worked more than 150,000 hours of overtime, and 70 additional pages were produced within one month to tell the story. Many of these pages were ad-free, and this extra newsprint and ink for the entire circulation area proved costly for *The Daily Oklahoman*. But it was worth it, Kelley said, to take the lead in covering this hometown disaster.

The story was deemed too big for the city desk alone, so editors called upon all members of the newspaper team. Each editor was assigned an aspect of the coverage such as crime, damage, casualties, and community and family support. One person alone was assigned the casualty list and, for 28 days, did nothing but report and write obituaries and life profiles of the deceased. Some of the bet reporting, Kelley said, came from its sports writers who obviously knew how to write about people. The disaster also tested the skills of its graphic artists who composed many unique "infographics" depicting the severity of the bombing. The paper also placed a copy editor to act as a liaison between the artists and the editorial side of the newsroom.

The first edition after the blast came the next morning, with an additional 50,000 copies printed. The number was not enough. Some people who bought them would later get from $5 to $10 per copy of what came to be a collector's edition.

The paper's extensive coverage catapulted it into a worldwide media spotlight. The editors received calls from television stations as far away as Germany and newspapers in Norway and Sweden, and inquiries in the form of 22,600 letters from all 50 states, every Canadian province and eleven other countries. There were also immediate pleas from magazines and the foreign press for the photos taken by *Oklahoman* photojournalists.

Kelley concluded, "I wish a lot of readers who at times are so very critical of our profession could have seen what I did. Powerful, precise stories, photographs and graphics that were written and developed with a collective soul from a group of talented and very caring people There was no blueprint for what we did. There was no way to measure ourselves. There had never been a disaster like this one before. Hopefully there never will be again."

But the *Oklahoman* was only one of a score of newspapers covering the bombing and its aftermath. The disaster also showed what a small daily could do in covering the scene as well.

Actually, the first newspaper into print with the story was the paper I was working for: the *Edmond Evening Sun.* It was a 10,000 circulation daily in this northern suburb of Oklahoma City, about 10 miles away from the blast site. Out of the 168 who lost their lives in the bombing, 21 of them were Edmond residents. Many others were among the approximately 500 who were injured. So, this was a huge story for the town.

At 9:02 when the bomb went off at the Murrah Building, the effect within the Sun's newsroom was the same as Ed Kelley described at the *Oklahoman*, which as two miles closer to the bomb site. The blast shook the suspended ceiling in the Sun's newsroom, shaking dust particles loose that came drifting down onto the staff below. In the weeks to follow, the staff of the *Sun* pulled out all stops to cover the bombing and its aftermath, despite having a much smaller and younger newsroom staff. Like the *Oklahoman*, this suburban daily also received many accolades for its coverage in the months to follow.

Checking with emergency officials, the *Sun* learned that the Murrah

Building had been bombed and moved rapidly into action, dispatching a reporter and photographer to the scene.

The newspaper had a great advantage over the much-larger *Oklahoman* because it was an *afternoon* daily that went to press around noon. Therefore, it was able to hit the newsstands and homes some 17 hours before the *Oklahoman* would the next morning.

Thus, by the afternoon of April 19, Sun readers had the newspaper in their hands that gave them a graphic look in front-page pictures and stories of what had happened just a few hours before.

In a story published on April 21, the *Los Angeles Times* described the rush by the world's television news media to get to Oklahoma City and report on this scene of domestic terrorism. In the heat of the first day or two, more than a few of these anchors and reporters were stating rumors and facts, overstating what they could prove was true, and sometimes reporting pure fantasy. These miscues underscored the need for paying attention to the first lesson of disaster coverage, discussed earlier in this chapter: Don't overstate the facts, nor needlessly panic the public. What can result is reporting like the following, described by *Los Angeles Times* reporter Howard Rosenberg, whose story, "Some Miscues as TV Races to Oklahoma Bomb Site," reads like this, in part:

Temporarily diverted from O.J. Simpson [whose trial was underway in L.A.], they raced to Oklahoma like settlers taking possession of free acreage during the great land rush of 1889.

From a Sacramento affiliates meeting came Connie Chung to anchor The CBS Evening News from Oklahoma City without Dan Rather, who was en route to Vietnam, which had its own carnage to memorialize. [It was the 20th anniversary of the end of the Vietnam War]. From New York came anchors Tom Brokaw, Bryant Gumbel, Harry Smith, and Charles Gibson. Joining them was Geraldo Rivera.

Network correspondents poured in, too, as did personnel from some of the nation's largest local stations, including KNBC-TV Channel 4 [in Los Angeles], which jetted anchor Chuck Henry and reporter Gordon Tokumatsu to Oklahoma City on Wednesday afternoon.

After touching ground, Henry got on the phone and checked in live during his station's 4 p.m. newscast.

Anchor Kelly Lange: "What is the mood of the people at this time?"

Henry: "Actually, I just got here ..."

By Thursday morning, just about everyone had "just got there," and the whodunit speculation was already swirling like an Okie dust storm, as observers began digging through the rubble of some of the TV coverage ...

On display once again was the amazing capacity of TV newscasters to swiftly mobilize their technological resources for horrifically difficult live coverage of major breaking news, and also the perils entailed by such instantaneous coverage as reporters and camera crews and their studio colleagues madly scramble for fragmentary information that they can rush on the air while the ashes are still settling.

Rosenberg continues his account by noting all the early speculation that the bombing was the work of Middle Eastern terrorists. One TV station even reported receiving a call from someone from the Nation of Islam saying they are responsible for the bombing. The reporter acknowledged he couldn't confirm that, but he just wanted to let the viewers know about it.

Other reports from TV reporters saying they were quoting the FBI that they were seeking three men with "Middle Eastern-type" looks. They didn't specify what those looks look like. Then there was an interview with Oklahoma Rep. Dave McCurdy who said on TV that the Islamic terrorist group Hamas was involved in the bombing. There was no evidence given and it was not true.

Add to this all the hyperbole of how dangerous everyday life can be, spewed out by anchors trying to fill time until real factual information floated their way, and you had trouble knowing what was true and what wasn't during the first couple days of the bombing.

There are always some snafus in reporting the immediate aftermath of disasters, and some of it is attributed to sources who are doing their own unsubstantiated speculation. In balance, there was much more solid reporting than there were miscues.

I found it interesting – but not too surprising – that most of the major media reporters and anchors left Oklahoma City as quickly as they arrived, and pretty much did it en masse.

The exodus began some 10 days after the bombing and continued for a couple more days. The number of known dead stood at 142 by then, although searchers would find another 26 more bodies over the next few days. The story had turned too routine for the drama-hunting television networks and local stations and, after all, the O.J. Simpson trial was drawing more viewer attention than the Murrah Building bombing. So the out-of-town TV crews decided to leave town.

"It's pretty much just a body-count story now," one TV engineer told me as he was packing up his satellite news van to pull out. "The big drama is over for us."

So, nothing but empty parking spaces remained after the vans from Texas, Florida, and Kansas exited the lot we all called "Satellite City," a block away from the Murrah Building. So were the elevated platforms the major networks had constructed for their news anchors. Only CNN's platform remained, but its coverage was reduced to occasional cut-ins and most of the cable station's coverage had returned to O.J. Simpson.

By and large, only the Oklahoma City, Tulsa, and Dallas media remained, keeping their coverage intact as we reporters continued out interviews and – at times still stood with our gaze transfixed on the two and a half walls and chewed-up remains of 9 floors that encircled a mammoth hole where the center of the building had stood.

As we watched it, we would occasionally talk with each other and some of us wondered out loud if we would ever be able to get that image out of our heads. As I write this, in the year 2022, I can still see it standing there before me.

Also remaining, still buried beneath the rubble, were the missing bodies. Estimates of their number continued to fluctuate between 25 and 35 and, as it turned out, that was an accurate estimate.

Searchers had begun their second full day of daylight-only work on Wednesday, May 2, after Tuesday's decision to abandon night searches because of safety hazards caused by the building's shifting remains.

Officials had told reporters that the east wall of the building was actually tipping 28 inches to the east since blast day on April 19.

This day had seemed to begin slowly, and the only thing that really came at 6 a.m. was a hard rain which followed an all-night drizzle. Reports came from a National Guard officer in the street that searchers would "probably not go in" due to the wet conditions. The remaining TV news crews scrambled for information as their early-morning cut-in times approached. Then, slowly, the eastern-most huge crane began to move over the building. High atop it, American and Oklahoma flags fluttered in the breeze which turned into a legitimate wind an hour later.

Also flying in the wind from the partially-remaining top floors were flags from nearly all the states from where rescue teams had come, along with banners of the Red Cross, ATF, and DEA. These flags were visible evidence of the nationwide support Oklahoma City had received from search-and-rescue teams across the country. But, in talking with some of those workers, I learned that the searchers had also wanted the flags to show how attached to the people of the Murrah Building they had all become.

Most out-of-state FEMA task force teams were sent home a couple weeks after the bombing, and the number of on-site searchers stood at about 55 per shift, down from some 225 per shift who had been working before. The work area on the rubble was becoming smaller, and fewer searchers were needed to assist the Oklahoma City Fire Department.

One of the last three teams to leave was the Puget Sound, Wa., FEMA task force which pulled out victim No. 133 Saturday afternoon. Members of that team staged their own memorial ceremony Saturday night at the foot of the Murrah Building rubble, laying a wreath at the site as other FEMA teams had done upon leaving.

"It's a tradition for us," Capt. A.D. Vickery of Seattle told me in an interview. "It was important for us to do this to remember the victims and those who have helped rescue others and search for bodies."

Vickery said his team wanted to stay until the end but he understood why Oklahoma City firefighters were designated to close out the search.

"It's only fair that they finish it up," he said. "These are their people."

Still, Vickery said this assignment had brought back memories for him and his team.

"We lost four firemen in an arson fire in Seattle recently," and I think this effort brought our group closer together," he said.

Vickery's comments were echoed by team member Lt. Thomas Miner who told me, "The people of Oklahoma City have been fantastic through all of this."

Across adjacent streets, teams of workers contracted by the state to clean up and help shore up surrounding buildings trooped west on Fifth Street to start another day of work. One of those construction workers, B.J. Powell, told me that the damage to the inside of the nearby Federal Courthouse and Post Office building had been severe. Powell said workers had re-hunt most of the ceilings and repaired damaged walls in those buildings. Plywood still hung in place of glass windows, however.

"The north face of the courthouse got it bad," Powell said. "A lot of glass was busted out and embedded in the oak paneling of the rooms. I went into one room, and there was a lot of blood in the carpet and on the walls."

Back at the Federal Building, track-hoe equipment carefully was picking up large pieces of rubble and swinging it around for workers to go through by hand as they searched for bodies and clues.

Just another grim day at the office for these hardhats.

I met some good people in covering the bombing and got to know some of the other reporters. One of the most dedicated is a woman for whom I developed a growing admiration, and even a fond attachment. She was a local crime reporter, and her name is Paige Osborne.

She and I found it easy to talk with one another about our reporting. She was doing a better job about being stoic, whereas my emotions were probably on my sleeve. Paige was very good at her job, as intrepid as reporters come. She was a good researcher and a good writer, but with an empathy for the suffering going on around her.

Our paths would cross from time to time as we did our daily jobs near the bombing site and, while the thought of seeing each other socially might have crossed our minds, I knew I was in town only temporarily and our jobs were keeping us busy. Probably busier than we would have liked.

It was not until a couple months later that we decided to explore our friendship more, apart from the journalism connection between us. But I remember sensing a feeling about her then, and it was good to know I could entertain such a feeling as I was still going through the long emotional goodbye from Selena. I wasn't ready to move to another relationship yet, but I hoped the time would come soon that I did feel okay about it.

It gave me some hope for the future where new flames of romantic passion might arise from the still-glowing embers of the fire that was Selena.

19

❧

Star Crossed and Starry Eyed

Every day that I spent covering the Oklahoma City story was a day to push Selena back into the corners of my mind. But the nights and weekends were another story, so I found different things to do to keep my mind on the present and future, and not the past.

I reconnected with some old friends, spent time with my cousin Bob who had, by this time, become more like a brother to me, continued jogging through the OU campus and let my mind return to happier college days. Those were the days before I became so intent on being someplace other than where I was at the moment.

After college, my wanderlust led me to look over one hill, then another and another, and mobility became a prominent part of my profile. I wondered if my desire to constantly try out new places hadn't contributed to Selena's death on the streets of Boston. I had, after all, once again uprooted her from another city she seemed very happy in. Now, in this new city, death had reached out and turned our marriage into a modern-day metaphor for the medieval German legend of *Ladyhawke.*

In that tale, a witch's curse is place upon Capt. Navarre and Lady Isabeau. That curse prevents them from going forward as lovers, as she becomes hawk by day, and he a wolf by night. Here I was alive, but Selena was dead. Going forward together was not an option.

Ladyhawke had a happy ending for Navarre and Isabeau, but not with Selena and me.

For now, in April 1995, here in Oklahoma was where I found myself, not knowing what tomorrow would bring. I certainly did not expect it to bring a very different kind of relationship into my life, but it did.

Looking for distractions from the pain, I decided to travel south from Norman to Ardmore, about an hour's drive, on a sunny Saturday morning in early April and check out a horse breeders auction. Even though I grew up in horse country, in a town where the Shetland Pony became a familiar sight because of a popular pony farm there, I had never attended a horse breeders auction. I was certainly not thinking of buying a horse, but I thought it would be enjoyable to see some of the finest horses in Oklahoma and Texas strut their stuff in the arena as buyers bid for the steeds.

Had I just gone into the arena, taken a seat, and enjoyed the sale for a couple hours, it would have been a pleasant-enough day. Just not the great one it turned out to be.

Arriving before the auction began, I veered off into the barn where the neatly bathed and groomed horses awaited their moment in the sale ring. As I walked the sawdust aisle past the stalls, I realized I'd never seen so many beautiful animals in one place before.

The horses all began to blend into one continual blur, like a LeRoy Neiman paining, until I came to the last stall on the left and a two-year-old Quarter Horse mare bearing the hip number of 153. Her name was Star, and I was struck instantly. Her sorrel coat was so fine and smooth, three of her legs bore gleaming white socks, her ears stood at attention, and it was all topped off by a white lopsided blaze smack in the middle of her face, and just between two of the softest brown eyes that seemed to peer right into my soul. In the vernacular of equine enthusiasts, Star sported a lot of chrome.

"How would you like to come with me, big girl?" I found myself asking her.

She didn't say no. So, to me, the deal was sealed at that point.

To the uninitiated, a Quarter Horse is a well-built animal bred for speed, and reputed to be the fastest horse over a quarter-mile. She certainly sent my heart racing on this April day.

Star

It was love at first sight and, I knew she was exactly what I wanted. She could make the pain go away, in time. Would she be expensive? Yes. Did I care? At that point, no. I reasoned, if you can call it that, I had just lost a beautiful woman, so why pass up this opportunity to share my life with a beautiful equine? Expense is one thing, but the value that a purchase like Star could add to my life could be, well, invaluable.

It would be several hours before we could ride off to the sunset, though, because she wasn't scheduled to show until late afternoon. And, of course, I had no idea how much I'd have to pay to make this new dream a reality. Nor, for that matter, did I have a trailer to get her back to Norman. Nor did I have a place to put her back in Norman. And, oh right: I had no real cash on me. But I did have a brand new Master Card with a $6,000 balance.

I would need all of it.

I went back into the sale arena and sat on my hands while horse after horse went up for auction, afraid I might get impulsive and be tempted to bid on a lesser candidate before Star.

As I sat through this parade, I realized this wasn't the first time I had lost a woman and opted to go forward in life with a horse instead. It had been my senior year at the University of Oklahoma: 1968. I had been dating Susan for some time, and was so sure we would be married, that I cobbled together enough cash to surprise her with an engagement ring.

I took her to dinner for the formal proposal and was so sure she would spill her soup in her rush to spit out "YES!", that I didn't even notice when she said "no".

After a few seconds of a reality check, my words came: "Not sure I heard that right, Sue. Once more, please?" After all, since "no" can sound so much like "yes," I thought I'd better check, and this time I heard the subtle distinction. For a couple reasons, the kind that don't make much sense to anyone beyond 21, she had -- in fact -- said no.

Although we've both since seen the wisdom in her saying no, it took a while for my sanity to set in and displace my shock and awe that night. But we made it through the dessert, and I took her home. Then I went home, talked it out with my big sister, went to bed and had a good night's sleep.

When dawn broke, I decided to push forward. Zales would not take the ring back, so I decided to trade it for something that caught my eye earlier in the week: a horse named Shorty. Surely this kind of relationship would be easier to handle, and everyone knows how loyal your horse can be.

Everything was going okay until the next evening when Susan called to tell me she *maaay* have been a bit too hasty with the "no." She wanted the ring, after all. I was about to ask if she would settle for a horse instead because that's what the ring had morphed into, but I took the high road and said, "Let's think about that, Sue. This day has been rainy, and maybe you're just overly depressed right now."

The subject was never revisited.

As I've taught Interpersonal Communication in college over the years, I have sometimes suggested that students use a line like that when they want their "no" to glide down easily. It certainly worked well for Susan and me and allowed us to have much better lives than a hasty "yes" would have handed us.

Back to Star, waiting eagerly in the barn to start a new life with me. It was approaching 5 p.m., and she was one of the last horses to enter the sale ring that Saturday afternoon. Watching her go through her paces, I resolved that no one was going to separate me from this magnificent animal.

The bidding began, and it was lively. A half-dozen of us were battling at the start but, after a series of $100 and $200 bumps, I leap-frogged a thousand over the last bid, and there were only two of us left. Another thousand later, and there was just one.

Star and I were now a twosome, my Master Card was obliterated, and I figured out the rest of the logistics before nightfall.

From that point on, this horse and rider spent several years happily exploring the hills and trails of Oklahoma and, later, Tennessee. She seemed to make it her mission to get me over the hurdles I faced. I like to think I did the same for her.

More immediately, in these few short months spent in reunion with Oklahoma that spring and summer, I stabled Star a couple miles south of Norman and I would see and ride her daily after driving back from the bomb site. She was a lifesaver on many of those days, lifting my spirits and reminding me that life is not all tragic and that even a horse named Star can bring a shot of sunlight back to my days.

Then, on Monday morning, I was back at the Murrah bombing site, churning out more stories of a people rebounding from this massive grief.

20

Finding the Killers

The Oklahoma City bombing was a jigsaw puzzle of a story, with the three biggest pieces being the ground zero search-and-rescue operations for victims, the reactions of Oklahomans to the carnage, and the search for the suspects responsible for the act.

I was focused on the first two of these pieces. I also covered a few of the funerals of Edmond victims (the suburb lost 18 residents in the bombing), for which we got permission from the families first. Then there were memorial concerts by entertainers such as Vince Gill, Garth Brooks, and Sandi Patti, who had personal Oklahoma roots.

The final death count would not be released until May 18, when the official search would come to an end. That figure was 164 dead, although another four would be added to the list later, making the total 168. The exact number of injured was hard to gauge because of how to categorize the cause of injury. For example, some motorists and passengers were injured in nearby traffic accidents, and flying debris from the building contributed to some of those. In the end, some 650 people were believed injured, many seriously, by the blast. An estimated 646 people were inside the federal building when the bomb went off. Five of the dead were outside the building and even in adjacent buildings.

It was Oklahoma's Day of Infamy.

Ironically, the easiest part of the whole puzzle to solve was the search for – and arrest of -- bombing suspects.

Just 90 minutes after the bombing, the Oklahoma Highway Patrol stopped a car being driven north on I-35 toward Kansas, because the car was missing a license plate. Upon a cursory visual inspection of the vehicle, the officer noticed a bulge in the driver's jacket and the butt of a Glock handgun protruding from a holster. That, plus the missing license plate and no proof of insurance for the car, were enough for the patrolman to arrest and detain the driver, who turned out to be one Timothy McVeigh.

Looking back on the role he played in arresting McVeigh, Oklahoma Highway Patrol Officer Charlie Hanger's story, reported in 2015 by native Oklahoma journalist Hailey Branson Potts of the *Los Angeles Times*, went like this:

Like all the local legends in this little town, Charlie Hanger has a portrait hanging on the wall of the Kumback Cafe, between the photo of outlaw Pretty Boy Floyd (said to have once eaten the biggest steak in the place) and the state champion wrestling teams.

"Town Hero," Hanger's photo says.

On April 19, 1995, Hanger — an Oklahoma Highway Patrol trooper so by-the-book that locals swore he'd ticket his own mother — arrested Timothy J. McVeigh, 90 minutes after a fertilizer bomb in a Ryder rental truck exploded outside the federal building in Oklahoma City.

Sunday marks 20 years since the bombing of the Alfred P. Murrah Federal Building, which killed 168 people and injured hundreds more in what was then the deadliest terrorist attack on U.S. soil.

Around these parts, Hanger —a quiet, unassuming man who now serves as sheriff of rural Noble County —will forever be known as the Man Who Caught McVeigh. To hear Hanger tell his story is to recall how skilled police work, but also luck, led to the arrest of the decorated Army-veteran-turned-radical who was later convicted and executed.

"I call the fact that I was put in the right spot at the right time divine intervention," Hanger said last week. "I've never sought attention for it. I'm not a person who likes a lot of attention."

On that cool spring morning, Hanger had been ordered to the disaster site and had driven just few miles outside Perry — a town of about 5,000 people 60 miles north of Oklahoma City — when he was told to stay in his area.

Hanger was driving north on Interstate 35 when he passed a rusting, yellow 1977 Mercury Marquis with no license plate. He stopped the car and found behind the wheel a clean-cut, 26-year-old Timothy McVeigh wearing military boots and a windbreaker.

McVeigh also wore a T-shirt with a picture of Abraham Lincoln and the words his assassin, John Wilkes Booth, shouted in Ford's Theater: "Sic semper tyrannis." ("Thus always to tyrants.") On the back was a quote from Thomas Jefferson: "The tree of liberty must be refreshed from time to time with the blood of patriots and tyrants."

McVeigh didn't have proof of insurance or a bill of sale for the car. He told the always-suspicious Hanger that he was on a long, multi-state drive — moving to Arkansas and on his way to get more of his belongings. But there was no suitcase in the car. No change of clothes, either.

As McVeigh reached into his rear pocket for his driver's license, his windbreaker tightened, and Hanger noticed the bulge of a shoulder holster under his left arm. McVeigh was wearing a loaded Glock pistol and had a 6-inch knife on his belt.

"My gun is loaded," Hanger recalled McVeigh telling him as Hanger grabbed the bulge under the jacket.

"So is mine," the trooper responded, putting his own gun to McVeigh's head before arresting him for unlawfully carrying a concealed weapon. If he hadn't spotted the bulge, he would have let McVeigh go with a ticket.

As Hanger drove back to the Noble County Courthouse, McVeigh, sitting in the passenger seat, rattled off the serial number of his gun, correctly except for a single digit. He asked Hanger how fast his car ran, what kind of firearm he carried, how he could get his own gun back.

"I thought it was just nervous chatter," Hanger said. "The radio was going. They were still sending units to Oklahoma City. I never made any comment

about it and he never made any comment about it. I thought, 'He's just passing through. He doesn't know what's going on.'"

Hanger booked McVeigh into the Noble County Jail, inmate 95-057, and took his wife to lunch. Like everyone else, he was glued to the TV news coverage of the bombing.

As the nation searched for the bomber and public speculation lingered on men of Middle Eastern descent, McVeigh sat in a concrete cell atop the aging courthouse.

McVeigh was supposed to go before a county judge the next day, Thursday, but his hearing was delayed because the judge got tied up in a messy divorce case. The hearing was rescheduled for Friday.

Hanger was at home that morning when a dispatcher with Highway Patrol headquarters called asking if McVeigh was still in jail. Hanger doubted it, since he could easily make bail, but to his surprise McVeigh was still there, his car still parked by the interstate about 35 miles south of the Kansas state line.

McVeigh's hearing had been delayed again, this time because the judge's son had missed the school bus and the judge had to give the boy a ride. McVeigh probably would be seeing the judge any minute, Hanger told the dispatcher. Put a hold on him for the FBI, he was told. Now.

The trail that led to McVeigh had begun with the discovery of the Ryder truck's rear axle.

Flung two blocks from the blast site, the axle still held the vehicle identification number, which led authorities to the rental agency and then to a motel where McVeigh had stayed, registered under his real name. Staff said he resembled a composite sketch of "John Doe No. 1," seen near the Murrah Building before the explosion.

Authorities had learned McVeigh was in jail because Hanger had run his Social Security number through a national crime database after his arrest.

Word spread fast in Perry that something was up.

Hanger was back at the courthouse when an angry crowd gathered on the lawn — some screaming, "Baby killer!" Hanger slipped out of the building in plain clothes and rode home with another trooper to avoid attention.

His role quickly got out and people wanted him — reporters for interviews, Oklahomans just to say thanks. Someone went to the local florist and tried to order flowers for Hanger, planning to follow the delivery driver to his home. Someone else sold maps to Hanger's house to reporters.

Hanger didn't do interviews, but that didn't stop locals from talking about the strait-laced trooper. No one seemed surprised it was Hanger who made the arrest. The assistant district attorney told a reporter that Hanger once testified at a trial, and when the 12 jurors were asked if they'd ever received a ticket, 10 of them had been written up by Hanger.

"He was always fair in the enforcement of the law, a no-nonsense type of guy," said Don Stoops, Hanger's former partner, now retired.

These days, Hanger says he was just doing his job, though he later realized that, had he made one false move, McVeigh could have shot him on that highway.

"Looking back later at who I was dealing with, what could have happened — that was more frightening than what happened that day," Hanger said. "I often run the whole scenario back through my mind to see if there was something I missed, something I should have picked up on, and I'm just glad I didn't let him go."

The arrest defined Hanger's career. He was elected Noble County sheriff in 2004 and barely mentioned McVeigh when campaigning. Around here, he doesn't have to.

Two decades on, McVeigh's co-conspirator, Terry Nichols, sits in prison while the pain and anger remain potent for Hanger and many Oklahomans. Hanger well remembers McVeigh's eyes. There was no emotion.

Hanger can recite all the minutiae of the arrest —but when he talked about the 19 children killed that day, the lawman in the black cowboy boots choked up, and his big, blue eyes turned serious. He can't bring himself to visit a memorial where victims' photos are displayed.

"The attention needs to be on the victims," he said quietly. He goes sometimes to the bombing anniversary events in Oklahoma City, but not always. When he's there in uniform, he feels like a distraction

"He's so humble about it," said Marilee Macias, owner of the Kumback Cafe.

"He doesn't like it when people call him a hero," she said. But that won't stop them.

So, as this story relates, on April 20, the day after the bombing, police realized they had arrested the man who blew up the Alfred P. Murrah Federal Building. FBI agents had found the rear axle of the Ryder rental truck McVeigh used to house the bomb. They traced the truck to the rental car agency and got McVeigh's name and physical description.

A composite sketch was made of him and circulated to the national crime data base, and that's when the FBI made a shocking discovery: McVeigh was already in jail in northern Oklahoma on the concealed weapons charge arising from his traffic stop by the Highway Patrol.

Within a few days the FBI would find and arrest his main accomplice, Terry Nichols, and one other accomplice, Michael Fortier.

Nichols would turn himself in for questioning in Herrington, Kansas, after hearing he was wanted as a material witness in the bombing. Two hours after his questioning, he was formally arrested as an accomplice to McVeigh. He went to trial in 1997 and was convicted for 161 counts of state murder, first-degree arson, and conspiracy. He was handed a life sentence without parole in a federal prison.

Fortier was arrested in Arizona where he worked in a hardware store and witnessed McVeigh test his homemade bomb nine months prior to the bombing. He pled guilty to railing to alert authorities to McVeigh's plot, lying to federal agents after the bombing, and selling stolen guns in order to raise money to finance the bombing. He would serve just over 10 years in a federal prison before being paroled. He and his wife Lori were then put into a federal witness protection program, given new identities, and provided with free housing, according to the Dallas Morning News.

The plan to carry out the Murrah Building bombing was hatched over the course of a year before McVeigh lit the fuse on April 19, 1995. He studied how to build and finance the bombing, built it, tested much smaller versions of it several times, and then put the final pieces of the plan together.

Evidence would later show that McVeigh rented the truck in Junction City, Kansas, drove it to a secluded spot in Oklahoma where he and Nichols filled it with 7,000 pounds of ammonia nitrate, an explosive mixture of chemicals and fertilize, and then McVeigh had driven it to Oklahoma City on the morning of April 19.

His destination was the Murrah Federal Building, and his intent was to kill as many people in that building as possible. His motive was revenge for the way the federal agencies – most notably the Bureau of Alcohol, Tobacco, and Firearms – had handled the Branch Davidian assault in Waco two years before. This was the anniversary date of that fatal assault on cult leader David Koresh who was, it was believed, posing a clear and present danger to his followers and to the federal government.

McVeigh had arrived at the Federal Building just before 9 a.m., lit the fuse to the bomb, then got out of the truck and walked to a getaway car he had parked a couple blocks away. He surmised he would have time to reach the car and drive out of town before the truck bomb was discovered and certainly before it exploded.

He was wrong on the second point: He got to his car alright, but the bomb exploded before he got out of the area, and the blast apparently had blown the license plate off the back of his yellow Mercury Marquis. He didn't know he was heading to the interstate without a license tag. Things went from bad to worse after that for McVeigh, Nichols, and Fortier, as they were eventually all convicted of their roles in this devastating attack that left so many dead and injured.

Tinker Air Force Base, in nearby Midwest City, served as the makeshift federal courtroom (in Building 460) to which McVeigh was brought for arraignment the day after he was captured. That arraignment would have happened in the Murrah Federal Building but, because McVeigh had blown it up, Tinker served in its place as the only other federal installation nearby.

"It was interesting to see his demeanor," said Henderson Ray, a sheet metal mechanic at Tinker and an Oklahoma County reserve deputy who was one of the first responders and who was on base when McVeigh was brought in for arraignment. "Tinker is and was part of the Oklahoma City community," Ray said. "It's unique in the way that Tinker has developed within the community and the amount of investment that the community has in Tinker. But this event showed that Tinker did and does step up for the community."

With these arrests, residents of Oklahoma City breathed a breath of relief. At least now they believed there no longer an active bomber threat crouching in the dark and waiting to replicate the horror of the Murrah Building bombing.

As for McVeigh, he would be convicted in federal court on all eleven counts related to planning and carrying out the Oklahoma City bombing and killing 168 people. He would be sentenced to death on August 14, 1997. Thus, would begin a series of appeals, all of which McVeigh lost, and he was executed by lethal injection on June 11, 2001, at the Federal Correctional Complex in Terre Haute, Indiana.

Nichols would turn himself in for questioning in Herrington, Kansas, after hearing he was wanted as a material witness in the bombing. Two hours after his questioning, he was formally arrested as an accomplice to McVeigh. He went to trial in 1997 and was convicted for 161 counts of state murder, first-degree arson, and conspiracy. He was handed a life sentence without parole in a federal prison.

Fortier was arrested in Arizona where he worked in a hardware store and witnessed McVeigh test his homemade bomb nine months prior to the bombing. He pled guilty to railing to alert authorities to McVeigh's plot, lying to federal agents after the bombing, and selling stolen guns in order to raise money to finance the bombing. He would serve just over 10 years in a federal prison before being paroled. He and his wife Lori were then put into a federal witness protection program, given new identities, and provided with free housing, according to the *Dallas Morning News*.

21

Farewell

The search for bodies at the Murrah Building came to an official end on May 10 when searchers came as close as they would to extracting all known bodies from the devastation. The final death toll from the April 19 bombing was 60 people fewer than the 228 that officials had feared were dead.

When the search ended that Thursday night, firefighters from Oklahoma City and 11 FEMA teams had pulled 164 bodies from the rubble, and 18 of them were children. Two adult bodies would never be found, Chief Jon Hansen said, and two more would die later from critical injuries sustained on the day of the bombing. Then there were the known injuries that numbered at least 645 victims.

"It's a miracle all but two of the dead were found," Hansen told our gathering of reporters in a midnight briefing. "But we have compared lists with the medical examiner, and are down to two out of the entire number of people lost. It's a sad relief, however. They (searchers) did it for the victims' families, for their communities, and for the state."

With the search over, the remains of the Murrah Building were turned over to police and FBI agents to continue their search for clues as to how the blast actually occurred and to gather more evidence for coming trials of the perpetrators. After that, the General Services Administration (GSA) was to get the building, and it would be their final decision to demolish it. There was some discussion of preserving the structure and restoring it, but polls were taken that showed 68 percent of Oklahoma City respondents favored tearing it down and building a permanent memorial on the site. Eventually, that's what would happen.

On Friday, May 11, a final on-site memorial was held at 2 p.m. in memory of the victims and in thanks for those who came from near and far to help rescue those who could be rescued, and search for the bodies of those who could not. I covered that story, and I will never forget what was uncharted territory for me as I reported on this outdoor memorial service, held on and around the rubble of the Murrah Building. It was also meant to be a show of gratitude for all the many first-responders from Oklahoma City and around the nation who came to help in the mammoth search-and-rescue operation. Another body had been found from the day before, leaving only one known body, a nurse who was still unaccounted for despite the best efforts of the search teams.

I showed up early for the service, and it was the first time most of the reporters were allowed to stand on the building's site. It was no longer deemed an active crime scene, and the building was set to be imploded a few days later, although there would be at least one delay before that was done.

My own emotional firewall I had erected three weeks ago had cracked a couple of times since then, and it would fall later this day. I could feel it coming when I stood on the building's bricks and mortar under a beautiful Friday afternoon sun. I had brought my Minolta 35mm camera along with a telephoto lens, and it helped immensely as I scanned the wide area looking for individual vignettes, facial expressions, or artifacts that would speak more voluminously than a thousand words. I wrote about them in the story that follows.

I knew there was a formal program planned as a stage and dais had been erected at the base of the building on which the Oklahoma governor and mayor of Oklahoma City would speak, along with others. But I also knew that the story I was going to tell would have nothing to do with those formalities or what might be said. Upon arriving, I knew instinctively that my goal was simply to bring my readers to this scene to see, hear, and feel some of what this rubble and these many mourners had to say simply by their presence and demeanor. It was going to be a story based almost totally on my observations of what lay out in front of me and memories of all I had seen and heard since the day of the bombing. Frankly, I didn't know where to begin.

I knew I had time to work it out, though, because this was Friday afternoon, today's paper had already gone to press, and the Sun had no Saturday edition. So, this story would be for Sunday, and deadline wasn't until tomorrow afternoon. Still, I wanted to write it while everything I saw, heard, and felt were still fresh. After the memorial service ended, I walked hurriedly to my car, parked a couple blocks away.

Along that short route, nearly a month after the Murrah bomb had gone off, after all the days and weeks of witnessing the carnage at ground zero, all the while dealing with feelings about Selena, my emotional dam broke. I was at my SUV, and I remember reaching out for the door handle, and then freezing in place while the tears flooded out. I leaned into the still-closed car door for support and just let my feelings out. The whole scene probably took less than a minute, but it seemed longer. The tears ceased about as abruptly as they had begun, but it was the cathartic moment I needed.

As I entered the car and sat down in the driver's seat, I instinctively pulled my cell phone from my jeans to call my Selena, just as I used to do after I had experienced an impactful event. While dialing her number though, the reality hit me hard that she, of course, could no longer answer. So I hung up and called my parents.

"Hi Mom, this is me and I just called to say I love you," I began. "I'm at the site of the bombing, and I had this overwhelming need to call you and Dad and tell you we all have to work to make sure nothing like this ever happens again. It's too tragic for words."

Mom waited and responded, "I hear you Luke, and I love you, too. Papa and I have been watching, and we can't imagine what it's like for you, being right there at the scene. But I agree it can never happen again."

I felt better after letting my emotions out and connecting with my folks that day. Then I turned the car toward Norman and my apartment to begin writing about what I had witnessed this afternoon. I couldn't wait to get to my Mac and start writing.

Once there, I launched into the story with all the zeal and adrenalin a writer feels when they know they have a story that must be written and they know it deserves a unique way of being written. I was glad that I would have a lot of time to collect my thoughts and rewrite the first drafts, because the *Sun* did not publish on Saturday, my deadline wasn't until the next afternoon (Saturday). As it turns out, I would not need the extra time.

On my drive to Norman, the afternoon sky had turned dark and it was raining hard now. As I sat down and began to write my story, I heard the first claps of thunder and saw a couple patented Oklahoma lightning streaks. Interesting background noise for such an electric story, I thought. The story wrote itself virtually as my observations, memories, and feelings coalesced into words that spread across the screen like soft butter spreads across warm toast. I was about five pages into the story, with the finish line in sight, when one of those lightning bolts hit the roof of my building and my Mac screen went instantly dark. This was the time before built-in surge protectors and automatic saves.

When I restarted the computer, my story was gone.

I sat there and stared at the blank screen, let out a loud moan and more than one "Shit!" but then regrouped and challenged myself to mentally recoup what I had just written.

As a professor of journalism, I've lost track of the number of "my-dog-ate-my-story" excuses students parried when they missed a deadline. But ever since this experience of losing my own story, in which I just started typing again and wrote what I think was an even better story, I am deaf to those student excuses.

"Then why didn't you just turn around and write it again?" I ask those students.

I submitted my story to my editor Carol Hartzog the next day, and I was not at all sure she wouldn't ask for a major rewrite, because this piece was told so unconventionally. One of the liberating things about writing a good story is that the form just seems to take its own shape as you move along. Writers sometimes speak of "opening a vein" as they pour their blood into a story.

Former *Baltimore Sun* reporter Jon Franklin, who won a Pulitzer Prize for a story about a woman battling cancer, recalled John Steinbeck talking about the feeling of holding "fire in my hands" when his writing is hitting the mark.

"I never knew what that meant," Franklin said. "[But] I started reading [my story] through and I noticed that my heart was racing. The piece was having a physiological effect on me. Whatever the hell it was, it was a moment you do not forget when you get a feeling from your own piece. God it was fun."

This is exactly how I felt writing this memorial story. It was having this kind of emotional effect on me, although I wouldn't call it fun. But it was what good writers are in the business for: to tell an important story in a way that will bring the reader to the scene. For this story, I was guided by the fresh memories of what I had witnessed, and my goal was simple: I wanted to bring my reader to the scene; to *see and feel* what we all were seeing and feeling.

My subconscious seemed to take over and glided me through the writing process and, when I was finished and looked back over the draft, I was surprised to see I'd written much of it in the second person. That was something I'd never done before, it was against a basic rule of Journalism 101 to stay in the third person, but I felt it hit my goal of allowing others to see what I had seen. I guess Carol saw that, too, because she approved it with no edits at all.

Here is how that story, headlined with a simple ***Farewell***, read:

You stand on Fifth Street in the shadow of what once was the Alfred P. Murrah Federal Building. The sun bathes the scene, and there is an official ceremony underway, but that story is dwarfed by what your eyes take in as you look around.

You can't take those eyes off the nine-story carcass in front of you and how it is affecting the many who have gathered here.

Hundreds of search-and-rescue workers come to pay their respects. They remember those 168 who died inside its walls, including the two women's bodies, yet unrecovered, and nurse Rebecca Anderson who lost her life after heroic attempts to rescue victims children from the building.

Six of those lost are still unidentified.

And they remember the many who did so much in trying to save the savable and locate the lost.

On Saturday, it would be the survivors and victims' families who would be doing on-site remembering. They would each be given a rose and allowed to pick up a piece of the rubble and take it home.

They would be allowed to meet individually with Gov. Frank Keating and then continue their mourning at the First Christian Church. It would be a much more private ceremony and run longer than this public, 10-minute rite.

But on this Friday, it was time for the rescuers, volunteers, and even journalists to remember and to mourn.

You look up and see this monument of man's inhumanity to man, it's hollowed-out section of floors, and the rubble pile remaining below. Yet you also know you are staring straight into a tower of love and self-sacrifice. You think instantly of the Oklahoma City police and firefighters as typified by Gary Marrs, Jon Hansen, and Sam Gonzales.

You think also of far-away firemen like Miami's Angel Machado, Capt. Greg Gerlach, and Skip Fernandez with his wonderful Golden Retriever, Aspen. The dogs like Aspen could have been anyone's backyard pets, but they were born to a greater mission of search and rescue, and they acquitted themselves brilliantly here.

Everywhere you look you see flow-ers, wreaths, teddy bears, and hand-painted signs of thanks. A rose juts its dark red head out of an orange high-way cone wrapped in duct tape that looks like it has been kicked more than once by a frustrated rescuer. Another rose dangles from the tripod belonging to a Reuters news photographer.

Elsewhere, two fatigues-clad Na-tional Guardsmen – like many of their comrades, -- bow their heads and clutch rose stems behind their backs. An FBI agent does the same.

There are those who insist that, in the battle between the eye and the ear, the eye wins every time. That seems true here today. There is so much to see, so much to take in. There is so much to remember for fear that – if you don't – you may forget your resolve to hate violence in any form.

You realize this is the legacy of violence.

Still, if you let your ears take over for a moment, you can hear the sound of bagpipes coming from somewhere down front, near the rubble pile ... near the infamous crater the bomb created. The strained music of the pipes seems a fitting memorial to those who lived and died and tried here.

If you can pull your eyes from the sight in front of you and pivot north, you see another moving image. In a blown-out window frame from five floors up in the Journal-Record Building, you see a team of hatless hardhats taking a break from clean-up and repair duties. They cluster shoulder to shoulder and lean out the space, gazing at the scene just south of them, across Fifth Street. They gaze at the Murrah Building's remains. They seem like men with hard jobs, but at this moment they are thinking very soft thoughts. [They are pictured on the back cover of this book.]

A rose juts out of a safety cone placed near the rubble.
Photo by Jim Willis

If you let your imagination wander as you survey that Journal-Record Building, with its windowless walls and top floor opening to the sky, you can almost hear it whispering to the federal building. It could be consoling its friend saying "I understand. I hurt, too. That was one hell of a blast, wasn't it?"

The same might be heard from the Downtown Y, standing just to the east of the federal building. Eleven million dollars. That was the Y's damage estimate. Like the 19 children who perished in the Murrah rubble, the Y stands as a symbol of innocence vastly underserving of such a fate. If ever there were a tribute to more peaceful things in life it is that YMCA.

You think to yourself, "I used to swim there as a child when I was in the Boy Scouts." But what you see now is a darkened cavern inside with headlamps of workers peering out, and miles of plywood windows blocking out the sun from this once-happy building.

Looking up again at the Murrah Building, you see spray-painted numbers everywhere, identifying the remaining columns. There is a gap between columns 20 and 22, where 24 once stood. This is the building's chief crater where so many of the innocents died.

You see the bracings put in place to keep the tilting columns from falling or caving in and bringing much of the remaining building down with them. Reporters were told earlier in the week that the entire east wall had tilted outward 28 inches since the April 19 blast. Oklahoma winds can do that.

As your eyes scan the floors and columns, you realize you are looking at a giant, hand-painted grid. You think of the grid paper you used back in high school drafting classes. But you know these grids signify missing structures; not planned ones. As you continue looking, your eyes are drawn into the remaining office spaces themselves, now open to the great outdoors. The walls are gone. You see rows of heaving filing cabinets, desks, coat racks, and rows of book cases. Some things have been untouched by the bomb. But, on the other side of an office, there is a hole where nothing at all exists. Your eyes pan downward and you can see the crushed debris below. And you can only imagine, in horror, that all of that would have fallen on the trapped humans below.

You remember the one terrific briefing where columns 20 and 22 of the Murrah Building were described, and of why they figured so prominently in the danger to searchers plowing through the rocks below.

You look at the sections of missing floors up above and remember the story of the man picking up his Social Security check and of the clerk reaching across the counter to give it to him. He lived, she died. And you realize that, on Wednesday, April 19, at 9:02 a.m., life or death for some was a matter of which side of the office floor you were standing on.

You recall first-responders like Jon Hansen saying how much the FEMA teams had waned to stay on the job past today and see it through to its end. Now, without any doubt, you understand why they feel that way.

After all, straight ahead in your line of vision is the pile of floors pancaked on tops of each other. And in between the first and second floor slabs were the bodies of 19 children in the Murrah Building daycare center.

And you pray fervently that no one will ever see anything like this again.

In reading through my story, I realized this had been an opportunity to reflect with the readers about much of what had occurred in the few short weeks since the Murrah Building exploded. And I was gratified when a woman wrote a note to me after reading the story.

It said simply, "Thank you, Mr. Jarrett. Your story made me feel like I was there at that memorial."

Since that was my intent in writing it the way I did, her comment reminded me that what I was doing was worthwhile. It was also an experience that writers crave: having the privilege to latch on to a story that tests you in every way possible and to feel you have applied your talents well to the challenge. It would not be for another year that I would come across writer Jon Franklin's comment about a writer's "holding fire in your hands," but – when I did read that – I realized that was exactly what I had done with the *Farewell* story. I had now been a journalist or journalism instructor for nearly three decades, and it had never been more exhilarating than it was after covering the Oklahoma City bombing.

After the *Farewell* story was written, there was only one major ground-zero assignment remaining for me, although most of the nation's journalistic core had pulled out and gone home a week or more earlier. I was still struck by their absence, because the story of how Oklahoma was recovering from this mass murder was much more than a body-count story. But I also understand the economics of the news business and the fact that, if it's not an event playing in your backyard, your station management wants you home covering those events that are. It's just not worth the expense of having you cover "someone else's news."

But there was still one major story yet to come, and that was the planned demolition of the Murrah

FBI agents stop with other responders to pay homage to the victims.
Photo by Jim Willis

Building, only a few days away. It would be delayed for weather and technical reasons until May 23, but Carol Hartzog assigned me that story and, as the day approached, I wondered how I would meaningfully fill this gaping hole on Page 1 that was reserved for the story of an event that would take only a few seconds to complete from start to finish.

On the night of May 22, I decided to go down to the reporters' parking area we called Satellite City, look at the Murrah Building on the eve of its destruction, and – strange as it sounds – see if it could be my muse and show me how to frame this story. When I arrived at the parking lot about 9 p.m., there were no other reporters around. I was glad, because I didn't want any distractions as I contemplated tomorrow's story. I knew that if the implosion were delayed an hour or two, I would be on a short deadline. Maybe I could even write some background material for the story tonight and just top it off tomorrow after the blast was done.

It was a warm evening, and I got out of my car, sat on the hood, and stared up at the remains of the building. I'm not sure how long I just sat there looking and remembering all that had happened over the past three weeks. At some point, it occurred to me that this building was not very old. Then, as I looked around to the neighboring structures, I realized the Murrah Building was like the new kid on the block. I decided to research the origins of the building later that night when I got home, and a frame for the story began forming in my mind.

I arrived at the implosion scene about 6 a.m. on Tuesday. The blast was to occur promptly at 7 a.m., and I was ready for it. I was one of a battalion of reporters and photojournalists who were standing in Satellite City, waiting for the go-moment. The charge exploded on schedule, and the Murrah Building crumbled before our eyes, landing in a heap of dust and smoke within a few seconds. It was over almost before it began. I turned to go back to my car, and head to the paper to write the story. But my focus was diverted by a young police officer, Julian Barden, in the same parking lot who stood by his squad car, just staring intently at the rubble. I was curious, so I decided to walk over and chat with him.

"Good morning, officer," I said. "I'm Luke Jarrett, a reporter for the *Edmond Evening Sun*, and I see you had the same idea I did about getting one last look at her."

He turned and smiled, and I was grateful he didn't just bark orders at me to leave him alone.

"Right. This sort of falls into the weirdness category," Barden said. " I hate to see it fall. There's a strange attachment to this building."

"I agree," I said. "I have felt that, too, over the past few weeks."

It turns out, Barden was one of the police officers on-site the morning of the bombing, and he said it was horrible working the northwest corner of the building where few survived. I could tell he was still envisioning what happened the morning of April 19 and, like Skip Fernandez who I met on my first day of coverage, Barnett seemed like he wanted to talk about it.

He told me he had actually been sitting in his squad car all night, just staring at the building's carcass. I didn't want to rush him, though, so we just stood there looking up at rubble. Then, quietly and pensively, he broke the silence.

"I was here from the beginning," he said, still staring at where the building had stood. "I think about that day of April 19. I think about the two bodies still inside the rubble. I would have given anything just to have found one person alive that morning. I keep thinking, what if there were a way to undo it? I drive by that building all the time. What if one of us had seen him and stopped him?"

At 7:10 a.m. Officer Barden stood alone by his squad car, staring into the void at Fifth and Robinson.

"It's done," he said.

I asked if I could quote him, and he said yes. So, Officer Barden wound up in my story that day, and I often wonder how he has dealt with his memories over the years since the morning of April 19, 1995.

As for my story itself, the framing that I feel the building itself gave me the night before was the one I went with. And if I thought my memorial story of a few days before was unconventional, this one probably topped it. Once again I was surprised that Carol approved it and didn't ask for a rewrite.

The story began this way:

Amid an immediate family of much older siblings, the teenager died just after dawn today.

Mortally wounded by assassins' explosives a month ago, the Alfred P. Murrah Federal Building was finished off by less than 150 pounds of charges that were detonated about 7 a.m.

Some 7,000 pounds were used on April 19 to turn most of the building into twisted and hollowed-out carnage. The inanimate giant, which has – in a strange way – come to life over the past five weeks, survived the firing squad.

But today, it seemed to await a single officer who stepped forward, pulled a pistol, and put a bullet into its brain.

When the end came, it was swift, sure, and even surprising to those trained observers who had been glued to their vantage points since 5:30 a.m.

The Murrah Building was 18 when it died. Nearby at its death were downtown's older, more venerable, buildings like the Journal-Record Building and the Downtown YMCA, along with the Southwestern Bell Building and others.

Under a partly-cloudy sky and with a brisk wind blowing from the south, the explosive charges ignited. The warm spring air was filled with several short, loud reports, and the building was gone within the few seconds predicted by Controlled Demolitions International.

It seemed much quicker, but the operation was surgically precise and was carried out as planned. The center and elevator shift dropped forward to the north, then the east and west wings toppled inward.

A cloud of dust rose from the debris and was carried north to Seventh Street by the prevailing wind.

The sound seemed as fitting a memorial as Oklahoma City has witnessed yet. The several short, curt blasts came within nanoseconds of each other.

They formed a sound strangely similar to a 21-gun salute.

When the smoke had cleared five minutes later, the building had disappeared. It was like watching magician Doug Henning in a television act where he jerks a jetliner or the Statue of Liberty from your conscious view.

But this was no stunt, and the Murrah Building is no more.

I have thought about that day and that story many times over the decades. What I saw and felt standing on the Murrah Building Rubble will always be a part of me. The fact that all that carnage, death, and pain was inflicted upon so many innocents, and that it was the work of two right-wing extremists carrying a two-year-old grudge against the government, still seems insane.

As I've told the story of the bombing to my university students over the years, I rarely get through it without feeling a catch in my throat as the emotions swell up inside me. Each year, the date of April 19 reminds me of the horror that was unleashed in downtown Oklahoma City in 1995.

Responders brought the flags of their agencies to hang on the
building before they left. (Photo by Jim Willis)

22

Leaving Oklahoma

I have made a few choices in my life that have proven to be the right ones, without a doubt. The choice I made back in Arizona to turn east to Oklahoma was one of them. It had, in fact, changed my life and prepared me to move on to the challenges that still lie ahead.

It was here I found a renewed purpose in life, began the process of regaining confidence in myself, even as I was providing a needed service for my fellow Sooners in finding and delivering answers to their heartfelt questions about the Murrah Building bombing.

In the ensuing years, I would be asked by various media and journalistic groups to reflect on Oklahoma City and what it meant to me to be able to cover this attack on my home state. Those reflections took both oral and written forms, as I would often speak about it to my students and write about it in my books and in two commissioned pieces for the *Edmond Evening Sun*. The first of those appeared on April 19, 1998, the three-year anniversary of the bombing, and it went like this:

I told myself I came back to visit my family, but I could have picked any weekend for that. For months in the back of my mind was this one weekend, especially Sunday, April 19. Coming back to the bomb site three years later.

183

Coming back to a pivotal point in my life. Coming back to remember ... and hopefully to feel again.

Three years ago, I had been visiting my parents in Midwest City, taking a leave of absence from my teaching post at Boston College and trying to put the wheels back on my life's Radio Flyer. A shattering personal tragedy had left that wagon in pieces, scattered across a thousand miles of grieving.

I was searching for a way to forget. Or at least to deal with the pain. Then, on Wednesday morning, April 19, 1995, my personal pain collided with a far greater collective pain that emerged from the dust, debris, and devastation that was the bombing of the Alfred P. Murrah Federal Building.

Hearing a distant, undefinable sound from a diner where I was eating breakfast in Norman, I didn't realize at first how this event would affect me personally. By the end of the day, that reality was streaming in like a door to a dark room opens slowly, allowing the outside light to seep in and gradually fill the room.

I have been in the news business for three decades and have seen a hundred faces of tragedy during that time. There was the sweet innocence of a 5-year-old girl who was killed by a falling beam as she sat in church one Sunday morning in Garland, Texas, 20 years ago. Ten years ago in Boston, Charles Stuart turned a gun on his pregnant wife, moments after emerging from a class on childbirth. Blaming it first on a black attacker, Stuart later took his own life after the police realized it was Stuart himself who had been the shooter.

Then, just a few weeks ago, there was the tragedy of four children and their teacher gunned down in a Jonesboro, Ark, middle school.

In between, there have been so many other stories of pain that they have faded, for me, into a collective blur over the years.

All except the Oklahoma City bombing.

As a journalist who now teaches future reporters and editors, I have trained myself to put distance between me and the pain of others. I have coached my students to do the same. Remember what you are, I say. Do your job first. Remain objective. Yes, there are times when that pain invades you personally. But it usually in the quiet, reflective moments after the tragedy – if, in fact, there is time for such moments.

Always, though, there are the exceptions. Thankfully, for me, Oklahoma

City was that exception in the spring of 1995. It may sound macabre to say I found a renewed energy and life force in the midst of such a tragedy. But I did. I needed a way to express my own pain, and I found it in joining with others who were grieving over something much more painful. What a privilege it was to have the chance to articulate their pain. What a catharsis it was to be able to release my own in the process.

I will always be grateful to the Edmond Evening Sun – the newspaper at which I began my career many years ago – for putting me at the bomb site and allowing me to report on its aftermath.

Over the years since the bombing, I have spoken to many groups, both in the United States and in Europe, about covering this tragedy. Always the thought is within me that I grew personally and moved beyond my personal grief as I watched survivors and families of the victims do the same.

In telling their story of survival, I was also telling my own. To myself, anyway.

On a professional level, I had been confronting burnout with this business of journalism going into Oklahoma City three years ago. I wondered if there was any real reason for us journalists to go around exposing the pain, problems, and perils of others. At the end of my first day of bombing coverage, I found a new meaning to journalism. I am sure the same has happened to reporters covering such tragedies as the assassinations of John F. Kennedy and Martin Luther King.

Such journalism puts all humanity on the same page in the hymnal of brotherhood, understanding, and support. Such journalism is washed clean of the manipulation and sensationalism of pseudo-news and trash reporting. Such journalism deals openly with the gut questions that friends and families of the dead and suffering are desperately seeking answers to: What happened? Why? And what can I learn from it?

Most of these questions are beyond the purview of journalism. The answers – or at least some clues – are found in discussions with loved ones, or in reading thoughts of those writers gifted at expressing consoling thoughts. But journalism can help. It can open the doors to the mind and heart as it shows all of us we are not alone in our grief. It can show us there are others who *can help. And it can make even the most objective of us feel the emotions that make us real people.*

Last Sunday night, with all ten fingers laced through the chain-link fence still separating mourners from the insanity of that bombing, with my eye fixed on the hallowed ground before me, and with the vivid memory of what that killing ground looked like three years ago, the feelings returned.

I know longer want to put distance between myself and Oklahoma as I once did as a young man. This is my state; these are my people.

I knew that in feeling for them and helping to articulate their grief, I was becoming whole again.

And two years later, on the fifth anniversary of the bombing, the *Sun* editor asked me to do a second reflective piece, and I have lost track of the number of times I have talked about the Oklahoma City bombing to my students and various other groups over the years. It has always been a privilege to do so and to keep the memory of that day alive and, along with it, the knowledge of what right-wing extremism/turned terrorism can do. I don't think I've ever spoken of Oklahoma City without feeling a catch in my throat somewhere during my presentation. I still feel it today

I allowed myself to feel the love being poured out by the three people who were my most solid supporters and cheerleaders in life: Mom, Dad, and Elaine. The folks were pushing 80 then but still very active. Dad had transitioned to retirement at age 65 but took up oil and pastel painting, won many ribbons at various art shows around the state, and was the driving force behind *Artisans 9*, a cooperative art gallery that grew to eight different stores in Oklahoma City and Norman. And Mom was there, helping him all the way and adding her own craft projects to the stores' mix.

But they always loved having me come home, and their pride in me was obvious. I quickly learned on this trip that Mom had been saving every story and photo I shot of the bombing and its aftermath, and had judiciously catalogued them into a series of scrapbooks to give me after my Oklahoma City assignment ended.

My sister was equally supportive, as she has been her whole life, and referred to me as "the golden boy" in my parents' eyes. That descriptor always produced mixed feelings in me. While I was pleased my parents were proud of me, I have always known that Elaine deserved much more praise than I because of her selfless nature and the lengths she would go to in denying herself and helping others. Often I was one of those "others." Still, with all I was going through in losing Selena who had been my life's foundation for the past 15 years, I was grateful my family's support and was happy to have them display it.

I stayed on at the newspaper for a few more weeks, covered a few more memorial events and concerts, then the Murrah Building story began winding down for Edmond. There is always new news to take the place of the old. So, I returned to my roots at the *Edmond Evening Sun,* covering local government stories and local controversies like the placement of a new megastore which had neighborhoods worried over increased traffic flow.

As important as this kind of local news is to the city's residents, it paled to me in significance when compared to the tragedy I had been covering for several weeks. I quickly became bored and had this recurring realization that I've been here before, covering city councils and school boards in my early years of journalism.

As a reporter, it is hard to leave the intensity of an all-consuming story like the Oklahoma City bombing behind and return to business as usual. That was happening to me, so I thanked Carol Hartzog for this opportunity to report such an important story, and I left the newspaper.

I had some money saved up, and I fantasized about doing international freelance work, going from hotspot to hotspot, chasing the adrenalin rush and the feeling that the reporting I was doing really mattered. I also considered just buying an RV, pointing it north, and heading for the Canadian wilderness.

Reality got in the way, though, and part of that reality was dealing with the emotional void created by Selena's death, deciding whether to return to Boston College or not, and, oh yes, there was that beautiful horse Star, waiting for me to ride her off into those wooded trails.

In any event, my next few years lay just ahead of me, and also the realization that the ride through them would be a bumpy one.

Part Three

*THAT WHICH DOESN'T
KILL YOU ...*

23

⚜

Walking in Memphis

I had learned from my time in Oklahoma that I could survive life's challenges, and my new mantra became, *"That which doesn't kill you, makes you stronger."* This would prove true, although I was carrying around enough PTSD inside to prevent that from happening anytime soon.

I still had to deal with all I had encountered over the past several months.

As my final days at the *Edmond Evening Sun* were coming to a close, I pondered what to do next and where to do it. Of course, I could return to my faculty post at Boston College, but that posed problems for me both on the personal and practical levels. Apart from the need to get away from BC to deal with my grief over Selena, I had not been particularly happy there.

The faculty in my department were on a cold war footing with each other, and I was in the middle of that and spent a lot of time refereeing the various personality disputes. Part of any department chair's unwritten job description is to manage all the conflicting egos that can be present among academics. The fact that Boston College is near the top of the food chain of prestigious universities means – among other things – that that many faculty members also consider themselves as elites and beyond the need of being managed.

When I took over the Communication Studies Department as chair, I inherited a divided faculty of self-proclaimed communication scholars who chose up sides over often-petty departmental issues and refused to have meaningful conversation with the other side. Despite the fact BC is a Jesuit school, the spirit of love did not evidence itself much in our faculty meetings or in hallway barbs tossed at targeted faculty, behind their backs. Several were aimed at me, since all did not welcome having a journalist lead their communication studies department. I was not immune and felt the arrows as much as other faculty did. Even in my dreams I would sometimes show up at school with a large bulls-eye painted on the back of my shirt.

The personnel issues and intramural debates focused on personal grievances were detracting me from my teaching and from focusing on more serious departmental issues. I have always valued quality of life over working at a prestigious place, and I wasn't finding much inner peace here.

Because of this, I was considering leaving Boston College even before Selena died. In March of 1994, I was offered the job of director of the University of Kentucky School of Journalism. It was a plum assignment and I was tempted. After I visited the campus and met the faculty, I said yes. A few days later, however, I retracted that after finding that I could be walking into an environment like the one I had at BC.

Helping me to decide against the job offer was a story from the *Lexington Herald-Leader*, sent to me by a UK faculty member, about my being hired there as director. Some of the faculty were openly critical of my selection. I had already spent too much time trying to play referee to some unhappy faculty members at BC, and -- where ever I went -- I wanted to be able to focus on developing a good journalism program.

Looking back, I also count that as one of my correct life choices.

Now, in the spring of 1995, I had to decide about returning to BC. Working against that idea was the knowledge of my own emotional limits, selfish as they were, of going back to a city that housed all the memories of Selena and me since we moved there in 1982 and left six years later for Cleveland.

In the midst of wondering where to teach or whether just to hit the road as a freelance reporter, I got a call from the University of Memphis. The school had just changed its name from Memphis State, and the chair asked if I would interview for a new endowed faculty position in journalism. I jumped at the chance, partly because Memphis is only a 7-hour drive from my parents and sister in Oklahoma City. Since I enjoy frequent road trips of that length, I knew it wouldn't be hard to come see the family a few times a year.

I followed through on the interviews at Memphis, met some fine faculty members who actually seemed to *enjoy* working with each other, and was offered the job. I said my goodbyes to Mom, Dad, and Elaine, packed up my belongings and made arrangements for Star to be delivered to a Memphis stable, and hit I-40 east to the Bluff City whose western border is the Mississippi River.

I had already told my dean at Boston College I would not be returning, and he graciously wished me well in my new chapter. I was excited about this new opportunity, and I felt the University of Memphis must have wanted me, because they not only paid for *my* move – which was a minimal expense since most of what I had could be hauled in my SUV – but also for *Star's* move. Since I hired an equine transport outfit for that, her move wound up costing Memphis more than mine.

That was something that the university's president Dr. Lane Rawlins liked to remind me of after I arrived. On three or four social occasions, when Rawlins was hosting all the endowed chairs on campus, he would remark, "In all my years as president, Lucas Jarrett is the only faculty member for whom we picked up the tab for his horse to be moved here with him!"

My emotions were being pulled in several different directions when I settled into Memphis life. The least of my worries was money, as the endowed chair job paid well and, coupled with what I had in the bank, I was freed of monetary worries. But that would only last a couple years.

The reason was a new battle I was about to wage in the then-new casinos that line the shores of the Mississippi River as I tried in vain to distract my thoughts from losing Selena. For the first time in my life, I was about to become obsessed with gambling.

But for now, in the summer of 1995, I knew I had begun a new chapter in my life and I hoped for the best. I moved into a new upscale apartment community and my neighbors were young-to-middle-age, often single professionals. I reunited with my tri-color collie Colby who I had adopted in Boston and who had been living with my sister in Oklahoma, and made a stab at being happy living the single life.

I still had my red Chevy Silverado pickup with my James Taylor, and Joe Cocker CD's in the windshield visor, and I also had a black Mustang GT. As a result, I could slip into town or country modes on any day of the week. I had dropped back to my college-days weight, and I knew a few women who were interested in me. No reason not to be happy, right? Wrong.

I did feel a sense of exhilaration at starting this new chapter and – perhaps – even finding a new life partner. At this point I believed I could simply patch up the hole left by Selena with someone else. I quickly found there was more than one fallacy in that logic, but I did my best to try and prove it true anyway.

Much of its fallacy was the impossibility of getting Selena out of my consciousness, and I would often fall asleep nights having these imaginary conversations with her wherein I would have said all the right things during those last days together when I was too emotionally tongue-tied to express how I really felt about her.

I found myself drawn to country music for the first time in two decades, mostly because the gut-level lyrics of failed relationships permeate so many country songs and there is no attempt to soften the felt pain. Absent a shoulder to cry on, these songs let you know you weren't alone in your grief. One such song was done by Earl Thomas Conley and it was called, *What I'd Say*. The lyrics seemed to fit my nightly plight perfectly:

Talking to my pillow, whispering your name,
Just like you were here, you'd think I'd gone insane.

Wasn't this exactly what I was doing for the first few months in Memphis? Was Conley my alter-ego or long-lost soul brother I never knew I had?

Alongside my stagnant depression, however, was the excitement of my new life in Memphis. Is there any chance it could actually be better than the one I'd left behind? I was so pleased to find that the University of Memphis – and particularly my department -- was a very friendly workplace where I enjoyed interacting with the faculty and staff both on and off campus. That was a night-and-day difference from what I had experienced at Boston College, and I gladly traded the national prestige of BC for a lesser-known regional university like Memphis.

What I didn't fully realize at this time was just how much of my identity of the past seventeen years had been wrapped up in my wife. I had made her the center of my life, and nearly everything I did had revolved around her and our relationship. Indeed, most of my writing (five books up to this point) was an attempt to show Selena and whoever else was looking, that I had professional value myself, even if I would never be paid for it at the level my celebrity wife was.

I had made her a central part of my being, doted on her, and my university offices were resplendent with many pictures of her. I recall one colleague coming into my office at Northeastern once and remarking:

"Wow, you've made this place a shrine to your wife!"

And it was true. I had. But what a visitor might see in my office was only a physical manifestation of how I had superglued Selena to my own internal identity. There was no me without her and now, as the marriage had died, so did half of my identity. The question lying before me was, could I rebuild that half-man into a whole one? Did I have the stuff to stand on my own two feet?

The answer would be both yes and no. I had gained a lot of self-confidence in my professional abilities in my coverage of the Oklahoma City bombing, and I also found that I had something to contribute to society; that there was value to my existence. But this was not Oklahoma City; it was Memphis, and I didn't have a bombing to distract me from my memories of Selena on a daily basis. So, whether I could grow those positive feelings into ones that would last ... well, only time would tell.

I was hired as a full professor, but the form of address was shortened on a daily basis to just *Dr. Jim*, which I found to be a favored southern way for students to address their profs. I liked that formal informality. Still do.

I had only driven through Memphis a couple times before in my life, and both times I found the city's skyline intriguing. The downtown area is perched right on the banks of the Mississippi River, and there is a long park right on the river that downtown residents use a lot for jogging and picnic purposes. It is also the scene of a fabulous Fourth of July concert every summer, topped off with fireworks and cannon sounds booming over the "Big Muddy."

The riverbank also comes alive also during the Memphis in May Festival and the big pork barbecue (a Memphis specialty) contest in full swing. Trolleys connect the tourist portions of downtown near the famous night club strip of Beale Street, which is Memphis' answer to New Orleans' Bourbon Street. But instead of Jazz, Memphis sees itself as the home of the blues. Many artists, including B.B. King who has a signature night spot on Beale Street, provide ample evidence that this city is the blues capital.

If this story were a feel-good novel, the enlightenment that came out of my reporting on the tragedy of Oklahoma City would have put my own personal pain into such an accurate perspective and minimized it so much that I would now be free of it. I'd be totally ready to embrace this new chapter of life. New town, new job, new friends. Maybe even a new love.

Life is not a novel, though, and it just didn't work that way. Not, at least for five more years. I had definitely rebalanced myself in Oklahoma and had regained confidence in myself in handling important challenges. They don't come any harder than covering a story like the Oklahoma City bombing.

I will always see my experiences in Oklahoma as the pivot point of my life after Selena was gone.

Still, in looking for ways to step totally out of my past and into a new life chapter, I would discover that pain is not that easy to jettison, and that a person could do some crazy things trying to ignore it, let alone rid himself of it. All I had now was a fighting chance to deal with it as I faced a new job, surroundings, and people. That would be the sum of what five years in Memphis would do for me, from 1995-2000.

Although I found Memphis to be what I call an acquired taste (I probably would have fallen in love with it earlier if I wasn't spending so much time falling out of love with Selena), the city's love of music finally hooked me. Ironically, it was hard to stay blue when I was in the presence of so much great *blues music* on Saturday night down on Beale Street. I spent a lot of time there, both to be close to the music and to the crowd. It was a way of being alone in the midst of a throng of strangers and the mix worked for me.

It's also impossible to think about Memphis without thinking of Elvis Presley, whose mansion was one of the biggest tourists draws of the city, situated on the south side of town. As a longtime closet Elvis fan, I liked being a part of the late legendary singer's city, although I waited a few years to tour Graceland myself. As it was when I lived in historic Boston, I seldom visited the tourists' spots unless I was hosting visiting family or friends who wanted to see them.

The first time I saw Graceland was in 1997 when I hosted a group of visiting journalists from Germany's Television Station ZDF. They were in town for a working seminar I had set up for them to learn more about the American form of journalism and to shadow reporters from the different Memphis stations to see how they worked. Germans have a great fondness for Elvis and his memory, because he had spent two years of his young adult life stationed there while in the U.S. Army.

So, the Germans and I spent a day at Graceland and, I must say, I was impressed. May I say I even felt his presence and ... hmmm ... the possibility that he *hadn't* left the Jungle Room after all?

From my perspective as a new *Memphian,* it appeared to me that music oozed from the pores of this city and that this answered more than the cultural need of music lovers. Music also brought people to-gether in a city that was historically racially divided.

Remember we're talking about the city where Dr. Martin Luther King was assassinated in 1968. And, although it had been some three decades since racial segregation and discrimination had been legally abolished with the Civil Rights Act and Voting Rights Act, a real kind of psychological racism still existed here. It appeared in more the form of unease about mixing races socially and both whites and blacks seemed to feel it. At least that was my opinion.

It was no secret that, at that time anyway, the population of the City of Memphis was more black than white, while Memphis suburbs composing the rest of Shelby County, were mostly white. The city and county leadership would often clash over the location of planned public sports and entertainment venues. Shelby County officials would want them placed in the suburbs, while Memphis city officials wanted them downtown.

The University of Memphis is an urban university located just a few minutes east of downtown in a nice, traditional residential neighbor-hood. It had a very racially and ethnically diverse student body, but it didn't seem to be very socially integrated at the time. Blacks mostly hung with blacks, and whites with whites. Comfort zones and tradi-tion, I reasoned. I noticed when I tried to get my mixed-race classes to talk about the issue of race, there was as much hesitation on the part of blacks as whites.

The point of bringing all this up here is that *music* was one of the few magnets that drew both whites and blacks together, and it happened every weekend down on Beale Street as the blues artists wailed away and party revelers danced in the brick street.

A couple weekends after I arrived in early July, got settled into my apartment and university office, I began thinking about my fellow re-porter Paige Osborne whom I'd met in Oklahoma City. I had been too rushed in leaving Oklahoma to follow through with what I detected was a mutual interest with this striking woman I'd met covering the bombing. I knew we had that disaster experience in common, but I felt there might be more. So, one Thursday night I picked up the phone and called her.

She seemed glad to hear my voice, and we chatted for a half-hour. Then I said impulsively that I was going to be in Oklahoma City the next day and I wondered if we could see each other? She said she would be working but I could come to the *Oklahoman* and we could talk over her dinner hour. I was elated, even though before that phone call I had absolutely no plans to go to Oklahoma City that weekend.

The dinner meeting was fun, and I became convinced I'd like to see her again. It became one of the most honest friendships I had up to that point. Paige let me know that she was already involved with a man in the Dallas area, but she said she would like for us to see each other socially as friends. I said I'd like that, too, although a part of me wished for more.

We both knew I was in a vulnerable state emotionally, though, and I knew that seeing her as a friend was better than not seeing her at all. So, we would get together a couple times a week for lunch or dinner or just to talk. Our visits often made me think of the 1989 film, *When Harry Met Sally,* which had asked the age-old question, "Can men and women just be friends?" I was pleased that Paige and I were answering that in the affirmative, although the "what if" question of a romance always seemed to linger over us like mistletoe.

When I left Oklahoma that summer, Paige and I said goodbye to each other or, more specifically, to any chance of a future romance between us.

My mission as the University of Memphis was to teach a whopping *one* journalism class per semester, and to organize and run the Lindner Center for Urban Journalism, and interact with journalists around the state. The center was meant to provide continuing education for journalists covering various issues of concern to the Memphis area. I jumped in and started doing that almost immediately, setting up and implementing several professional workshops for journalists and other professional communicators in the area.

I was eager to take on the issue of "Covering the Disaster Scene" for the first of those workshops and, as speakers, I brought in Paige from *The Oklahoman* as well as that newspaper's managing editor, Ed Kelley. Clearly, the reporting on the Oklahoma City bombing was our main focus, although we also studied other disaster scenes. One analyzed reporting on the transportation of hazardous waste, a topic especially relevant to Memphis, since the transportation industry is so key to this crossroads city with the only two bridges across the Mississippi for a long way north or south. Also, FedEx is headquartered there, and their trucks often carry different types of dangerous materials.

During the first two or three weeks, I became aware of a couple large grief recovery programs underway in town. One was affiliated with a Methodist church and the other with a Presbyterian church. I decided to give one a try, and I would soon sample the other one as well.

I was in search of what might hopefully be a quicker fix to grief than I could manage on my own. Truth be told, however, I also knew there would be a lot of now-single women in these groups who might be interested – as was I – in the thought of starting over with a new partner. That proved to be a spot-on reality, and I'll never forget going to the first meeting at the church where I was one of two guys in a room full of a dozen women.

We all exchanged our sad tales of lost love, and I remember one forlorn guy finishing his long story by noting all this had happened four years ago and he still wasn't over her. Wow! I thought. I sure hope I'm past this quicker than him.

After the meeting ended and I was getting up and going to the door, I was approached by two women from the group who not only walked me to the door, but also down the hall and outside to my car, competing for my attention. I remember a lot of giggling, and I wondered what I'd gotten myself into. That didn't stop me from asking one of them out a little later, though. We had a nice chat over lunch the next day, but I could tell neither of us was ready. All she did was talk about her ex, whom she claimed she hated now but whom she kept talking about.

As the summer moved on in Memphis, I spent more time with Star every day at her barn in the Germantown suburb. She seemed to like her new residence, and we had plenty of land to ride and explore together.

That's when my life took yet another unexpected turn. It also offers an example of why I love the line from the film, *Prince of Tides,* when Tom Wingo looks back at his life and says, "It is the mystery of life that sustains me now."

24

⟨✤⟩

At War with Myself

Ever feel like you are three persons in one, and that two of those seem totally different while the third tries to mediate between them? In Memphis, this is exactly how I came to feel. I knew I had achieved a good sense of who I was from my Oklahoma City experience, only to see a part of that person morph into someone new and hell bent on trying to destroy the other. I theorized it could be a form of delayed trauma I was going through from what I had been a part of in Oklahoma City. I wasn't in the building when it exploded, but I did work daily in its rubble for several weeks while bodies were being carried out. Maybe there was even some survivor guilt, as if I needed any more of that. Still, I walked away alive, while 168 others did not.

My muse from Boston, Dr. Sandhu, said that this inner battle often works like this example:

*When someone harasses you and tries to pick a fight, the **id** would respond by punching the person, whereas the **superego** would just walk away, but the **ego** would find a balance and instead confront the person, not in an aggressive way, but ask them why I irritate them so.*

This is an example of Freud's theory of the human psyche. The part of the unconscious mind, the id is concerned with instinctual impulses. It wants to satisfy basic needs, such as sex (libido) and aggression (death instinct, called Thanatos) and (in my case) gambling. It is not rational but impulsive. The superego is concerned with what is *morally right*. It learns from society what is socially acceptable behavior, in order to control the id and its impulses. It is reasonable and tries to keep you out of trouble. The ego is what *mediates* between the id and the super-ego, it tries to follow society's rules and expectations, while also trying to satisfy the id.

In a nutshell, that was the makeup of my psyche in Memphis, as well as the fight I waged among the three parts of it. My attempts to fill the emotional pit left by the loss of Selena was much more than a craving for sex, but it was just as powerful, if not more so. And, as mentioned earlier in my story, there was a curious symmetry between *that* desire and my desire for gambling: the odds against winning in both battles were stacked against me, but I continued to pursue the brass ring anyway.

Assisting me in my fight to right myself, was my job which was becoming more of a passion for me. The German experiences brought a new dimension to my life and a new focus to my university teaching. The Center for Urban Journalism, which I was hired to direct as Chair of Excellence at the University of Memphis, was created to serve working journalists reporting on important urban issues of the day. The workshops that I organized did that, but increasingly my interest turned to international issues and to setting up international partner-ships and taking freelance reporting assignments in Germany.

With a class load of only one or two classes per term, I had a lot of unstructured time on my hands, and I put it to good use in developing ideas for workshops, planning, and implementing them. I also contin-ued my prolific work in writing books that focused on different aspects of journalism and the news media. For a while, I was turning out about a book a year.

I was also working with the National Newspaper Association (NNA) and agreed to start an online continuing education program for staff members of the NNA-member newspapers. The NNA is the largest newspaper trade association in America, with over 2,000 member newspapers, most of which are small dailies and weeklies that focus on community-level journalism. Their newer staff members are sometimes not trained as journalists, so the NNA offers workshops and programs to give them additional training. I agreed to teach online reporting classes, starting in the mid-1990s on some of the first platforms (like Blackboard) created for online education. I taught these classes for a couple of years, and it was a good experience. I always enjoyed teaching, and having students who were already working as reporters made it even more meaningful.

I was proud of my contributions to the profession during these Memphis years, and I would have felt even better about myself had I not been increasingly putting some of my free time to use in the worst possible way: gambling in the casinos just a few miles away.

The emptiness of losing Selena was still there for me, and I used gambling to fill the hole. This was a life I tried to keep secret from my family, friends, and colleagues, letting only a trusted few know what I was up to. Ironically, I was living a secret life while I was on a mission to teach my journalism students how to pursue and report the truth.

This dual life was taxing, both mentally and physically, as sleep came hard and keeping my stories straight with others became even harder. Then there was the inner turmoil of dealing with a side of me that seemed a total stranger. I had never been in the grip of something so dark before, and had never lived life as a double agent, serving opposing identities and values.

As an introspective person, I spend a lot of time trying to figure myself out, especially when I feel I am not living the life I want to live. As a movie buff who enjoys films that are good character studies, I have often learned things about myself in watching wonderfully etched characters on the screen. During my time living this double life in Memphis, I remember watching the 1960s David Lean film, *Lawrence of Arabia*. I have seen it decades before, but I was young and this time I found myself focusing mostly on the angst the real-life title character was experiencing. I was watching the movie while prepping for a lecture in my intercultural reporting class.

The film is drawn, in part, from the 1926 autobiography of Col. T. E. Lawrence (the famed Lawrence of Arabia), called *Seven Pillars of Wisdom*. I was trying to show the students how difficult it is to truly assimilate into another culture and, in a real way, another identity. The young Lawrence was an adventurer and intellectual who was disillusioned with his own English culture. The Army deemed a good man for the assignment of going to Saudi Arabia to organize the Arabs in their fight against the Turks. That was beneficial to England, because Turkey had joined forces with Germany in the First World War.

While in the desert, Lawrence quickly became transfixed by the Arabs and their culture and tried to replace his own English identity – with which he had become disenchanted -- with an Arab one. Here is how he describes that attempt, and its results, in his book:

"The efforts to live in the dress of the Arabs and to intimate their mental foundation, quitted me of my English self and let me look at the West and its conventions with new eyes; they destroyed it all for me ... At the same time, I could not sincerely take on the Arab skin; it was an affectation only. Easily was a man made an infidel, but hardly might he be converted to another faith. Sometimes these selves would converse in the void. And then, madness was very near, as I believe it would be near the man who could see things through the veils at once of two customs, two educations, two environments."

Although my situation was vastly different from Lawrence, the principle of living in two different cultural identities at the same time – the compulsive gambler and the esteemed college professor holding an endowed chair of teaching – was, in fact, maddening. I wondered how long it would be before madness would indeed befall me as it nearly did Col. Lawrence, or when I'd be discovered and have to face a reckoning. There were times, when I actually wished that day would come soon so the double life would end. If I was going to be a career gambler and live in and out of my car, so be it. At least it would be an honest life.

In my saner moments, however, I knew I had to keep fighting my gambling addiction and work toward the time when my honest life as a positive force in society would win out.

I had been stacking up too many nights at the casinos losing money I could now not afford to lose. My nest egg I had saved was nearly gone, and I was hitting the credit cards too hard, maxing out their available cash limits. Then I opened a casino credit account and had to scramble to pay that off before scary guys in sunglasses, driving big black SUVs, starting showing up in my neighborhood demanding I pay up or else. I made those accounts a priority to pay off, just in case my imagination of rough back-alley nights began to materialize in real life.

But I couldn't shake the siren call of these damned Tunica haunts, no matter what I did. I lost count of the number of nights I had tried to beat the odds by simply shoving more money at them, but the more I shoved, the more I lost. Then the times I would win $8,000 or $10,000 or whatever seemed like a winning sum, I would often turn around and lose it later that night. Some nights I did feel strong enough to pull myself away from the tables, take my gains home with a false sense of victory and a false promise to never return. But over the next couple days, I'd be back, losing all those winnings and more. I was scraping the bottom of the barrel to pay my living expenses and, on occasion, sunk to the point of borrowing from high-interest payday loan storefront operations.

I knew I would have to reach the bottom of the pit before mounting a sustained effort to repair the holes in my sinking ship. I took a few spins at attending Gamblers Anonymous meetings, but the group therapy concept didn't work for me and, in fact, made things even worse for a while. I realized that the last thing I needed then was to sit in a room listening to other compulsive gamblers talk about the ill-fated excitement of gambling and how it had become the most important thing in the world to them. My mind seemed to dismiss the "ill-fated" part and focus instead on the "excitement" part instead, and that triggered my own memories of how great the dopamine high of winning felt.

Most compulsive gamblers learn to minimize the memories of the losses, and that was true with me. Time after time, I would be feeling so good driving to the casino, willingly risking the cash I had on me in the expectation of winning much more. Time after time, I would be feeling so low driving home, having lost what I brought and then gone to the ATM to withdraw even more to lose. Although I was making a fine salary at the university, money went through me like water and I would start frequenting payday loan stores in strip malls around town to borrow a few hundred dollars to get me through the month, realizing I would have to pay sky-high interest rates on it, which would only put more financial pressure on me the next month.

I don't know what kept me from taking my own life on some of those days and nights. I began putting more desperate hope into finding relief from gambling at the Gamblers Anonymous meetings. I remember one GA meeting in particular, where a gambler recounted a tale that propelled me back to the Grand Casino immediately after the meeting broke up that night. His story went something like this:

"I couldn't wait to get down to Tunica that night after work, and I was so excited I didn't notice when I drove through a red light at an intersection a few blocks from the casino. As luck would have it, another car was entering from the left, and we collided. His right front fender came right into my driver door, and I felt my leg break instantly. Fortunately for me, the guy must have had some outstanding warrant on him, because he just backed up and sped off into the night before the police arrived.

So, there would be no citation against me for reckless driving; only for running the red light. The police called an ambulance, and a wrecker came and hauled off my car. I was taken to a local hospital and my leg was reset. When I was done at the ER a couple hours later, my leg was in a cast, and I was on crutches. Out in the waiting room, I called a taxi. Despite the pain pills I'd been given, the leg was still aching. Even so, I couldn't wait to tell the taxi driver to take me to the Grand Casino instead of home. When I got there, I hobbled into the casino on my crutches, took a seat at a slot machine, and stayed there the rest of the night.

The only thing that guy's story did for me was to kickstart my own craving for the anticipation that comes from watching four aces or even a royal flush magically appear in the cards I was holding. So, I headed south for another night of gambling, bidding adieu to Gamblers Anonymous.

To be fair to this fine organization, I must admit to never getting into its program all the way. And if you don't go all in, you're not going to benefit from it. I never spoke myself at the meetings I did attend nor – more importantly – did I ever seek out a personal mentor to help walk me through recovery and serve as my safety net. Actually, the last thing I wanted in my life was someone calling me up or coming over to my place to encourage me to stay away from the casinos.

It was on one of these dismal nights of losing at Tunica that a strange thing happened, which proved to be the first rung on my ladder up out of the seemingly bottomless gambling pit. I had just lost another bundle and was feeling the utter desolation of emptiness and self-loathing. I was driving back home when I pulled over to the side of an isolated stretch of country road in northern Mississippi five miles from the Memphis line.

It was around 2 a.m. as I sat there staring at nothing but the field of clinging kudzu and thinking what an apt metaphor for the grip that gambling had on me. Then, out of total exasperation, I began pounding the steering wheel and screaming, *"I can't take this anymore, God! I've tried so many different ways to get this monkey off my back, and I've pleaded with you for help! I've asked you for a partner in life to help fight this with me. I've tried it on my own and it's not working. What the hell do you want from me?!"*

I don't mean this to sound any way other the way it sounded that night, but immediately I *felt* a quiet but genuine response saying, "I want *you*." In my mind at least, this was audible, and it stopped my ranting cold. I sat silent for a couple minutes, but it was if I had just been able to take a deep breath for the first time since my eruption began. Just the fact there was a response that felt so unmistakable, and caring was enough for that moment.

Was it a manifestation of God? I suppose that's so, although my faith in such a personal supreme being has always ebbed and flowed. There have been times when I have found it easier to believe than others, and

I know I've taken a lot of unearned graces for granted in my life when I should have been more thankful. I've sometimes felt like the Israelites who were rescued from Egypt by Moses, but who then turned their back on him in the wilderness, demanding he do more miracles to get them through their current rough patch of the journey.

I have no sure answer for where that response came from this night; I just know it was there, and it calmed me and gave me a sliver of hope that help was not far off.

I knew this was a battle I would have to fight myself, but I also knew I only felt I was only half the man I could be if I had a loving partner in life. At least such a person would give me someone else to focus attention on and, in adding my strength to her weakness and she to mine, this all might work out after all. So, in the days and weeks to come, I continued chatting with that mysterious responder in my car about it

I vowed that until I found my other half, I would make what strides I could on my own, and I managed at least to minimize my number of gambling days each month. I knew that to be rid of it, however, I'd have to give it up altogether. All addictions, I came to believe, work like that. It is impossible for most mortals to give a monster control over just a *part* of your life. Monsters tend to be greedy.

With the gambling losses eating away my disposable income, I decided to downsize on my expenses. I had purchased a home in the Germantown suburb but decided to lease it, live in a less-expensive apartment, and pad my bank account with the rental income. That plan worked for a year or so until I rented it to a tenant who had little intention of paying his rent. I struggled with him for months before finally taking him to court for back rent and to have him evicted. I was successful in getting him out of the house, but not in collecting the lost rent payments. He declared bankruptcy in the middle of the litigation, and he got a pass from paying up.

I had lost so much money on that real estate deal, coupled with the gambling losses, that even I had to declare bankruptcy in 1999. It was the first time I had ever done that and, while it gave me some financial benefit, it also took my self-esteem further down into the same pit that sucked in my gambling losses.

Bankruptcy did make life less stressful for me for a while. The pressure of paying what I couldn't afford, was gone, but so was my credit rating. On a scale where 850 is seen as a perfect score, mine had hit a low of 387 which meant I was about the worst kind of credit risk there was. I would have to go on a cash-only basis for at least a year, if not two. But for someone trying to kick gambling, that actually turned out to be a good thing. Less credit meant less money to lose at the casinos.

As I assessed my situation, I began to see a ray of hope although it came at a cost to my self-esteem. I was responsible for the fix I was in, but I felt somewhat better as I continued my white-knuckled resistance to losing my life to gambling. And I still felt the bedrock experience of seeing the determination of people after the Oklahoma City bombing, and how they endured to rebuild their own lives as well as the city.

I knew the answer to my current problems was to be found in focusing more on others and less on myself.

25

Germany and Beyond

It was my new Memphis environment, coupled with the growing self-confidence that Oklahoma City instilled in me, that led me to believe I needed to move forward in life instead of living in the past. Selena would always be with me in spirit and memory, but the reality was I needed to move on.

I met several women in Memphis and began a relationship with a an attorney named Marian that looked promising. We dated for several months but, I think we both feared we would be using each other as a band-aid for our lost loves, since Marian had just recently come out of a divorce. So we wished each other well and decided to go forward alone, at least for a while.

Life after Marian seemed doubly hard, because now I had two sets of lingering regrets and emotions to handle. And, of course, I was still trying to add to that list by going out with other women, always wondering if this new one could be the one. If ever I doubted I was a romantic optimist, these days were putting that doubt to rest.

Happily, however, I had also become involved in a new venture, that would expand my interests past creating a new Hallmark Television episode of a lonely college professor on a middle-age quest for love. My new interest took my career in a different direction and to a distant land. It had begun with a government invitation to lecture there in 1995, but it would continue for many years after that.

My exposure to Germany began shortly after I began working at the University of Memphis. I received a letter one day from the Bonn office of what was then the USIS, or United States Information Service in Germany. The USIS was the European name the State Department gave the United States Information Agency, which was a huge public diplomacy division, tasked with the work of – essentially – global public relations for America. It was begun under the Eisenhower Administration in 1953, who set it up to operate as an agency officially independent of the State Department.

Ike believed it would have more credibility, free of political propaganda, if it were not just seen as another department of the federal government. The USIS operated until 1999 when it was subsumed by the public diplomacy wing of the State Department.

The cultural affairs specialist for the USIS in Germany had come across a book I'd written a couple years before called, *Turbonews*, which was a study of the changing technology of mass communication and what might be in the offing for the next few years. The subject matter fit with that year's speaker program's theme of the USIS and its *Amerika Haus* program, and I was asked if I could do a lecture tour in Germany on that subject.

Amerika Haus was the name given to one of many public-access libraries the USIS created around the world. Altogether, there were 100 of these information resource centers, and one of the first was in Berlin. The U.S. government would keep them going until shortly after the 9/11 bombing in New York, when security became a huge concern at American facilities on foreign soil, and public access was cut off to these libraries except for special-invitation programs held there. The Berlin Amerika Haus was shuttered, then given to the City of Berlin in 2006. Groups of Berliners, concerned with keeping international understanding alive among Germans, opened it back up for public use.

That would all transpire later, of course. In the fall of 1995, the cultural affairs specialist who invited me to Germany was Dr. Martina Kohl, a woman who would become a lifelong friend and who would invite me to do several other lectures in Germany, Spain, and Latvia over the coming years. It would open up a whole new international phase of my career, and it was a welcome addition and distraction from my days of pining over lost loves.

My first lecture trip came in the winter of 1996, after Marian and I had started dating. A second trip would come the next fall. The first trip had me jetting to Frankfurt, and then traveling in country to Giessen, Mainz, Dresden, and Nuremburg to deliver lectures about major news stories in America (the Murrah Building bombing and O.J. Simpson topped the list).

It was my first time in Germany, and it was an exhilarating experience. There was a touch of foreign intrigue to it, since I was there on assignment for the USIS and I had a "control officer" with me every step of the way. In reality, I was just an American college professor doing his bit to further cement good will and understanding between the United States and Germany.

I found the German people to be very friendly, and I was surprised to find many of them -- especially in the cities and on university campuses -- had a nice command of the English language. I would soon discover, however, that this was more the case in the former West Germany than in East Germany. The reason was simple: East Germany had been a Soviet-controlled state, isolated from the West, from 1961 to 1989 when the Berlin Wall came down and European Communism fell apart. The second language in East Germany during those years had become Russian and not English. Now that East and West Germany were reunited, it was taking years for the East Germans to catch up with the West in language and in economic development.

My audiences were mostly college students and faculty, although one of my lectures was to news staff members of the German television giant, ZDF, headquartered in Mainz, not far from the Rhine River and Wiesbaden.

I was in-country for ten days and met several individuals who would be responsible for future invitations back to the country. One was a department chair at Giessen University, about an hour north of Wiesbaden. After lecturing to two of his classes, he took me to dinner and asked if I would consider coming back for eight weeks during the following fall term as a guest professor of American journalism. I said yes, and that was the reason for my second trip to Germany several months later. My fourth book, *German Images in the American Media,* came out of that trip as I came to see the role that both the news and entertainment media play in how the people of one country perceive people from another.

The other man I met proved to be an even more important contact and one who become a good friend for many years. His name was Dr. Fritz Hattig, and he was a recently-retired vice president of ZDF for documentaries. Fritz also had the distinction of being a former athlete who was a key member of the German national handball team in the 1960s. Then, in 1972, he became a personal advisor to Willi Daume, the president of the West German organizing committee of the 1972 Munich Olympics. That, of course, was the ill-fated Olympics where a group of Arab terrorists broke into the Olympic Village and took eleven members of the Israeli team hostage before killing all of them and then dying themselves in a shootout with authorities at a nearby airport.

As much as I liked and admired Fritz, everything from his size to his energy, to his dominating nature made him a handful to get along with at times. Gregarious, passionate, self-assured as he was, however, he was also sensitive, very polite, and seemed to enjoy my company a great deal.

He would be hurt over the times I came to Europe but didn't take time to travel to Mainz to see him, even though I was usually on a tight itinerary in another part of the country. Then, on the times I did see him, he would begin by showing his indignation that I hadn't stopped by the last time, and then follow that with a bear hug and assume I would rearrange my schedule to spend most of *this* visit with him.

An American friend who had spent a lot of time in-country told me once, "Some Germans are either at your throat or at your feet." I wondered if that guy had met Fritz and, if so, if he had developed that overgeneralization from knowing him.

Personae aside, Fritz and I worked together well and, together, we set up a series of workshops for ZDF staff members in the United States to broaden their understanding of journalistic decision-making by shadowing American journalists as they reported their stories and by participating in a series of presentations and discussions about journalism at the University of Memphis. A side-goal of these discussions was especially important to Fritz: immersing ZDF staffers in an English-speaking environment for a week at a time where they could hone their English language skills.

Fritz and I deepened our mutual respect during these years, and we would both be honored for our program by a dinner at the U.S. Consul General's residence in 2001 and each receiving a Certificate of Appreciation from the U.S. Embassy for furthering German-American understanding. It would be a highlight of my professional career.

It was on one of my first visits to the large ZDF Television campus that I met a woman named Suzanne who was a news reporter and executive in charge of children's programming. She was an intellectually curious, sensitive, and consummate professional, had the looks of the sophisticated on-air talent that she was. We connected instantly, and I found myself wondering if I'd found the German equivalent of Selena. Suzanne and I went out a couple times, and she would be one of the first staffers to make the trip to Memphis for the workshops I organized. We became good friends and saw each other socially both in Germany and in Memphis for a couple years.

Like nearly everyone else I met, both on university campuses and at ZDF, Suzanne spoke English as her second language and, although good at it, would often slip into her native German for a word or phrase when she couldn't locate the English equivalent. I would jump in and translate it in English if I could understand what Suzanne was saying in German. My own facility with the German language never rose about a basic level, and I could get lost quickly if the conversation went on very long in *Deutsche*.

Over the three-decade span of what came to be at least 20 trips to Germany, both as a guest lecturer and a freelance news correspondent, my German improved incrementally, but the ability of most educated Germans to speak English improved much more. Case in point: By the year 2005, the German students I spoke with would be speaking English readily, with only their German accents reminding me I wasn't speaking to American friends.

On that first trip, in 1995, one of my stops on that first lecture tour in Germany was in the former East German city of Dresden, where I spoke to an evening class of journalism students at the University of Dresden. It had been only six years since the Berlin Wall had come down and East Germany gained its freedom from the Soviet Union and rejoined West Germany and western democracy. English was a relatively new language for most of these Dresden students, having taken the place of Russian, which had been the proscribed second language.

Long story short, my talk that evening required a translator for the students who were still speaking and listening in very broken English.

I still had a memorable evening, and I was invited out to a local *bier garten* by some of the students after my lecture. I began asking them about their experiences the night of November 9, 1989, when the Wall was breached and Communism crumbled along with it. The students were only in their early teens when that happened, but they remembered it vividly and described their utter joy of tasting freedom for the first time as they joined the all-night, massive street party going on in West Berlin. Although that was just a few blocks from where some had lived in East Berlin, yet an unfathomable distance given the Berlin Wall and *death strip* separating them.

But one student then pointed to the next morning and recalled his reaction to the new reality, promising as it seemed.

"I remember waking up and, when my senses cleared and my head cleared a bit from all the beer the night before, I was struck by the question: What comes next?" he said. "My question was, how will I make a living since we will no longer be under a socialist economic system where so many of our basic needs were provided us by the State?

I realized I would soon have to for a job in a capitalist economy, and it was exciting, yet worrisome at the same time. But more than anything, I was glad to be free."

One of my more memorable trips to Germany – as well as my first trip to Berlin itself – came in November, 1999, when I accepted another USIS invitation to do a lecture tour and also when I agreed to go and report on the 10th anniversary of the fall of the Wall – *Mauerfall* as the Germans say it – for one of my former employers, *The Oklahoman.* I was still with the University of Memphis, where I had put an international focus on my duties there as director of the Lindner Center for Urban Journalism. By 1999 I had already done three or four lecture trips to Germany and had established German Television ZDF as a viable internship opportunity for our U of M students. I was fortunate in having a young German woman as my graduate assistant, Simone Notter, and she would prove invaluable to my task of interviewing former East and West Berliners on how they viewed their new life in a unified country.

It was a wonderful trip. This was the first time I'd met Martina in person, since none of my previous lectures had all been in Berlin, and we had communicated via email for those three years. And it was my first time to see Berlin, which was the buckle of the belt that had been the Iron Curtain, separating western democracy from communism. Berlin was the epicenter of all the tension created by that divide, and so much drama, death, and heartache had unfolded here in Berlin from 1961-1989 as so many East Europeans tried to flee the Communist rule by breaching the Wall – or *The Monster* – as it came to be known, during those 28 years.

Portions of this Wall have been left standing as a permanent reminder of this tumultuous era and a memorial to the lives lost on and near it. To stand at the base of remaining sections this 14-foot-tall structure is to feel the lust for freedom that these East Berliners or *Ossis* felt and to realize that freedom is a universal desire in people, no matter what their country or culture. I still feel East Berlin's pain and ultimate victory whenever I return to Berlin and walk along Friedrichstrasse near Checkpoint Charlie, one of the main armed crossings from East to West Berlin during the years of the Wall.

"I love going to Berlin to keep from taking liberty for granted, and to get my freedom batteries recharged," is a comment I've made to my students many times in America. "Every time I cross the line of embedded street bricks upon which the Wall stood, I realize so many East Germans were shot for trying to do the same thing. Now you cross it without any worries at all."

In 1991, the German government had begun returning Berlin to its previous status as the capital of Germany. During the years of the divided Germany, the west Berlin capital had been in the city of Bonn about 600 kilometers southwest of Berlin. The capital had been moved there after World War II ended and the city of Berlin was divided into East and West Berlin, with the former under the German Democratic Republic (or Communist) rule. West Berlin became an island of freedom surrounded by the Wall that had been built by the GDR. In the words of the East German government, it was an "Anti-fascist barrier" designed to protect its citizens from the corruption of West Berlin, which was under the control of western Democracy.

When most of the government ministries returned to Berlin, so did Martina and her cultural affairs division, setting up shop first in downtown offices of the United States Information Service, which was purposely separated in function from the State Department and in presence from the American Embassy. Forty-six years after the founding of the USIS, its staff was still trying hard to convince Berliners it was independent of the Embassy.

It was important for Germans to believe that the Amerika Haus libraries and programs were factual presentations and not American propaganda.

From what I saw of Martina, she pressed hard to keep this independence alive and, like many of her colleagues, she was sorry to see it disappear. The Amerika Haus libraries invited local residents and government officials to their lectures and programs, and served as the touchpoint to America for Germans interested in learning more about the U.S. and even studying at American universities. The libraries were walk-in facilities, no appointments necessary, and security was either downplayed or non-existent at all. I delivered several of my own lectures at various America House libraries.

Things changed for the Amerika House in the fallout after the 9/11 terrorist attacks, however, and the State Department subsumed the program, stepped up security at – or shut down – the walk-in libraries, and the staff and programs were moved into the secure U.S. Embassies.

It was a great privilege to cover the 10th anniversary celebration of the *Mauerfall* on November 9, 1999. Although the city had held previous commemorations, this was the first of three celebrations marking the 10th, 20th, and 25th anniversaries, and I would be there reporting on all of them for *The Oklahoman*. I'll always remember the 1999 event best, however, because memories among all Germans were fresher about conditions they confronted on a daily basis during the Cold War between East and West. Yes, 10 years later the memories were less vivid, and many of the young children born after the Wall come down in 1989 saw the event as more of an abstract history lesson. Not so with those who were teens and adults during the Cold War years, however, and I assumed all of them would share in the elation of the anniversary; so happy they must have been to live in a free society now.

As my editors had warned me years before, however, "Never assume anything when reporting a story," and that was true as I interviewed former Ossis in 1999.

While most of my interviewees were indeed happy, some were not. These were the ones who clung to memories of some good times, shutting out the bad. I shouldn't have been too surprised, though, because we all do that to some degree. It's a defense mechanism. As the student at Dresden had told me in 1996, East Germans were perplexed about their economic future when the Wall came down and they became part of unified Berlin. Competing for jobs could be challenging, and the infrastructure of the former East Germany paled in comparison to West Germany.

The spirit of reunification was felt before the economic benefits were. East Germans had to learn how to function under capitalism, and the subsidies their former system provided were gone now. Simone and I conducted these interviews near the path that the Wall had taken and at the ceremony itself beneath the Brandenburg Gate in Pariser Platz: the zone which had been a no-man's land between East and West Berlin when the Wall stood.

I wrote about both of these emotional reactions among the Ossis in the story that Simone and I produced that night for publication the next day in *The Oklahoman*. As she and I sat huddled over a computer in a Berlin newsroom, I realized I had never been so excited about writing a story in my life. I was feeling the echoes of John F. Kennedy's famous line, "*Ich bin ein Berliner!*" On this night, I was one with the people of Berlin.

In part, that story would read like this:

To the "Ossis" it was a monster standing menacingly between them and freedom. To the "Wessis," it was a constant reminder that a third of their homeland had been abducted, possibly forever.

Feared and loathed for years by East Germans and West Germans alike, it was one of the defining symbols of communism, whose collapse 10 years ago stunned a nation and a world.

The monster was the Berlin Wall, a concrete barrier that had divided a nation but also served as a reminder of a barrier between worlds. Tuesday night, a crowd of some 40,000, including 1,000 youths who were in town for a European Youth Festival, helped mark the anniversary of the collapse of the Berlin Wall as they gathered beneath the historic Brandenburg Gate.

"The process that brought together what belongs together cannot be stopped," German Chancellor Gerhard Schroeder said in the Reichstag earlier in the day. "The wall did not fall only because of Bonn, Moscow or Washington. It fell because the people made it happen."

Former President Bush, who was in office when the wall collapsed, agreed: The sweetness and harmony that exists in this chamber today is something I'd like to bottle ... and take home."

Like a singer who labors for years in obscurity and then lands the break making her an overnight success, the menace of the Berlin Wall vanished Nov. 9, 1989 in the blink of an eye that took almost three decades to shut.

During the 28 years of its existence, the wall created a lot of heroes among Easterners who refused to stop seeking freedom. Such stories were part of the legacy that spirited Germans commemorated in Pariser Platz Tuesday night in the drizzly, 40-degree weather. Despite mixed feelings of some Germans, those gathered on this cold night were glad the wall was gone.

The big party included floodlights at the Gate and red flares attached to light posts illuminating the path of the wall from Checkpoint Charlie to Humboldthofen. Smoke from m the flares shrouded the area in a fog reminiscent of the scene at the wall 10 years ago.

But Tuesday was a day of celebration, and the city that has once again become the nation's capital was in a party mood. Still while Germans celebrated the reunification, many are disturbed that reconciliation has been expensive, time-consuming, and frustrating.

Many compare it to a marriage. Ten years ago, two lovers came together to start a relationship. They knew, despite their differences, that they belonged together. After the euphoria of the wedding and honeymoon, problems arose faster than they could be solved. Much work was needed to keep together wht belonged together. This week, some ordinary Germans spoke about the relationship now, 10 years after the wedding.

"For me, nothing really changed," said Katharina Borgmann, an employee of the Deutsce Bundesbahn, who is originally from the former East Germany. "To be honest, now I might be able to buy everything, but the price I pay for this luxury is the fear I could lose my job. The unemployment rate here is just so high. The freedom to travel; that's all we actually needed," she said.

Her comment stood in stark contrast to the many exhibits on display at the Checkpoint Charlie Museum that depicted the deadly risks so many East Germans had taken to cross the wall and find freedom in West Berlin.

Nevertheless, another former East German, Thomas Behrends, agreed with Borgmann.

"Well," he said, "if you can buy everything, nothing is special anymore. Back in the old days, everybody had to stand in line to get some oranges for

Christmas. That didn't only make Christmas something special, it also made you belong to a community."

This is an interesting comment, especially when compared to U.S. press attache' Peter Claussen's feeling that some East Germans felt this closeness to each other because of the common enemy of the GDR leadership that they faced.

Among Western Germans, feelings were also mixed.

It was good that the wall came down," said Wolfgang Kaedng, a native of West Berlin. "It really had to happen sooner or later." But he added, "Financially, I did much better before the reunification. Now we have to pay so much money out our own pocket to solve damages that we aren't even responsible for. I guess this sometimes causes a lot of frustration.

Happily, this would not be the last of these freedom celebrations I would be able to cover in Berlin, because I was back reporting years later on both the 20th and 25th anniversaries of the Mauerfall. Each was distinctive from the one before. In November 2009, the 20th anniversary took on an even more festive tone, and the crowd in Pariser Platz was 100,000 on the night of November 9. It was more of a carefully and comprehensively staged event wherein the wall was made a symbol for all "walls of oppression" that still exist around the world.

To depict that theme visually, hundreds of huge rectangular obelisks – each painted with impressionistic designs of freedom by German artists – were set up along the path the wall had taken around the city. At the appointed hour when the wall was first breached on November 9, 1989, Polish freedom activist-turned president Lech Walesa tipped over the first "domino," which fell on the next, toppling the next, etc., etc., until all the simulated walls of oppression had fallen through the streets of Berlin.

The 25th anniversary was no less impressive, as messages of freedom were released in thousands of white, lighted helium bags into the night sky across the city.

While I loved all the lecturing I was able to do in Europe, courtesy of the State Department and various host universities, nothing could top the feelings of exhilaration I received by being in the midst of these celebrations, reporting on them for American readers, and feeling the warmth of freedom flow anew though my veins.

Over the course of all my German experiences, I made so many good friends with whom I will stay in contact until I die, gained a new understanding of post-war Germany and its passion for world peace, and I added an entirely new and unexpected dimension to my professional portfolio and career. Much like my coverage of the Oklahoma City bombing had done, it gave me something larger to think about and involve myself in, than myself and the ongoing emptiness that lingered from my personal loss of Selena and the added disappointment that Marian was now out of my life, too.

Germany, and all the European trips that followed, helped to get me reoriented to the important things in life, broadened my view of America's role in the world, how the world views us, and – most importantly – gave me hope for a better tomorrow.

<h1 style="text-align:center">26</h1>

A Little Silliness, a Lot of Work

The introduction of a new country into my life helped immensely in broadening out my worldview and adding an international dimension to my professional career. With that addition to my life, saner and more patient men might have been content to let love come to them rather than actively pursue it. But I was still that hopeless romantic who felt real wholeness would happen only with a significant other in my life. So, I stayed open to the possibility of a new love.

In the process, I ushered in what I often call my "silly season" of cross-country travel to find a new Selena. Some of these stops turned out to be more like loony *Saturday Night Live* skits than fruitful endeavors at netting the elusive butterfly of love.

The only Memphis candidate of note would be a bona fide Choctaw Indian princess named Naomi who was a graduate student at the University of Memphis and who helped pay for college by performing magic tricks and doing native dances, in full regalia. She had great talent for both. I had met her on the *One and Only* dating site I decided to join, even though she lived only a few blocks from my campus. She was a beautiful woman with long black hair, a sweet smile and personality, a 5' 4' svelte body, and could have been readily cast in a movie as a real-life Disney Pocahontas.

Since I was from Oklahoma, which the federal government had labeled Indian Territory before it became a state, Naomi was not the first Native American I had dated in life. Back in college I dated a member of the Choctaw Tribe in Oklahoma City. She was the sister of the Air Force officer my sister dated, and it was really more of a friendship than anything else. But I did learn from both women how seriously Native Americans are about their heritage and culture.

I was so taken with Naomi in our initial online chats that I looked up some Choctaw language online and dropped a few basic words and phrases into my emails. I even told her (without any basis in fact, by the way) that I was one-quarter Choctaw myself and knew some of the language. I didn't bother to rationalize any of that lie to myself, other than to say I had grown up in Oklahoma for 20 years, so some Choctaw must have rubbed off on me. Fortunately, I never had to prove any of that because I had no idea how to speak Choctaw or pass off my mother or father, whose ancestors had immigrated from England and Germany, as anyone looking like they were Native Americans. And then there was the matter of explaining my own sandy blonde hair ...

Still, I found myself beginning my emails to Naomi with "Osigwatsu" (How are you) and closing them with "Osdaigo Heda" (Have a great day) to add substance to my claim of Choctaw heritage, even though those were only transliterations of the mysterious Choctaw alphabet.

I've sometimes wondered how Naomi took those feeble attempts. As it turns out, it didn't make much difference. My relationship with her never really took root, although we did remain friends.

I had other zany episodes that season, but the one online dating episode that convinced me to cool my jets happened in Nashville, about 190 miles east of Memphis. I had answered an email from a woman there, named Belinda, and she invited me over to her home for a Friday night dinner. She had read in my dating app ad that I had a dog, so she said to bring Maggie along, too. "I love dogs! So please bring her along!" she beamed.

As the night would play out, that was good.

If Belinda had played poker for a living, she would have gone bust within a short time, because she inadvertently showed her *desperation hand* so easily. It was hard for me not to see it. I was checking the logistics of our scheduled 5 p.m. meeting when she said something I wasn't expecting.

"Oh, I'll be working a little late, so I left a key under the doormat for you," she said. "Just let yourself and Maggie in, make yourselves ad home, and I'll be home soon afterwards!"

Now, given that Belinda and I had never met face-to-face and had only exchanged a couple online messages, I found her arrangements odd and unsettling. I quickly totaled the number of women I knew who would have offered a key to her home to a total stranger, then told him to go in and wait for her arrival. The sum came to zero.

So, the prospect that I had made a date with either a very desperate woman and/or an unbalanced one began to concern me. I thought about all the safety measures I'd read concerning online dating, and Belinda's invitation seemed to run counter to all of them. In fact, if there were an "AVOID DOING THIS" section, her plan would be listed there in second-coming type.

Always up for an adventure, however, (and possibly exhibiting some of my own desperation), I pushed forward, located her home, found the key, and Maggie and I made ourselves at home and awaited the arrival of this mystery woman.

The attractive 40-year-old Belinda arrived about 6 p.m. and greeted me effusively like a long-lost lover, with no hint of nervousness. What I felt inside was something different. As for Maggie, she was enjoying the treats that her host dispensed liberally. Belinda was gracious and talkative, but there were times I caught her out of the corner of my eye, staring at me with a kind of hungry look. I thought of a scene from *Seinfeld* where Newman fantasized that Kramer, who had taken in too much sun using butter as a tanning lotion, and morphed into a delicious, cooked turkey lying on a silver serving platter.

Still, believing the shortest distance to a man's heart was through his stomach, she prepared an elegant dinner set to candlelight as the fire warmed the January night. I was friendly, but felt I kept some personal filters in place until the time my doubts might evaporate, which they never did. I was vague about where I taught, never mentioning the University of Memphis, and I also never mentioned my address or phone number.

After dinner, she hurriedly cozied up with me on the couch, and my mind was racing trying to figure her out. We had known each other for only a couple hours in life, and she was already moving in for the romantic kill.

A half-hour later, she was asking me to sleep over. When she saw me hesitate, she offered up the guest room instead of her own bed. That helped a little, and I was really tired after being on the road all day, so I agreed. I just wanted to be sure my door had a lock on it and that I could keep Maggie inside with me.

A couple hours later, after more wine, more heat from the fireplace, and more heat from Belinda, I was so drowsy I called it a night. I wasn't sure I could even make it up the stairs to the bedroom. But I did, comforted by the fact it was at least down the hall from *her* room. We finally said our goodnights and Maggie and I moved into our quarters. I shut the door, simultaneously locking it, and headed for the bed. I sat down and was starting to untie my shoes when I realized I did *not* want to spend the night in this house with a woman down the hall who was really worrying me. I'm told I have a vivid imagination, and it was working overtime now. Had I encountered the knife-wielding Glenn Close character of Alex Forrest from the film, *Fatal* Attraction? Probably not but, at the least, I didn't feel we were a good fit as a couple.

I stopped untying my shoe, laid back on the bed, fully clothed, to rest while Belinda went to bed and fell asleep. The plan was to then get up, pick up Maggie and slowly tiptoe down the stairs and out the door to freedom.

Some 90 minutes later I arose, looked over to find Maggie lying on the floor, eyes wide open, staring at the bedroom door.

"Good girl, Maggie," I praised. "Good watchdog."

I arose, took off my shoes, put them in the small bag I'd brought, then picked it up with one hand and all 35 pounds of Maggie with the other. One quiet step at a time, thanking God for the sound-deadening plush carpet beneath my feet, I quietly unlocked the door and opened it slowly, peeking out to make sure all was clear. I saw no sign of human movement, and Belinda's bedroom door was shut; no light shone from under the door.

"Coast is clear," I whispered to Maggie, nesting quietly in the crook of my right arm. "Let's go!"

Just before I took the first step into the hallway, though, I saw Maggie's eyes dart downward in front of me. I followed her gaze, and saw a sleeping *Belinda* lying on a pillow just outside my door, and just under where my left foot was about to come down on her head.

My raised foot froze in mid-air and, gratefully, Maggie didn't move or make a sound either.

"Jesus!" I exclaimed under my breath. "What the hell is this?"

I swung the outstretched leg backwards and put it down to regain my balance, missing Belinda who was still asleep.

Whatever resolve I had made about leaving the premises that night was only solidified by realizing this woman of uncertain temperament had decided to pitch her bedroll right outside my bedroom door because ... why? My mind raced. Was she hoping I'd change my mind and invite her into my bed after all? Did she sense that I would be leaving in the night, so she turned herself into a human trap to stop me? Was she planning to unlock the door with her passkey and become my bedmate?

If ever an answer didn't make a bit of difference, this was it. All I wanted to do was leave as fast and quietly as I could. With regained composure, I reached out again with my left leg, only this time arching it far over her prone, sleeping body. That worked, so then I pulled the right leg up and over her. A few steps to the top stair and then 12 more steps down to the front door, and I was a free man. This would all be a memory no one back in Memphis would believe, even if I had the nerve to share it.

It all worked, and I stood facing the door. I put Maggie down quietly, leashed her and reached into my pocket for a note I had jotted down an hour ago. It was for Belinda and it read simply, *"Sorry I had to leave in the middle of the night. I got a call on my cell phone that my son was in a wreck and I need to drive home to see him. Best wishes!"* I signed it, put it on the hallway desk, opened the front door slowly and got the hell out of there.

On my walk to my car, grateful I had parked out on the street and not in her driveway where she might have heard the motor start, I half-expected Belinda to come bursting through her front door, demanding that I stop and come back inside. No such scene materialized, however, Maggie and I jumped into the car, I started the engine, and crept out into the street headed West.

As I left Nashville, I realized I could avoided all this by simply being honest with this woman. To wit,I didn't think we were a good match and I'll just leave now and say thank you for a lovely dinner. I guess I felt that wouldn't be polite, so I said yes to the sleepover, and then pulled off this escape, leaving her to think and feel who knows what? In doing this, I exhibited my chaotic state of mind at this time in my life.

Either way, I never looked back as I headed home to Memphis.

Contrary to what could be presumed from these tales of romantic misadventure, my life in Memphis did also include some work I did for the university. And actually, there was quite a lot of that work. Although wallowing too much in my emotional travails, I did manage to teach my classes, and was probably the only prof at the U of M that asked his chairman for a larger-than-required load. The reason? Not only did I miss spending more time in the classroom, but I also knew it would keep me from heading down to Tunica more.

By this time, I had managed to help my cousin Bob get a job in a nearby university as advertising director for the school newspaper. It was a good fit for him and his PR/advertising background, and we had a good time continuing our friendship in Memphis.

I did my part to advance the cause of journalism in and out of the classroom. I developed and carried out several professional workshops and seminars for journalists and even PR practitioners, set up and led the international seminars for several groups of German news people from ZDF Television.

That international partnership continued to blossom, and I made friends with all of them, hosted them at my home in suburban Germantown, and took them on local tours to see the sights. They *all* wanted to visit Elvis' home, Graceland, on the city's south side, and they loved it. So did I, actually, closet Elvis fan that I am.

On one occasion, I decided to introduce them to another piece of Americana by taking them a few miles south into Tunica, where the Beach Boys were doing a concert at one of the casinos there. Most of them already knew of the legendary boys from Southern California, but none of them had heard them in person. I'll never forget the sight of seeing a dozen middle-aged German adults led by my good friend Fritz Hattig, dancing, clapping, and singing along with this famed American band. It was a great night of German-American friendship.

I hosted them back at my home after the concert for beer and pizza. While still in the kitchen, I heard strains of singer Karen Carpenter coming from my bedroom and I went to check it out, because I had not turned that music on. There I found one of my German guests, whose nickname was Abbi, standing over the DVD player and wiping tears away from his eyes.

"I'll never forget hearing the news that she passed away," Abbi said when he saw me enter. "Karen Carpenter was such a wonderful gift to music, and I loved her so much!"

How about that, I thought: these stoic Germans can be just as sentimental as we Americans. I had long suspected that on my trips to Germany, but not so much because of emotional effusiveness springing forth from the Germans themselves. Rather, it was in the American music that was so popular there, the most popular genre being romantic ballads and soft rock. While it might be hard for Americans to imagine Germans swooning over American power ballads like Melissa Manchester's *The Power of Love*, I saw it happen. Seeing the tearful Abbi that night, mourning the loss of Karen Carpenter, only confirmed it.

I was also doing a lot of writing during these years, knocking out an average of one book a year focusing on some aspect of the news media, journalism, and journalists themselves. In only a couple of what came to be seventeen books, did I write about the actual process of writing or reporting. I instead focused on what I perceived as the nature, ethics, and impact of journalism.

That impact was not only limited to the readers or viewers, but also studied the effects – often the trauma – of it on *journalists themselves.* My Oklahoma City bombing experience took that aspect out of the realm of the abstract for me and showed me firsthand what that impact can feel like. Two of my books, focused on how journalists feel and think about what they do and how it effects them and their stories.

I've also believed journalists have an unwritten contract with readers to provide accurate information, point out how those verified facts become the building blocks of truth, and to also present their findings in an engaging written style that – when appropriate – puts a human face on the story; shows the reader why he/she should care. I innovated some ideas, but I also borrowed from gifted writing coaches like Walt Harrington who championed the term, *"intimate journalism,"* which immerses the reader in the story, fleshes out the individuals (characters) in that story (plot), and never sways from factual accuracy in the process.

That's a tall order for any journalist but an important one. And, if it's not readily apparent, that definition of journalism does not rest on simply writing what sells. It doesn't have to, if the public is paying attention; good stories, well-told, should automatically sell. Too few media executives forget that when they slash newsroom staffs and beef up the marketing department instead. Too many of them wind up selling sizzle, because the budget steak itself has been gutted.

27

A Stormy Trip Home

As the year 1999 moved into May, I received a very nice and un-expected honor for the work I'd done as a journalist. That recognition came from my old school, Midwest City High School. I was to be the latest inductee on the school's Wall of Fame, which is comprised of alums who have made a name for themselves in their professions. I was invited to the Wall of Fame induction ceremony, to be held the evening of May 3 on the campus of Midwest City High School. My parents and my sister Elaine would both be there, and I looked forward to it. Little did I know it would be an evening impossible to forget, and not just because I was being honored. In fact, I would come to call it, the ceremony that wasn't. The story goes like this, as I would later relate it in print:

Two signal events provided the drama in my Oklahoma hometown on Monday night, May 3, 1999. One was an awards ceremony at Midwest City High School where six of us alums were being inducted onto the school's Wall of Fame.

The other was the tornado.

The first ceremony would have been one to remember — if it had actually taken place. But it was blown away by the second event: the one that still raises goosebumps when I recall it. Left in the wake of this massive twister was a city devoid of electrical power but loaded with storm debris. Some of it landed very close to where the 300 of us were huddled at the high school.

Although located in the center of a geographical strip known as Tornado Alley, Midwest City had not suffered a serious tornado in 50 years until that night.

For those of us gathered at Midwest City High School, the school's jazz band was just finding its groove, old friends were embracing, and the fun was just beginning when Principal Rick Bachman took to the lectern in the cafeteria. His calm voice belied his concern when he made what seemed a strange announcement.

"Our great band reminds us of the music played by the ensemble aboard the Titanic, but we don't want to be like the passengers on that ship, so let's quietly and orderly leave this building and walk over to the field house," Bachman said.

At table after table, smiles dissolved into quizzical looks. Bachman went on: "We have just received word that a tornado has been spotted on the city's west side, so just to be safe, let's move on to the field house."

Most of the 300 did exactly as Bachman asked.

As we walked, I was chatting with Mom and Dad about how this wasn't a total surprise for us.

"This must be that same twister that started up down in Chickasha an hour ago, and was headed north," I said. "Remember how the weatherman said it was one of the biggest the state has seen? But Chickasha is about 35 miles south of here."

Dad replied, "Right. Tornados usually stay on the ground only a few minutes at any one time. How could that funnel still be touching ground an hour later?"

In this case, it did. This was the same storm.

In the field house, some guests mingled in the hallways, others took seats. A few moments later, the court was lit, and a few hundred spilled out into it. Some students found a basketball and began shooting hoops.

"This is pretty eerie," one teacher said. "It's like we're in a bomb shelter waiting for the blast."

Many huddled around a television featuring a live account and video of the approaching tornado. Midwest City and the adjacent Tinker Air Force Base were in its sights.

"Oh my God," uttered one parent who had shown up to see a friend's daughter honored. The sentiment was repeated several times as you passed through the huddled masses.

"Fifty years and no real tornados; now this," another woman whispered to her husband.

My sister Elaine, who came to see me be inducted in the ceremony, appeared in the locker room with a chunk of hail the size of a tennis ball. "Just for your information," she said, "this is what it's doing outside."

At that moment, the television blurted out the news: "Residents of Midwest City should take cover immediately! This tornado is headed straight for the downtown area."

Hearts sank.

Out on the basketball court, school officials made the announcement: "Everyone must leave the court and move to the hallways or underground locker rooms. The twister will be here in a couple minutes."

There was no panic among the hundreds huddled together. Only the dread of what was coming. You don't grow up in Oklahoma without getting used to this dance every spring.

Some embraced loved ones; others held hands; many just waited and stared into the blackness.

"Midwest City, take cover! Tinker Field, take cover!" the radio said again. We listened from the locker room as the storm winds howled above us. We waited for what seemed the inevitable, and I realized my parents' home was between us and the twister. I was glad they were with me at the school, because their home would be hit before it swept over us.

Our eyes were glued to the TV, watching the tornado approach us, creating electric sparks, pops, and flashes as it took down power transformers on telephone pools in its track toward Midwest City. Then suddenly, the TV screen went dark and, a second later, the locker room was plunged into darkness, too. The storm had taken out the power lines. A few people had transistor radios and turned them on.

Over those radios came another message.

"Wait a minute," the announcer said, "the funnel seems to be making a left turn, going north toward Oklahoma City. It is missing Tinker."

In the darkness, hearts were buoyed.

"It now seems headed north between Air Depot and Sooner Road," the radio voice continued. If that was true, it would miss us at the high school by a few blocks.

"Pray for Del City," one voice said in the dark, referencing the adjacent town that began at Sooner Road. Although the twister would miss our street, it did wind up venting its fury on Midwest City's west side, as well as Del City.

As word of the storm's new path filtered through the crowd, a new worry began. A strong odor of natural gas began to fill the field house so, once again, we were all evacuated to the main school building. But once outside, the feeling of relief spread through the crowd as the danger seemed over for us. Most headed not back to the school but to their cars for a drive home to assess wind and hail damage.

A drive through the city's traffic-congested west side showed downed power lines, especially along Air Depot, lost power across most of the city, and limited or no phone service. Debris, probably blown from the west and the funnel track, littered the city's west side. Many cars were showing the hailstone damage. One image that stuck in my mind for years to come were three new Chevrolets that were picked up by the funnel from a car dealership and deposited in the swimming pool of a motel across the highway. They were now at the bottom of that pool.

I drove to Oklahoma City to see if *The Oklahoman* needed some help and to let them know I could write a story about how the storm hit Midwest City. The managing editor, Ed Kelley, welcomed my contribution, and I pounded out the story I had just lived through in the Midwest City Field House. I filed it with the city editor and was leaving the building when Kelley stopped me and said, "You know, Luke, it's really great to see you again, but I have a favor to ask. The last two times you've come home, we've had huge disasters hit. First the bombing, and now this twister. So, could you start coming home fewer times please?"

The next day we all realized how lucky we had been at that high school ceremony. The twister was officially labeled the Bridge Creek/Moore Tornado, measured as an F5 tornado, the most powerful grade a twister is given. In fact, meteorologists said it registered the highest wind speeds ever measured globally, with winds recorded at 301 mph. It was the strongest tornado ever recorded in the Oklahoma City metro area. It had covered a path of 38 miles from its point of touchdown, staying on the ground for 85 minutes.

The death toll from the tornado was 41, with many others injured. More than 8,000 homes were destroyed, as was much of the city of Moore located just south of Midwest City, and loss damages topped $1 billion.

It was the first storm to ever use the tornado emergency tracking system of the National Weather Service, whose severe storm headquarters is located 20 minutes south of Midwest City in Norman.

Oh, and that ceremony I had come home for? I got my gold watch in the mail a week later, back in my Memphis home.

That was fine with me. I realized the 20th Century was going out with a loud and violent bang, and my family and I had just dodged a very large bullet.

28

I've Got Mail

I was making greater strides toward living in the moment instead of the past, and I found great peace in going out to the stable to see Star, then saddle and ride her off into the hills while my new dog Maggie raced along at our side, occasionally veering off to chase a rabbit or squirrel. They had become clutch partners in a life that I was otherwise living mostly incognito because of an embarrassing obsession with casino gambling. I'd been at it a year now, making too many trips to the new casinos just south of Memphis in Tunica, Mississippi. I knew I had to give it up, and I knew I had begun gambling on weekends to distract me in my free time from living in the past with Selena.

Not only were the 1990s fading into the past as December, 1999 set in, but the whole 20th Century with it. I was now teaching two and – sometimes three -- courses each semester, and the added structure of that second one was causing me to stay in Memphis more and visit the Tunica casinos less. I knew I was only treading water, though, and I realized how fragile the daily recovery from addiction can be. It truly is a matter of taking one day at a time, and sometimes taking each hour of each day one hour at a time.

I was also continuing to write books and was currently immersed in researching and writing more books, as well as working with the program the Germans called, "The Memphis Opportunity." That was the one Fritz Hattig and I developed for ZDF staff members to learn more about how American journalists work, and increase their English language skills in the process. It would soon evolve into an ongoing student- and faculty-exchange program that is still in existence today.

I had been focusing less on pursuing new love interests, not for any special reason other than feeling that would work out in time. For some strange reason, the audible/inaudible voice I had heard in my car a few months before was still helping provide a calming feeling. I had this feeling that I had *not* come this far in life and in my work only to be derailed in my early 50s.

So, I pushed ahead and tried to focus on the present tense. Dwelling on the past had already cost me too much and was wasted time. I had also spent too much time on the backroads of dreams and fantasies, thinking if I just kept scouring the country, I'd find my soulmate.

As the year 2000 approached, bringing with it the 21st Century, we were all wondering how New Year's Eve 1999 would play out. The big question was what – if anything -- would happen to our personal computers and the data they carried. They both had become indispensable to our lives over the span of just five years since we figured out the Internet and began using email enough to become dangerous with it.

There was a scare going around that had some merit to it, and it was called the "*Y2K Problem.*" It was related to our digital world housed inside those desktop computers in our offices and homes. The issue referred to potential computer errors related to the formatting and storage of calendar data for dates in and after the year 2000. Many computer programs represented four-digit years with only the final two digits, making the year 2000 indistinguishable from 1900. Computer systems' inability to distinguish data correctly had the potential to bring down worldwide infrastructures for industries ranging from banking to air travel. If this could happen to giant industries, it could certainly effect all individual computer users.

There was an open question about what might happen to the data stored in each desktop computer. Would the changeover to the 2000s scramble our stored data? Make it inaccessible? Would it all be too much for the computer mother board to handle? Would there be a loud pop at midnight coming from inside our desktops, followed by a plume of smoke coming out the ventilator slits? All of the above? None of the above?

Looking back, it all seems silly but it wasn't silly as the year 2000 approached. Most of us were only digital semi-literates at the time, and we didn't know what to expect. After all, some American company executives had predicted the global damage resulting from "the Y2K bug" could cost as much as $600 billion to fix. For some Americans, the unknown extent of danger was similar to a coastal town receiving hurricane warnings. In the case of the Y2K scare, a lack of agreement and clarity about how real the danger was, caused some Americans to stock up on food, water, and even guns. I never figured out why we'd need guns but, hey, this *is* America after all.

The scare also caused people to buy backup generators and withdraw their life savings from banks, fearing some meltdown the country's banking and economic system.

At universities like mine, faculty were advised to back up computer data and monitor their computers as much as possible during the millennial transfer period to see if there were any signs of damage caused by the sweep of the clock's minute hand past midnight 2000.

Many of us didn't attach that much certainty to the problem occurring, but I had no plans on New Year's Eve, so I decided to go on down to my office that night and babysit my desktop Mac through the last harrowing hour of 1999. Contrary to the expectations of those warning of Y2K problems, the night passed safely for the computers of the land and the precious data housed in them. It seems there had been enough global preventive action taken way ahead of time by computer programmers and IT experts that helped prevent the dire consequences of the night that many had predicted would occur.

I breathed a sigh of relief when midnight arrived and passed quickly, realizing things would be fine. But I didn't realize *how* fine until my AOL flag popped up about 12:05 a.m. with its friendly message, "You've got mail!" Who, I wondered, would be writing me just after midnight on New Year's Eve? Could there be someone else as foolish as me at the university who was nursing their own computer in their office and saw the light from mine through the window?

I clicked the message open and was surprised to find a woman had written me telling me she loves to bake chocolate chip cookies and has been told they are the best in the country. It took a minute for this introductory line to make sense until I realized she was responding to the post on my *One and Only* dating site profile, wherein I had mentioned that I love chocolate chip cookies.

Wow, I thought. Looks like I have a date on New Year's Eve after all, albeit a virtual one! Her name was Kathryn she lived in Louisville, and she had found my profile interesting enough to write and say hi. She liked the fact I was a journalist and an educator, she joked about my references to my world travel and to the fact I actually had an Indiana Jones snap-brim fedora hat. She said any man who seemed that rugged yet still had a soft spot for chocolate chip cookies must be okay.

I remember that Kathryn, a name I would often shorten to Kate, did not post a profile picture, which usually lessens the chance for a response on dating sites. But she seemed so sweet and intelligent that I wasted no time in responding.

"So, your bakery must be open all night," I wrote. "Since I live in Memphis, it's unlikely I can swing by to sample your cookies, but maybe we can talk awhile online, anyway. Are you up for that?"

So, yeah, we did talk more. A lot more. And, for the first time in a long time, I was actually thinking something was going right in my life; something which I absolutely did not deserve. But I resolved I would gladly take it, anyway.

A couple days later she did send me her photo, and she was as pretty as her online personality predicted she would be. The photo showed her dancing with her father (who bore a striking resemblance to Jimmy Carter) at her oldest daughter's wedding. She had a smile that brightened up the dance floor, and I predicted – correctly, as it turned out – that Kate and I would be talking a lot more. She told me she was a musician, with music degrees from the University of Kentucky, and that she was volunteering with her local community theater and was about to play the role of Miss Hannigan (obviously against type for such a pretty actress). She was recently divorced and had three daughters, the youngest of which was just finishing high school.

Kate was getting under my skin, and life was looking much better. The month of January passed, and I felt a new breeze blowing through my daily life. I was buoyed by the possibility that she represented, and wondered if she was supernaturally sent my way by the voice in my car out in the Mississippi kudzu several months before. Either way, I was actually happy for a change.

About a month into our online exchanges, Kathryn and I felt confident enough to set up an in-person Kentucky meeting in Louisville We agreed to meet at a wonderful bookstore which had a pleasant cafe' on its first floor.

We set the meeting for the night of February 14. Valentine's Day seemed appropriate. I arrived about 6 p.m., and Kate was already there. I had written her I'd be wearing a burnt orange barn coat, and when she spotted me, she came to the front of the café to greet me, holding out her hand. We shook and she directed me back to our table.

I cannot remember what we ate, but I will always remember feeling so comfortable talking with her. She spoke of her daughters, her community theater work, and of what it was like growing up in Kentucky. She was a very young-looking 47 and I was surprised to find her oldest daughter had already graduated from college. There was no hint of desperation about her; quite the contrary, she was very self-possessed, independent, and secure in her womanhood. She was also straightforward and, she had already let me know in an email what she would like the ground rules to be of our face-to-face meeting.

"Luke," she said, "I look forward to meeting you in person but, in case we don't feel a connection, let's have an understanding that we chalk our meeting up to a nice dinner conversation and then go our own ways in life."

Wow, I thought to myself, as the relief flowed through me. This is not going to be another Nashville experience with another Belinda! This woman does just fine on her own – better than I'd been doing myself – and maybe she just wants what I want: to feel even more complete by developing a symbiotic relationship with someone who could be a complementary mate for their soul.

We must have talked about three hours straight, because it looked like the café was getting ready to close up. So, we each paid our own check (another of her ground rules) and went into the lobby of the connected Hilton hotel where I was spending the night.

Thus far, our new relationship was off to a good start. I had learned years ago about the value of being able to converse easily and go deep into it with a woman. I knew I would not be asking her up to my room, and I sensed even more certainly that Kate would not accept even if I did. This dinner meeting was not a prelude to sex, and we both knew – without saying it – that we'd better stick to the plan of seeing if we might be a match. And we knew it was highly unlikely we would know that after our initial meeting or meetings, for that matter. So the protocol seemed to be that we just take it slow and see what developed.

Kate had a great sense of humor and reminded me a lot of comedian Carol Burnett's persona when she really got going with a story to the point of impersonating other accents and personae. But she could also be serious and thoughtful, was a champion of civil rights and equal rights for women, and she leaned left in politics. This latter trait put her at odds with many other Kentuckians who leaned hard right. But Kate really didn't care, and she made friends with them anyway.

She told me stories about her needing to take personal retreats, however, just to get away by herself to think and absorb nature. Her destination was usually Bardstown, Kentucky, the site of a monastery and village of nuns who did agrarian work on the farm. She would take her favorite books and head there, sometimes for as long as a week, living at a retreat the nuns supervised.

I would come to see Kate as a real-life version of the character Belle from the story of *Beauty and the Beast.* As the townspeople followed their traditional thinking and daily routines, Kate would be off sitting under a tree, eating an apple and reading a book. She would wonder about the world outside the village, engage friendly animals, and stretch her boundaries of her mind and curiosity as far as possible.

As I reflected later in the evening, I realized two things: first, I liked this Kentucky woman very much, and second, that while the idea of taking things slow was different for me, it was best if we did it that way. Neither of us was sure we'd found the one we'd been looking for, but we did sense that this was a promising relationship, and we wanted to see each other again.

So that's what we did. I drove back to Memphis a couple days later and we talked on a regular basis by phone and chatted by email. We set dates for future meetings in Kentucky, and it was easier for me to make the six-hour drive than her because of her weekend job as a church organist.

We wound up seeing a lot of each other that way and about a month later we set up a rendezvous in New York City. Kathryn had been raising a guide dog for the blind and was due to return him to the organization's training center in Long Island. She was going to stay with one of the benefactors of the group, Mrs. DeAngelo, and I took a hotel room for myself in midtown Manhattan. We met at Penn Station on a Saturday afternoon, toured the Empire State Building, and had dinner at a cozy restaurant in the Theater District. I had purchased tickets for the famed musical *Les Miserables,* and we departed the restaurant about a half-hour before curtain and walked over to the theater.

As we strolled from the cafe to the theater, I broke through my hesitation about touching Kate. I didn't want to seem too presumptuous, but it felt like the time was right.

I prefaced my touch by saying, "I'd better hold on to you, Kate because I wouldn't want to lose such a pretty woman to some vagabond on these city streets!"

With that preamble, I reached out and found a welcoming hand reaching back, and it felt like first-time love all over again.

We found the Broadway Theater, took our seats, and I felt the same enthralling grip from the opening numbers of *Les Mis* that I had felt in *A Chorus Line* two decades before. Only this time, that grip was tighter because of the woman sitting next to me, and because the casual handholding we felt on our walk to the theater had become a vise grip involving all four of our hands.

We were so close to each other, I wondered for a moment why I had even bothered to buy two seats.

The words and music of *Les Miserables* had helped Kate and me overcome our initial fear of getting involved again, and transported us — right in that theater — to the next level.

The show's lyrics had a lot to do with that. *"I Dreamed a Dream," and "One Day More"* were words and phrases that took on new meaning for us that night, as Kate and I each realized neither of us was no longer *"On My Own."*.

For me, that did it, and I was sold on this Kate Hammond from Louisville. She was starting to feel the same way, I could tell, but her moment of certainty would not come for a couple more weeks when she made her first trip to see me in Memphis. I picked her up at the airport and took her to my place where I had made up a bed for her in the guest room. As the night turned out, that bed went unused and we spent a blissful night embracing beneath the sheets of my bed instead.

We had a great weekend together, and I drove her back to the airport Sunday afternoon. There, at the terminal gate during our goodbye kiss, she whispered, "I love you, Luke." My heart leaped, and I confessed my love for her as well. She then followed that up with email telling me there was no doubt now: she had fallen hopelessly in love with me.

I knew this was a woman I wanted to spend a great deal of time with, and I made plans that spring to take an apartment in Louisville to be near her. I was back to teaching just the one class at Memphis, and I received permission to take it online, teach it from Kentucky, and work on my research there, too.

I did have one remaining on-campus commitment for the semester, however, and that was to host the group of journalists from German Television ZDF for about 10 days. I asked Kathryn to come down for a couple days of that workshop and to interact with the Germans socially. I was glad I did, because she enjoyed it immensely and became friends with a couple of the Germans. She liked Fritz, too, and loved how the group referred to him as the "Pope," but she also could see how I had my hands full with his mercurial personality. Personally, I also think she enjoyed the experience because it was further evidence that I really did have a job!

I drove Kate back to the airport on Sunday afternoon for her return flight to Kentucky, and we were both knew that soon there would be no need for anymore goodbyes.

We were going forward together.

29

A New Life

For five years I had been trying to complete a very long pivot in my life, charting a new course away from the loss of Selena, then away from gambling, and away from the double life that I was living in the classrooms and the casinos. That effort was a very long process and often was characterized by one step forward and two back; sometimes more.

But I had learned a few things over these five years, chief among them that hammering my thumb by moving into a destructive addiction and moving too quickly into the wrong relationships, had not worked to erase my pain. Indeed, it had only led to more of it.

I also came to grips with being a flawed individual and even admitted as much in speaking at my father's funeral. But I was working hard to be a better man, and that became my daily objective. I was making strides toward that goal, and Kate's entrance into my life helped immensely. I now had even stronger reasons to leave Selena and the Tunica casinos behind permanently. I didn't want to drag Kate into all that, I was tired of lying about myself to people I cared about, and I knew I would have to put more geographical distance between me and the gambling houses of Northern Mississippi.

Today, as I write this, I have not entered a casino in many years.

As for my experiences with love ... well ... the fact I'd lost Selena was the reason I was seeking escape in these casinos in the first place. I had lost in my pursuit of an unattainable and lasting love, even though so many of these experiences with Selena had – in our opening chapters – strongly hinted the story would go on forever. Now, five years later, the pain had diminished greatly, and I no longer felt captive to it. As for the hit-and-run driver who had ended Selena's life, he or she was never found.

Although the reason for my losing Selena was different from subsequent failed relationships, the end result was always the same. This guy who was meant to live life with a soul mate, was left standing alone when the music stopped

Until Kathryn came into my life.

It was during one of Kate's visits to Memphis in the spring of 2000 that I received an offer from the University of Oklahoma to become their McMahon Centennial Professor, starting in the following fall term. I readily accepted, partly because the inference I received was that I would be a strong candidate for the dean's position which was opening up in the school of journalism that year. Kate was excited for me, and we knew we would work out the logistics for both of us, because we both knew by then that, where ever either of us was headed, we would definitely be going there together.

Kate and I saw each other almost daily in Kentucky, and she would spend many of those nights with me at my apartment. On one of those nights I asked her to marry me, she said yes, and we set the date for July 16. I felt my grip on life had strengthened enough to make that move, knowing I wanted to be able to stand on my own two feet before asking her to spend her life with me. So, for the first time in a long time, I felt I was regaining control of my life. Early on in our relationship, I told Kate of my gambling problem, and she must have thought I was worth the risk, which is something for which I am eternally grateful.

We married in Kentucky as planned. Our new chapter in life was now formalized into an unbreakable union. As is obvious, I'm still the romantic optimist! Kathryn and I have both come to experience a love like we had never known before. It took a while for it develop to the even-deeper state that it would in years to come, but that's the best kind of love, no?

The wedding was held on the evening of July 16 in a small Episcopal Church, and a couple weeks later Kate and I were packing up to move to Norman, Oklahoma, for my new job at OU.

It was a new experience for her is every way possible: she had never lived outside of Kentucky, in all her 47 years; she had only been to Oklahoma once, to meet my parents; she was leaving her three grown daughters behind in Louisville, and she was doing all this with a brand new husband who she knew was bringing some heavy baggage into the marriage. She knew I had been fighting sadness from the experience with Selena, and she knew that I had resorted to gambling in a way an alcoholic tries to drown his sorrow in booze.

All in all, it took an extremely brave and confident woman to do that, and those are two of Kathryn's shining traits. It was an undeserved stroke of good fortune for me that she did it out of genuine love for me.

Kate helped me leave gambling behind and forge ahead in my profession and personal life. The OU experience lasted only one year, but it was a memorable one for both of us. It was good being only a half-hour away from my parents and sister, and Kate got to know both of them well by the time the year was over. She also was able to broaden her career resume' by working as a musical accompanist for the OU School of Dance where she had to play a variety of impromptu pieces to fit the kinds of dances the instructor would be teaching each day. Kate has often told me it was the most stressful job she has ever had.

When I took the OU job, I was excited and had idealistic visions of returning to the school I had loved as a student there. But a couple months after arriving, I learned the wisdom of the saying by the poet Heraclitus: *"No man steps twice into the same river, for it is not the same river, and he is not the same man."* The University of Oklahoma was a different river by this year of 2000-2001, and I missed the old river that I had known in the mid-1960s. Coming back to it as a 54-year-old man caused me to see it differently than had the 22-year-old man who graduated decades ago.

As for Kate, she was hoping for a less stressful job than the juggling act she was called on to perform every day in the school of dance. Add to all this the Oklahoma weather which was extreme this year, going from ice storms in the winter to 104 degree temperatures and tornadoes in the spring and summer, and we were ready to seek greener pastures for 2001-2002. I was asked to return to the University of Memphis, and I said yes right then and there. Sealing the deal for Kate and me was the fact we spent one of our last nights in Norman dodging a tornado.

We decided to return to Memphis for what would be a two-year stint which began with my being credited with a new student- and faculty-exchange program with two German universities that grew out of my partnership with ZDF television. Kathryn and I were invited to Frankfurt for the ribbon-cutting of the program that was overseen by newly-appointed U.S. Ambassador Dan Coates. Two decades later, that program is still going strong and I was invited back to Germany in 2023 to help commemorate its founding. It is the only German-American journalism school exchange program like it, and I am proud of my contribution to getting it started.

After a few months' back in the Bluff City, however, I realized that gambling still held too much of an allure for me, despite a year's abstinence while living in Oklahoma. It got to the point where Kate and I knew I could not live in such close proximity to casinos, so I began searching for other universities and found one in Southern California that invited me out to an interview.

That school was Pomona College an elite private liberal arts college in the city of Claremont, known by locals as "the town of trees and Ph.D.'s." It had so many of both, and the latter because of the five private colleges and two graduate schools that make up the Claremont Colleges Consortium. The campuses were all adjacent to each other, each more beautiful than the next. I got the job as chair of the Department of Communication Studies, and we entered into the West Coast phase of our life and marriage.

It felt good to be finally offering some tangible help to Kate in her unfolding career by securing free tuition for her at Pomona Using that benefit, she was able to complete two Masters degrees and expand her interests beyond music into college student affairs management and teaching English to international students. This latter TESOL Master's degree gave her entry to teach internationals at the university level for several years. Along the way, we served as homestay parents for the international students she taught. At one point in our four-bedroom home, we were housing four different international students from three different countries. A real United Nations, and it was a lot of fun.

I came to admire my wife so much and the love I felt in the early days together has deepened to immeasurable levels since then.

Nearly a quarter-center later, with Kathryn right beside me all the way, I know she is that person. I am indeed happy and have found my peace and my love. It has been years since I've walked through and out of a casino's door, I have rebuilt my life and finances, made good friends, and Kate and I share a beautiful home that's not far from our kids and grandkids, a home that's filled with a half-dozen loving animals.

What more could a guy ask for?

As I write this, all these years later, I know I did have enough resolve left inside to fight my demons and move forward with hope. And I managed to salvage and build a life of value out of the trail of faux diamonds and rusted memories of Selena's passing. I moved on to some 17 years of service at a values-centered university in Southern California, and I will soon celebrate the 25th wedding anniversary to a woman who I love madly. I have recovered from my financial losses and have taken my credit score from a dismal 387 to a perfect 850. The man who once had to visit payday loan storefronts in strip malls, now gets a half-dozen invitations a week from large financial houses to borrow money. I pride myself in turning them all down.

I will always look back to the Oklahoma City bombing as the pivot point in my life. In my darkest days of losing my beloved wife Selena, I encountered a much darker day thrust upon the people I grew up among; my fellow Sooners. It was an undeserved and cruel act that turned a vibrant city into a city of mourners. And it was a privilege for me to be able to tell their story of heroism and resilience in responding to that bombing. In articulating their pain and the way they dealt with it, I was also articulating my own grief. I hoped I could match the resilience and pluck that my Oklahoma friends exhibited. It became my challenge and gave me enough inspiration to deal with the fight still to come in my own life.

I continue to grieve for the victims of the Murrah Building bombing, and I realize that as I write this in 2024, the youngest of the 219 children whose parents perished in that blast have now neared or reached the age of 30. Those who went -- or are going -- to college could do so for free in-state tuition, thanks to a multi-million-dollar donation fund set up in a foundation for that purpose.

As for me, I count the patience, love, and support Kate has given me to be among my greatest gifts in life. As is the case with many journalists, I experienced some ongoing trauma from being so close to the bombing. But my career as a writer and educator has given me the creative and linguistic abilities to imagine and express my feelings. As a professor and writing coach, I've been able to pass some of my knowledge along to many young writers.

Loosely translating a line I once heard, again from Tom Wingo, *"I am a writer, a teacher, and very much in love. That is more than I deserve, and it is certainly more than enough."*

Afterword: The Field of Empty Chairs

I have often returned to the Oklahoma City National Memorial and Museum. It was built as a lasting tribute and remembrance to those who suffered and died there, those who endured, and those who came to save lives, recover bodies, and console grieving family members and survivors. Each time, my visits have inspired me to stand stronger against violence as an answer to problems in the land. Each time, I am swept back to the heartbreak which I witnessed – and felt myself -- in April, 1995.

Between the minutes of 9:01 and 9:03 a.m. on April 19 of that year, life ended for 168 innocent people in the Alfred P. Murrah Federal Building in Oklahoma City. So it is appropriate that the Outdoor Memorial surrounding a long reflecting pond are bordered on the east and west ends by large golden gates with the inscriptions of "9:01" and "9:03." The beauty and serenity of the memorial grounds and pond stand in stark contrast to the deadly brutality that took place there when Timothy McVeigh blew the building apart with his homemade truck bomb.

The rectangular reflecting pool is bordered on the south by 168 glass straight-back chairs that illuminate after dark. They are ordered in nine rows, each corresponding to a floor of the nine-story Murrah Building. Each chair represents the location on each floor where the person killed was working or visiting when the bomb exploded. The chairs are further grouped by agency and in alphabetical order within that agency, whether the person was employed or just conducting business that day. Additionally, there are five chairs in the column furthest west that represent the five people who died in the vicinity of the building. One of those five chairs represents nurse Rebecca Anderson who lost her life rushing into the building to save children from the nursery. She died a few days later in the hospital from injuries received in the building. Three unborn children also died in the blast and, although not officially counted in the 168 killed, their names are etched on their mothers'

Silent chairs stand for the 168 bombing victims plus the three unborn children of women killed in the blast.

Photo by Jim Willis

chairs. On the second row, there are 19 smaller chairs, denoting the children and infants who died in the building's day care nursery.

On the north east side of the reflecting pool stands a tall Elm tree that has been dubbed "The Survivor Tree." Prior to the bombing, this tree was the only thing giving shade in the downtown parking lot, and employees would often arrive early so they could park their cars beneath its shady branches. Despite its close proximity to the blast zone on April 19, 1995, the tree somehow survived destruction. But it was nearly intentionally cut down by investigative teams that needed to retrieve crime-scene evidence that was blown into its high branches. But it also survived that threat, partly because its roots had stretched back to the earliest days of Oklahoma statehood. Today it stands as a symbol of strength, resilience, and hope. The branches on the tree have grown even larger over the years, and there is more shade now than ever. Visitors often sit near those branches to reflect on what happened in 1995 just the other side of the reflecting pool.

Not far from the Survivor Tree stands the Oklahoma City National Memorial Museum, at 620 North Harvey. welcoming visitors 365 days a year, The museum is a highly rated attraction in Oklahoma City, and it transports visitors back to the tragic day of the Murrah Building bombing, given them a real sense of what that day was like and the impact it made on so many lives. Its many visitors have left page after page of comments about the experience. One simply wrote, *"Stunning, simply stunning. Should have visited a long time ago. It truly moves you."*

I agree.

Author at the Alfred P. Murrah Federal Building, April 1995.

About the Author

Jim Willis is a career journalist, professor emeritus, and author or co-author of 21 books. He is a graduate of the University of Oklahoma, East Texas State (now Texas A&M), and holds the Ph.D. in journalism from the University of Missouri. He reported on the bombing of the Murrah Federal Building and its aftermath in April and May, 1995. He has reported on the fall of Berlin Wall and its impact, and has lectured many times in Europe for the U.S. State Department's Foreign Service. He now lives in Kentucky with his musician wife Annie, whom he calls his live-in muse and forever partner. The couple have five children, six grandchildren, and six dogs and cats.

www.ingramcontent.com/pod-product-compliance
Lightning Source LLC
Chambersburg PA
CBHW070454300726
48975CB00007B/2173